DEADLY CHOICES

DETECTIVE ZOE FINCH BOOK 2

RACHEL MCLEAN

press

Catawampus Press

catawampus-press.com

READ ZOE'S PREQUEL STORY, DEADLY ORIGINS

It's 2003, and Zoe Finch is a new Detective Constable. When a body is found on her patch, she's grudgingly allowed to take a role on the case.

But when more bodies are found, and Zoe realises the case has links to her own family, the investigation becomes deeply personal.

Can Zoe find the killer before it's too late?

Find out by reading *Deadly Origins* for FREE at rachelmclean.com/origins.

Thanks,
Rachel McLean

CHAPTER ONE

"Mum, she stole my Curly Wurly."

Alison looked down at her son. His mouth was ringed with chocolate and his curly brown hair was smeared with it.

"It was a free Curly Wurly, Ollie. I'm not sure you can steal something they gave us free."

"Wan' it back."

Alison turned to Ollie's big sister. "Maddy love, give it back please."

"He doesn't like Curly Wurlys."

"That's not the point."

"Why should I give it back when he won't eat it?"

A man brushed past Alison. She flinched, her nerves frayed. They were standing on the walkway leading to the outdoor play area at Cadbury World. She knew they were blocking the route.

"Come on, you two. There's a stall over there selling hot dogs. Let's get some lunch."

"Don't want lunch," Ollie huffed.

Alison sucked in her cheeks. "You need to eat something. Balance out all that chocolate."

In the last two hours the kids had eaten one Curly Wurly (Madison), two Dairy Milks, two Double Deckers (did they still make those?) and four pots of melted chocolate. Plus one of each that Alison had given them from her own haul of freebies.

"Don't want hot dogs."

Alison checked the food stall. "OK. There's burgers too."

Ollie wrinkled up his nose.

"Look," said Alison, "Let's just grab a table and I'll see what they've got. OK?"

Madison shrugged. Ollie thumped her.

"What was that for?" Alison asked.

"Nicking my Curly Wurly."

"We don't use words like 'nick'. She stole it."

Ollie poked his sister. "See. Mum says you stole it."

Maddy flicked her head and flounced off to an empty table on the other side of the picnic area. Anxious not to lose her, Alison grabbed Ollie's hand and dragged him along to follow. They stumbled past other mums trying to convince their kids to eat something that wasn't chocolate. It was a Friday lunchtime and there weren't a lot of dads.

She reached the table and helped Ollie onto the bench. "Stay there while I investigate. And Maddy, don't go running off like that again."

"I wasn't running, I was—"

Alison raised a palm. How much of this outing had been enjoyable? Maybe five minutes, on the chocolate-themed ride. She'd enjoyed watching the old TV ads for chocolate bars that didn't exist anymore. But the kids had soon pulled her away from that. This would be so much easier if Ian had showed up.

"I don't want to hear it, Maddy. Just sit down and make sure your brother doesn't wander off. Alright?"

"Yeah." Maddy folded her arms across her chest and scowled at her brother, who was squishing a line of ants moving across the table. Alison swept a sleeve across the table to wipe away the crumbs that had attracted them.

"Mum!" Ollie gave her an exasperated look then sank to the ground to find the ants.

Alison dashed across to the food stall and gave the guy inside a nervous smile. "What've you got?"

"Hot dogs, burgers, cans. Baguettes. Tea. Coffee." He shrugged. He had an Australian accent and blonde hair that looked out of place on an October day in Birmingham.

"Is that all?"

"Sorry, I don't decide the menu."

She gave him a smile and rushed back to the kids. Madison had pulled a wedge of hair in front of her face and was plaiting it, her eyes crossed as she focused. Ollie was on the ground, following the ants away from the table.

"Right," Alison said. "Ollie, they've got hot dogs. There's plenty of ketchup, you like them with ketchup. Madison, you can have a tuna baguette."

"Euugh."

"You like tuna baguettes."

"Since when?"

"Since I bought you one in Greggs yesterday."

"That was yesterday."

"Well, I'll buy one anyway and if you don't eat it, I will."

Maddy shrugged, her gaze not leaving her hair. Ollie giggled at the ants.

"Ollie, get up off the floor."

He ignored her.

"Please?"

Nothing.

"Ollie! Your trousers are filthy."

He looked up at her with a wide-eyed smile. She bit her lip, guilt washing over her. October half term, an unseasonably sunny day. This was supposed to be fun. Ian had only needed to pop into work, they were going to have a nice day as a family. And here she was, shouting at her kids and making it miserable for all of them.

She crouched to kiss the top of Ollie's head.

"Stay here, both of you. I'll be five minutes."

Ollie returned to the ants. So his trousers were mucky. That's what washing machines were for. Madison had moved onto another section of hair. Her tongue poked out between her lips and she hummed under her breath.

Alison took her phone out of her pocket. Twelve messages to Ian, none in return. *Where are you?* He was doing far too much of this lately. Taking time off work but then telling her there was an emergency. Coming home after midnight. Being married to a police officer was never going to be easy, she knew. But couldn't he manage one trip to Cadbury World?

A queue had formed at the food stall. Alison shifted from foot to foot, needing the toilet. Madison was twelve, only just old enough to be left alone. And Ollie would object to going into the Ladies. She watched them as the queue shunted forward, wondering if either of them would acknowledge the other's presence. Did Madison even know she was supposed to be watching her brother? If he wandered too far in pursuit of those ants, would she notice?

Alison reached the front just as Madison moved onto the third section of hair. She turned away from her daughter to the Australian man.

"Hello again."

"Er, hi. One hot dog and one tuna baguette please. And a large Americano."

"One shot, or two?"

Her nerves jangled with fatigue. Olly had woken her at three am and she'd only dozed from then until the alarm went off at six.

"Three, please."

"Three? We don't do three."

"I'll have two."

"Coming right up." The man turned to his gleaming coffee machine and started pulling handles and turning knobs. The sausage for Ollie's hot dog sizzled on the grill.

Alison felt her eyelids droop. If Ian had been here, she could have squeezed in five minutes' rest, just a moment to recapture herself. But it was relentless, this married lone parent business.

"One Americano." He leaned across the hatch and winked. "Three shots."

She grinned. "Thanks."

"No worries." He lifted the hot dog sausage into its bun and wrapped the whole thing in paper. He turned to a fridge behind him and pulled out a baguette.

"Enjoy."

"Thanks." She shuffled along to a gingham-covered table and splashed milk in her coffee then smothered Ollie's hot dog in ketchup. She rearranged the items in her grip and turned back to the kids.

Her stomach lurched. The table was empty.

She hurried towards it, bending to see if Ollie was behind it, on the floor. She scanned the picnic area and the playground beyond, searching for Madison.

She reached the table, her heart racing.

"Ollie? Madison?"

Don't shout. Don't panic. Not yet. Ollie had followed those ants and Maddy would had gone to get him. Good girl.

Alison placed the food packages and coffee cup on the table, telling herself to move carefully. To be calm.

She scanned the tables. About half of them were in use. She blinked, willing her vision to clear.

"Madison?" Her voice was strangled. She cleared her throat. "Madison!"

A woman at a nearby table looked up. Alison felt her limbs shaking.

"Madison, Ollie. Your food's here. Stop messing about."

She stepped towards the play area, leaving the food behind. Children roamed the pirate climbing frame, bundled up in winter coats despite the sunshine. What had Ollie been wearing?

She closed her eyes and searched her memory of the morning. His blue anorak, and pale grey trousers. She'd been worried about him getting them dirty.

She felt a hand on her arm and almost collapsed in relief. She turned.

"Is this yours?"

The woman from the nearby table was holding out a blue bundle. An anorak. Alison let out a strangled sound.

"You OK?"

Alison nodded, her eyes prickling. "Yes. No."

The woman glanced back at her own kids. They were

tucking into hamburgers, oblivious. Why couldn't her two eat like that?

"You sure? You look sort of grey."

"My kids. Have you seen them?"

The woman's eyes narrowed. "Sorry. Are they over there, on the climbing frame?"

"I can't see them."

The woman gave her a smile, the kind of smile you give to someone who's told you they're terminally ill. "You go and look. I'll keep an eye on your stuff."

Alison nodded. She breathed something that might have been thanks and ran to the climbing frame.

"Ollie! Maddy!"

She circled the frame twice. No sign of them.

Her phone buzzed in her pocket. She grabbed it. Ian was here. He was with them. Everything was going to be OK.

It was a text from her mum. A problem with her boiler. Alison wanted to throw the phone to the ground. She clutched it, her palms sweaty.

Where were the nearest toilets? She ran back to the table. People were quiet as she passed. Watching her. Wondering.

The woman hovered by her table, scanning the area although she wouldn't know what she was looking for.

"Is there anywhere they could have gone?" said Alison. "Toilets?"

"None out here. They're inside."

Alison turned back to the factory building behind her. She'd been in the queue five minutes, ten at the most. Madison would have told her if she was going to the toilet.

"They've gone," she said. Her legs felt soft and her hands shook. "My kids have gone."

CHAPTER TWO

"WHAT THE HELL?"

DI Zoe Finch slumped to her chair, her teeth gritted. Around her, colleagues were cursing, and raking hands through their hair. One DC thumped a table.

Beside her, DS Mo Uddin shook his head. Zoe's boss, DCI Lesley Clarke, was up near the TV, a few rows ahead.

"That sucks," said Mo. He put a hand on the back of Zoe's chair. "Sorry."

Sorry wasn't good enough. Zoe stared at the screen. A thin man in a navy suit spoke to camera, his eyes dancing. Next to him, on a lower step and looking suitably contrite, was Jory Shand. He wore a dark suit and a grim expression, his grey hair combed neatly. Behind him was a heavily built man with light blond hair, his expression more forceful. Howard Petersen. Two of the three defendants in the Canary trial.

All three had abused children. She knew it, Mo knew it, they all knew it. It was Zoe who'd found the evidence linking those two to Robert Oulman, the other lowlife she'd watched in the dock as she'd given her evidence. And they'd all been part of the group that had abused vulnerable kids. But the three of them each had his own barrister. Oulman's, it seemed, wasn't as good at his job.

"Bastards," Zoe hissed. Mo leaned forward, his hands clasped on the chair in front. The briefing room was full, over twenty people in here. Normal activity had been suspended to await the outcome of the trial they'd all worked so hard to bring about.

Lesley turned towards them. She wore one of her trademark beige skirt suits and a green brooch that clashed with the jacket. She pursed her lips for a moment then slammed her hand on the table.

"We're all angry," she said. "You are. I am. But don't let it consume you. It has no bearing on the cases you're all working on right now. Alright?"

A murmur came from the front.

"I asked a question," Lesley said.

"Yes, ma'am," muttered Zoe. Twenty other voices followed suit.

"Those men," Lesley waved a finger at the screen, "will have committed other crimes. They'll have hurt other children. They'll have left evidence. We will take them down eventually. But we do it by the book. We gather evidence, we build a case." She sheeshed out a harsh breath. "But for now, focus on your jobs. Let me deal with this."

Zoe leaned back, her chest heavy. Frustration, anger, fear maybe. Fear for the kids those men would prey on now they'd won their freedom. Suspended sentences, both of them. For money laundering. The irony that they'd been convicted by the evidence she'd uncovered wasn't lost on her. But Jory Shand and Howard Petersen belonged in jail. Cowering in the nonces' wing of a high security facility, as terrified as those kids had been.

Mo grabbed Zoe's arm and nodded at the TV. The bastard's solicitor had been replaced by another, more familiar figure. Detective Superintendent David Randle. Head of Force CID.

"Turn it up, ma'am," someone called. "The Super's on."

Lesley grabbed the remote. Zoe watched, her fists clenched.

"Disappointed we weren't able to build a stronger case," Randle said. "And gratified that one of the defendants has been sent down. My colleagues in West Midlands Police worked hard on this case. I'd like to salute their hard work."

Zoe stared at the tight-faced man on the screen, barely able to recognise the David Randle she knew. He was linked to those three men, she was sure of it. She just hadn't been able to prove it. And Lesley Clarke was a stickler for building a watertight case. If she'd been in charge on the Canary case, there would have been three jail terms. More.

"Right." Lesley flicked the TV off. "Back to work."

Zoe approached her as the room emptied.

"Zoe."

"Ma'am."

"You'll be just as disappointed as the Super is."

"More so."

"Hmm. Tell me something, DI Finch."

"Tell you what, ma'am?"

The last of their colleagues left the room. Lesley called for them to turn off the light and the two women were plunged into a relative gloom.

"What have you learned from this?" she asked.

"From those bastards going free?" replied Zoe.

"Uh-huh."

"I've learned that the system's broken. Justice goes to the man with the most expensive legal team."

Lesley shook her head. "Nope." She bit her fingernail and spat. "What else?"

"That we needed more evidence?"

"Bingo." Lesley spat again. "We build a case, DI Finch. Watertight. Evidence, proof, thoroughness. That's how you take criminals down. Chain of evidence, proper procedure."

"Yes, ma'am."

"Good. Now bugger off and leave me to punch a wall or two."

CHAPTER THREE

ALISON STOOD at the entrance to Cadbury World, her arms loose at her side. Around her, people were leaving. Making their way to their cars. With their children.

She hugged herself, willing warmth into her body. She cast her eyes around the car park, back to the outdoor play area.

"It really is best if you go home, Mrs Osman," the female PC next to her said. "If anything changes, we'll tell you immediately. And they might come home."

"Ollie's four." How would a four-year-old find his way home without her? Even Maddy, mature for her twelve years, didn't know how to get all the way across the city to Erdington.

"There must be somewhere you haven't looked. It's a big place."

The PC gave her a tight smile. "We've locked it down. We've searched the whole building, but we won't stop until we find your children."

"Hmm." Alison's body felt hollow, like someone had

scooped out her insides. A car pulled into the car park, against all the traffic. People whose days had been cut short.

It lurched to a halt next to her. She tensed as the driver's door opened, her eyes filling.

"Where were you?"

Ian hurried to put his arms around her. She shrugged him off. "You said you'd be an hour. Where were you?"

"I'm sorry, love." He exchanged a glance with the PC. "What's happening? Have they started a search?"

"Yes, they've started a bloody search," Alison said.

"Good. Where are CID?"

"On their way," said the PC.

"Right. Who else is here?"

The PC nodded towards the car park. Three police cars sat at one edge. Two uniformed constables talked into radios next to them. "There's four more inside. Security are helping with the search."

"Where were you when they disappeared?"

Alison realised he was talking to her. She waved towards the picnic area. "Getting lunch. I turned my back for five minutes..."

He rubbed her arm. "No one's blaming you, love."

She yanked it away. "Who said they were? You should have been here!"

"Sorry. I had to..."

"*Work.* I know. You told me you'd be here at half past ten. There should have been two of us with them."

His body dipped, like she'd punched him in the ribs. "I know. I'm sorry. Look, I'm just as worried as you are. Let me talk to the officers, work out what's going on. There are procedures..."

She shook her head. "Stop. Please. Be a dad, not a detective." She shoved her hair out of her eyes and blinked at him. "Where are they?"

He grabbed her hand and looked onto her eyes. "We'll find them, love. I promise you. We'll find them."

CHAPTER FOUR

THE OSMANS LIVED in a modern terraced house in Erdington, north of the city centre. It was miles away from Cadbury World and Zoe could imagine how hard it would have been for them to come home without their children.

Two squad cars sat outside the house, filling the narrow street. Opposite, a woman with a blue rinse stood outside, hanging onto a Yorkie on a short lead. Pretending to walk her dog, but in reality nosey-parkering.

Zoe indicated the woman with a jerk of the head as she and Mo reached the front door. "Someone for us to talk to later."

"You think she might know something?"

"Busybodies like that can tell you a lot about a family."

"I'll go see her now, if you want. Get an address."

"No. I want you with me." She walked up the narrow path to the front door, where a male PC stood, looking uneasy.

"Can you get that woman's name and address? Tell her

she'll make an important contribution to our investigation, or bollocks like that. Flatter her."

"Right, ma'am."

Zoe looked up at the front of the house. It was covered in scaffolding.

"And whatever work's going on here will need to pause. Turn any workmen away, OK?"

"Yes, ma'am."

The front door was open. Zoe gave it a gentle push.

"Hello?"

A female PC stood in the narrow hallway flanking a tiny kitchen.

"PC Bright. We must stop meeting like this."

"Good to see you, ma'am."

Trish Bright had been Family Liaison Officer on Zoe's last case, the murder of Assistant Chief Constable Bryn Jackson. She'd been stationed in a considerably bigger house.

"Where are they?"

"She's in the living room. He's upstairs, on the phone."

Zoe approached the open tread staircase and listened. Above, a man was talking indistinctly.

"We need both of them downstairs."

"Right." PC Bright headed up, her footsteps echoing in the still house.

Zoe flashed a look at Mo and took a deep breath. He gave her an encouraging nod and she pushed open the door to the living room at the back of the house.

Beyond the door was a large space, clearly extended. It made the kitchen they'd passed on the way in feel like a box room. At the back of the room, in front of wide patio doors, was a purple floral sofa. Two women huddled together on it. One had thin dark hair and eyes that were red-rimmed but dry. She wore outdoor clothes: a grey fleece and a green scarf. The other had the same pointed jawline and flat cheekbones but grey hair. The grandmother.

"Mrs Osman?" Zoe asked.

"That's me," the dark-haired woman said. She dragged the sleeve of her fleece across her face. Her mother patted her shoulder, looking into her face with concern.

Zoe wondered what it felt like to have a mum who looked at you like that.

"My name's Detective Inspector Zoe Finch. This is Detective Sergeant Mo Udin. We'd like to ask you some questions, find out what we can about Madison and Oliver."

"Maddy and Ollie," the older woman said, her eyes narrow.

Zoe kept her gaze on the daughter. "Is your husband available?"

"I'm here." A prematurely balding man with sallow skin pushed past Mo and threw himself into an armchair. He stared out at the matchbox-sized garden.

"We need to talk to the two of you alone," said Zoe. The younger woman nodded at her mother who rose from her chair, giving Zoe a look that would melt steel.

"Thank you," said Mo as she passed him.

"I'll make tea," the grandmother said.

"I'm sure PC Bright can do that," said Zoe.

"I want to be useful."

The woman clattered out of the room. Seconds later the sound of a kettle being switched on and mugs being banged together came from the kitchen.

Zoe approached the couple. "Mind if I sit?"

The woman shrugged. The man pointed at another chair.

Zoe took it and Mo stood to one side. She frowned at him and he pulled out a chair from the dining table.

Zoe leaned towards the woman. "Can I call you Alison?"

A nod.

"Thanks, Alison. Please, call me Zoe. I'm the senior investigating officer assigned to you. It's my job to find Maddy and Ollie and get them back to you as soon as possible."

Another nod. Ian shifted forwards. "Why have we got you? Why not my colleagues at Kings Norton? It's closer to Cadbury World."

"We're with Force CID. If your children have been kidnapped – and this is only an if – then it's a serious crime. And you live in a different part of the city. It's better this way."

"Kings Norton know me."

Alison's head was lowered, her eyes closed. Zoe shifted a little closer to her.

"Can you tell me what happened at Cadbury World, please?"

"She's already told them," said Ian.

"Alison?"

Zoe knew that Mo would be watching Ian while she focused on Alison. In possible abduction cases, the obvious suspects were always the parents. Seeing their reactions, and the dynamics between them, would help establish their honesty. And as the dad hadn't been at Cadbury World, there was no issue with cross-contamination of witness statements. They could speak to the couple separately later on, get background. See if it matched.

Alison clutched her hands in her lap. Next to her on the settee was a box of tissues. Crumpled balls of white paper lay on the carpet at her feet, along with a half-empty cup of tea. Trish Bright's work no doubt.

"What do you want to know?" Alison's voice was thin and breathy.

"Tell me what happened from the last point you were with Maddy and Ollie."

She was using the children's names deliberately. She had to build a rapport with this woman. Alison needed to believe Zoe was on her side.

"They were arguing. Maddy took Ollie's Curly Wurly. Or it was the other way around. I'm not sure." She looked up, her eyes wet. "I should remember."

"You're in shock, it's OK. Go on."

"I thought if I got them something to eat that wasn't chocolate, it might calm them down. There was a hot dog stand. An Australian guy... sorry. You don't need to know that."

Mo would be taking notes. The guy on the hot dog stand would be questioned, along with anyone else who'd been near the family.

"I knew they probably wouldn't eat it but I bought it anyway. A hot dog for Ollie and a sandwich for Maddy. She said she didn't like tuna but I could have it if..." Alison's hands twisted together. The skin on the knuckles was raw. "I left it there. The food. They might be hungry."

Zoe leaned in. "Don't worry about the food, Alison. So you went to the hot dog stand and...?"

"I paid for the food. A coffee for me too. Proper barista coffee, it took a while. Oh God. I shouldn't have ordered the coffee."

"It's not your fault, love."

Alison shot her husband a look of confusion. Zoe watched her, waiting.

"I headed back to the table and they weren't there." She took a shaky breath. "I thought they'd gone to the play area. Ollie was chasing some ants. But I couldn't..."

She looked up, her bottom lip caught between her teeth. "I need to go back. They could still be there."

"We've got officers and security searching the attraction, and the factory. If Ollie and Maddy are there, we'll find them."

"I want to do something. I feel so useless."

The grey-haired woman slid past Zoe and placed two mugs on the coffee table. She handed one to Alison and took one herself. Ian shifted in his seat but said nothing. Zoe moved back in her chair to make space, but the woman lowered herself to the floor next to Alison and placed a hand on her daughter's knee.

"I'm her mum," she said. "I live nearby. I came straight round as soon as I heard."

"That's good," Zoe said. "Can I ask your name?"

"Barbara Wilson. I'm a widow."

"Have you thought to ask what the kids were wearing?" said Ian. "Are you going to do an appeal?"

Zoe scraped her palm with a fingernail. "Ollie was wearing a blue coat and Maddy had a purple hoody and blue jeans. We've been given a physical description."

"No," said Alison. "He took the coat off. He was wearing..." Her face clouded over. "A red hoody. With dinosaurs."

"Thanks," said Zoe.

"What about the appeal?" said Ian. "There were a lot of people there."

"It's an option. But we need to know what we're dealing

with first. Sometimes a TV appeal can do more harm than good."

"Bollocks," he replied.

Barbara hissed under her breath. Alison stiffened.

Zoe focused on Alison. "Are there any friends or family who might have been there, who Maddy and Ollie might have recognised and gone to?"

"No," said Alison. "There's just Mum. No other family."

"What about friends?"

"My mums' group are all working today. Or we'd have gone together."

"It was a family day out," said Ian, his voice low.

Alison jerked her head up. "Without you."

"I'm sorry. Christ, love, how many times do you need me to say it?"

"Ian," Zoe said. "I'm sorry to ask you this, but we have to consider it. You're a DS. There might be someone with a grudge against you." She flicked her gaze to Alison. "I don't expect you to remember right now, but make sure you tell us anything that could be relevant."

He shook his head. "I don't deal with the kind of things you do. Burglaries are my staple diet. Car crime."

"I'll need both of you to think hard. Tell us if you think of anything, doesn't matter how trivial. We'll keep in close touch with you, so you know what's happening. But meantime, we'll be heading back to Cadbury World to find out what we can there. We'll speak to any witnesses."

"I'll come." Alison stood up.

"No, sweetheart." Barbara grabbed her hand. "You're in no state."

"I can't just sit here."

"You're not just sitting here," said Zoe. "It's important

that you're at home. When Maddy and Ollie are found, this is where they'll be brought. You'll be here to welcome them."

Alison slumped into the sofa. She shifted her weight onto her hands then threw her head back to stare up at the ceiling. "Find them."

"We will. If you think of anything that might be important, anyone who they might have gone to or who might want to hurt either of you, you tell PC Bright. Straight away. She's got my mobile."

Alison wiped her face with her sleeve. Barbara had shifted onto the sofa and had an arm around her daughter. Ian stared at the two of them, his face blank.

CHAPTER FIVE

"He wasn't happy," said Mo.

Zoe leaned back in her car seat, watching the male PC talking to the old woman. "His kids have disappeared."

"You know what I mean. The atmosphere in that room was so thick you could eat it."

"Yeah. Not a happy family. Still, I don't think it's suspicious." She started the ignition.

"Certainly not her. Him I'm not so sure about."

"He's a DS."

"Yeah." Mo held onto his door handle as Zoe sped around a traffic island, heading into the city centre. "Take it easy."

"I want to get back there before the witnesses have buggered off."

"Uniform will have their details."

"Still." She pressed the accelerator and her Mini sped through traffic lights.

"You know anything about him?" Mo asked. "Ever worked with him?"

"Nope. We need to find out what we can about what he's working on."

"Kings Norton. Maybe Carl Whaley can help."

"Let's keep Carl Whaley out of this."

DI Whaley had been part of their team for the Jackson case. She'd worked out that he'd been an undercover officer from Professional Standards, spying on their bosses.

"Fair enough," said Mo. "I'll call Connie."

"Put it on speaker."

Zoe passed two vans as the call connected. One of the vans swerved into her path as she passed, narrowly avoiding it. "Numpty," she muttered under her breath.

"Sarge?" Connie sounded out of breath.

"Everything alright, Connie?" Zoe asked.

"Boss. Yeah. Sorry, I was talking to Forensics."

"What have they got?"

"Nothing. They've got the boy's jacket, nothing from the girl. Nothing useful on the jacket so far but they'll send it off for analysis."

"What about the scene?"

"Still being searched. No sign of anything left behind."

"Damn. We're heading over there now. See if we can get to some witnesses. There'll be CCTV, I'll get it sent to you."

"Already got it."

"Already?"

"The security boss at Cadbury World is sharper than most. I'll tell you if I spot anything helpful."

"Thanks Connie. How much of it is there?"

"Just two cameras on the play area. One on the route to it from the front of the building."

"OK. You go through that now," said Mo. "Where's Rhodri?"

"Right here, sarge."

The two DCs were on speakerphone too. Maybe they should do all briefings like this, thought Zoe.

"Rhod," she said. "You help Connie with the CCTV. Take a camera each, then swap. Fresh eyes. And I want you to find out what you can about DS Ian Osman. He works out of Kings Norton."

"I've got a mate works there," said Rhodri.

"That's good," said Zoe. "But go easy. Don't make it too obvious we're checking up on him. See what you can find about anyone who might bear Osman a grudge. Old cases, unusual sentencing, people recently released. That kind of thing."

"Don't worry, boss. I'll be subtle."

Zoe exchanged a look with Mo. DC Rhodri Hughes was many things, but subtle was not one of them. But she had to trust him. "Thanks, Rhodri."

"Boss," said Connie, her voice shaky. "Do you think they might just have wandered off?"

"I hope so," said Zoe. "It's a big place. But we've got to be prepared for the worst."

"Yeah," came the reply. "Poor things."

"You alright there Connie?" asked Mo. "I know it's not easy, this kind of case."

"I'm fine, sarge. Want to do my job."

"Good. We need you to be alert, in case there's anything on that CCTV..."

"Don't worry. You can rely on me."

"Thanks."

Mo ended the call. They were in the Queensway tunnel under the city centre, almost halfway to Cadbury World.

"OK," said Zoe. "So we've got the grudges against Ian

Osman angle. There might be someone who's got it in for Alison that she hasn't thought of."

"Trish Bright can jog her memory."

"Yeah. And Ian might know more than he's telling us."

"He might have the kids, you mean."

Her stomach clenched. "God, I hope not. He's a copper. But he was mighty pissed off about something."

"Not the happiest of marriages."

"Let's hope that was the only thing bugging him."

"And that Rhodri gives us something useful."

She pulled out of the tunnel, momentarily blinded by the low sun. "Even if we find out he's squeaky clean, never pissed anyone off in his life, dotes on his family. That's something."

"Chances of that?" said Mo.

"Hmm." Ian Osman was a serving DS. There'd be plenty of people pissed off with him. "There's that old lady too. And the neighbours. We'll get Uniform knocking on doors, finding out what they can."

"They were miles away when it happened," said Mo.

"If you were going to abduct your neighbour's kids, wouldn't it be safer to do it away from home?"

"You're making my blood run cold."

"Sorry. Just considering possibilities."

Mo leaned back in his seat as Zoe accelerated through the lights at the inner ring road.

"I know," he replied. "Let's hope it turns out to be nothing."

"That those kids wandered off and got lost."

"That the worst that happened to them is eating too much chocolate."

"Yeah."

Zoe squeezed the steering wheel. She didn't need Mo to

tell her that neither of them really thought that was going to happen. It had been three hours now. If those kids had turned up, they'd have had a call.

They drove along the Bristol Road, traffic bunching up at the lights near the university. The two of them stared ahead, both absorbed in their thoughts.

"Nearly there," said Mo.

Zoe nodded, her skin bristling. She pictured Alison Osman's eyes, sunken into her face. If the woman knew Zoe had never been SIO before...

She shook herself out. "Who's the senior officer at the scene? Who's coordinating the search?"

"You really want to know?"

"Helps if it's someone we've worked with before."

"Oh, you know him alright."

She flicked him a frown. "Go on then."

"You're not going to like this," Mo replied.

CHAPTER SIX

ZOE SIGHED as she got out of the car to see a familiar figure approaching. "Jim."

"DI Finch. How are you?"

"Inspector McManus." Zoe slammed her car door and followed the uniformed officer towards the Cadbury World building. It was dark now, the lights of the foyer shining over the car park. "Mo tells me you're coordinating the search."

"I can hand over to you if you like, now you're SIO."

"It's fine. Have your guys pulled together a list of witnesses?"

"Of course we have, Zoe. This is what we Uniform plods do."

Mo sucked in a breath behind them. The officer in charge at the scene was Inspector Jim McManus, whom Zoe certainly did know. He was her son Nicholas's father.

They reached the building and Jim stood back to let Zoe pass.

"Thanks."

Jim nodded then let the door swing back for Mo to catch behind them. Mo made a spluttering sound.

"Be nice, Jim," Zoe said. "I know you don't like working with me..."

"I never said that."

"Good. Well let's keep things professional."

"Never anything but."

She surveyed the space at the entrance to the attraction. Normally it would be full of visitors. Stopping for photos, munching on free chocolate, queueing for tickets. Today it held half a dozen police officers and a row of temporary tables.

She went to the first table. A constable sat behind it, his face pimply. She gave him a smile.

"Constable, is this the list of witnesses?"

"Er, yeah." He looked up at Jim, his Adam's apple bobbing.

"Good," said Zoe.

"We've kept a few of them here," said Jim. "There's a woman who spoke to Alison when she was looking for the kids."

"Maddy and Ollie," interrupted Zoe. "They have names."

His eyes narrowed. "I know that. There's also the guy in the hot dog stand, who she was talking to when she lost sight of them. And a security guard, who says he saw her leave the play area with her children."

"I'll speak to him first," said Zoe.

"Over here."

Jim ushered her towards a burly man in a tight-fitting uniform. At about six foot four, he was trying his best not to look as huge as his body dictated.

Zoe turned to Mo. "Can you take the hot dog guy?"

"Sure, boss."

She raised her eyebrows. She and Mo were old friends and she preferred him to call her Zo. But he was never doing that in front of Jim.

The security guard stood up from his perch on a slender purple bench that didn't look strong enough to take his bulk. It shifted as his weight left it.

"I'm DI Finch. You've told my colleagues you saw the children leave the play area."

"Yes. Two kids, and a woman. The ones in the photo."

"When was this?"

"About twelve fifteen. I'd just switched places with Sam. Came from my stint on the front door." He gestured the way they'd come in.

"And you saw them enter the play area?"

"No. I saw them leave."

"All three of them."

"Yes."

"There are lots of families that come through here. How d'you know it was them?"

"Your officer showed me a photo. I've got a good memory for faces, like."

"Are you sure you saw them leave? Not come in?"

"Yeah. I saw them leave."

"Where are the nearest toilets? Could they have come out and gone in again?"

He shrugged. "There's a couple in the play area, for kiddies. Some bigger ones in here, by reception."

"Right." If Alison had left with the kids, she must have gone back to the outdoor area. Unless she was lying.

"Did you see her after they disappeared?"

"No. Sorry."

"There would have been a woman panicking because her kids had disappeared. You didn't see?"

"Sorry, didn't see nothing. There was some kids climbing the wall down the side of the factory, I was dealing with them I reckon."

"You reckon."

"I'm not going to tell you I'm sure of something if I'm not. But it makes sense that's when it happened. I were looking the other way, over the railings. Can show you if you want."

"No need. Have we got your contact details?"

"We have," muttered Jim, still hovering next to her.

"Good. Here's my card. Call me if you remember anything else, or if one of your colleagues does. Day or night."

The guard pocketed her card and gave her a nod, scratching his nose. A woman in a grey jacket and purple shirt bundled him off, talking to him as they walked away.

"Who's she?" asked Zoe.

"Duty manager," said Jim.

"I want to speak to her too."

"She's busy helping with the search effort right now. But yes, her details are on the list."

Officers were coming and going behind them, heading for those tables. Reporting back from the search.

"Who's searching?" Zoe asked.

"Twelve of ours, six security staff. They've got plans of the building and are sweeping it so the teams converge on each other. The kids can't slip away, if they're in here."

"If they're in here. Is this place operational these days, or just a museum?"

Zoe had grown up within the smell of the Cadbury factory. You could tell by sticking your nose out of the window whether they were roasting, grinding or pressing out. But she'd all but forgotten the place existed since she'd last brought Nicholas ten years ago.

"Still operational," Jim said. "They've paused work. Health and Safety."

"How easy would it be for the kids to get into the factory?"

"The manager says nigh-on impossible. They don't want tourists wandering in there, you can't get in without a swipe pass."

"If you're small, you might be able to slip past someone."

"There is that.'

"There is. Thanks Jim. I can handle it from here."

He gave her a *you'll change your tune* look but withdrew, heading towards a uniformed sergeant who'd come from the direction of the cafe. A place like this would have a million and one hiding places. And kids could find spots that no adult would even consider. She had to hope they'd run off in search of treats and that now they were hiding out, scared.

The duty manager was with Mo and the hot dog guy. Her purple shirt hung out the top of her skirt and her hair was escaping its ponytail.

"Hello," said Zoe. "I'm DI Finch. Senior Investigating Officer. You're the manager here?"

"Nisha Grange. Just the duty manager. The manager's on his way."

"Do you have a standard procedure for this? You must have had kids go missing before."

"We do. They tend to go back to the spots where they've been given freebies, or to the rides. We check those first, then work outwards. This time, we've started a sweep of the factory floor."

"You think they could have got in there?"

Nisha blushed. "We make it very hard for the public to gain access. But you can't be too sure."

"No." Zoe turned to Mo. "How's it going?"

"Mr Jakes says he served Alison Osman, but never saw her kids. Didn't see anything."

"Right. Have you spoken to the other witness?"

"Not yet."

"Come on."

Zoe nodded thanks to the manager and approached a woman standing to one side, a young boy in her arms. Tear tracks ran down her face.

Zoe flashed her warrant card. "Hi. Thanks for staying. I'm DI Finch, this is DS Uddin. I hear you saw Alison Osman, when she was looking for her kids?"

The woman gave her son a light kiss on the top of the head and nodded. "I minded her stuff, while she was looking. I didn't see them, though."

"You didn't see Maddy or Ollie?"

"Ollie." Another kiss to the head. "My boy's called Ollie too." She paled. "Sorry."

"It's OK. You sure you didn't see the kids? Didn't see them talking to anybody?"

"Sorry. First I knew about them was when they'd gone."

"What was Alison doing?"

"She'd gone off to get food. I saw her chatting to the guy on the stall. I'd been there just before, he was flirting with me. I wondered if... sorry. Yeah. She came back and she almost dropped her stuff. She ran around the playground a couple of times then she came up to me, asked me if I'd seen her kids."

"Then what?"

"I told her I hadn't, then said I'd watch her stuff while she looked for them. She said something about ants. Her son had been following them or something. We had some on our table, I'd shoved them all off."

"So you watched her things, and then what?"

"She came back. She was a state. Well, you would be." She tightened her grip on her son. "Then she ran round again. I said they might be in the toilets. There was a man, he offered to go and look in the main building while she looked in the loos. Pretty much the whole place was watching by then. People started calling their kids back, they looked worried."

"Did Alison go to the main building looking for her kids?" Mo asked. Zoe thought of the security guard who'd seen her heading that way.

"No. She stayed put. That's what you do, isn't it? You stay where they last saw you. Bloody pain, there was one time my eldest wandered off at Alton Towers and if I'd just walked round the corner..."

"Thanks," said Zoe. "Make sure you get in touch with us if you think of anything else. And we'll need your contact details."

"I gave them to the good-looking chap over there." The woman pointed at Jim. Zoe sensed Mo's surprise.

"Thanks. Don't forget, tell us if anything comes to mind." Zoe pressed her card into the woman's hand.

Jim was behind her again. "Sergeant Taylor can give you the list of all the witnesses. There were a lot of people there."

"Most of them won't have seen anything. But we'll need your help with the lower priority ones."

"Unless the search finds them."

"Yeah." She checked her watch. Six hours. A long time to hide in a factory. "I'm not holding out much hope."

Her phone buzzed. She raised a hand to keep Jim from speaking and answered it. Lesley.

"Ma'am."

"You left your team without leadership, DI Finch."

"Mo and I wanted to interview the witnesses while events are still fresh in their minds."

"I've had DC Hughes in here asking for permission to go digging into cases at Kings Norton nick. What have you told him to do?"

Zoe blew out a breath. "Sorry. We'll come back."

"Those kids'll turn up somewhere at Cadbury World, I'm sure of it. You don't want to go pissing off Ian Osman's senior officers because of some hunch you have."

"Yes, ma'am. Which is why we came here."

"I thought you were questioning witnesses."

"That too."

"Get back here. We can't have your team running around the place willy nilly, you know. You need to give them direction."

"We won't be long."

Jim's eyes sparkled as she ended the call. He would be enjoying her dressing down, the reminder that he was a more experienced Inspector.

"Don't," she said, making for the doors.

He shrugged. "Not the best start to your DI career, is it?"

"None of your business."

"I bet you're mighty pissed off about Shand and Petersen."

"Understatement of the century."

"Is that case going to come back and bite you? Is my son safe?"

She stopped walking.

"Nicholas is perfectly safe. Leave it, Jim. Please."

"Give him my love."

"Hmm."

CHAPTER SEVEN

"Sorry, folks."

"What for, boss?" asked Rhodri.

Zoe slung her bag on the desk. "Leaving you alone. I hear you had to go to DCI Clarke for help."

"We were fine," said Connie. Rhodri rubbed the back of his neck.

"Next time, call me, huh?" Zoe said. "I'm here to help."

"You were busy interviewing witnesses, boss," said Rhodri.

"Not too busy," said Mo. "Not if it's urgent." He gave Rhodri a look. Rhodri tugged at his collar. "Sorry, sarge."

"Right," said Zoe. She perched on her desk. The inner office was officially hers now that she was a permanent DI, but she still didn't want to use it. In the Jackson case they'd filled it with boxes of paperwork. More use to have a secure storage space than for her to hide behind a closed door. "What's been happening?"

"I got onto my mate at Kings Norton," said Rhodri.

"Subtly, I hope," said Mo. He sat at his desk and plugged his phone in to charge.

"Yes, guv. Height of discretion."

"Good. What did you get?"

"Not much," said Rhodri. "Keeps himself to himself pretty much. Not got a lot of mates, comes in, does the job, goes home."

"That's not the impression I got from his wife," said Zoe. "There was definitely tension about his hours."

"Maybe he does a lot of overtime."

"Hmm. I think we need to ask him. I'm reluctant to push any more buttons at Kings Norton until we know we've something to go on."

"Right, boss."

"Anything else? Any cases that turned nasty? Old grudges?"

"He used to work in Organised Crime."

"That's more like it. When?"

"Until three years ago, when he married Alison."

"Maybe he wanted something a bit more steady, with the kids and that," said Connie.

"He married Alison three years ago?" asked Mo. "Maddy's twelve."

"Nine," said Rhodri.

"Sorry, Rhod?"

"She'd have been nine. The girl."

"Maddy," said Zoe. "Maddy and Ollie. Those kids have got names. Don't you forget it. But it's not unusual for parents to get married after the kids come along."

"Still," said Mo. "Worth checking. They might not be his."

Connie brushed her cheek.

"You alright, Connie?" said Zoe.

"Just want to get them back. Can't be easy on the mum."

"Or the dad," said Mo.

"Let's see about that," said Zoe. "We have to consider the possibility that he's responsible."

"How so?" asked Rhodri.

Zoe shifted position. It was awkward perching like this, but she was here now. And she didn't want to hide behind the desk. "He was supposed to meet her at Cadbury World. Family day out. He didn't show up, and then the kids go missing."

"Maddy and Ollie," whispered Connie.

"Yes. Do we know if he showed up eventually?"

"Yes," said Mo. "Uniform told me he got there about half an hour after they did."

"Half an hour?"

"Yeah." He frowned. "Works at Kings Norton station which is, I guess, ten minutes away from Bournville at most."

"So how come it took him so long to get there?"

"Maybe he didn't know," said Connie.

"It's possible."

"She was in such a state she didn't call him?" said Mo.

"Difficult to say what people'll do in a situation like that. And chances are she was already pissed off with him."

"Yeah, but not so pissed off she wouldn't call him after what happened."

"No." Zoe tapped her front teeth with a pen. "We need to find out when he knew the kids were missing and why it took him so long to get there."

"You want me to get onto that, boss?" asked Rhodri.

Zoe smiled at him. "Initiative. I like it. No, we can ask him next time we're at the house. I'm going to head back there. Let's not go sniffing around Kings Norton unless we really have to. Not yet, at least."

"Right. You want me to keep checking his old cases?"

"Yes. And both their social media profiles. See if there's anything unusual, anyone singling them out. Trolling.

"What's her job, boss?" asked Connie.

"She works at a school in Erdington. Teaching assistant."

"We'll need to talk to them too," said Mo. "Find out if there's anyone who might have a grudge. Parents."

"That's a depressing thought," said Connie.

"Depressing, but realistic," said Zoe.

"It's really possible that a parent would be so annoyed with their kid's teaching assistant that they'd do this?"

"It's a long shot, I know. But we have to consider every possibility. But we can't do that till tomorrow now. Mo, can you head back over there, keep an eye on things? I want to know as soon as they find anything useful. And call Adi Hanson. I want to know what's going on with Forensics.

"You want them to go over the spot where the kids were last seen?"

"I don't know if that'll do us much good. But if they find anything belonging to them, it'll be worth examining."

"Right, boss." Mo slung his coat over his shoulders and unplugged his phone.

"Right," said Zoe. "How's it going with the CCTV, Connie?"

"Dead end. There's footage of Alison sitting at a picnic table with Maddy and Ollie. Not much of it, either. The camera feed switches between the two positions and they're only visible in one."

"They didn't have a continuous recording from either of them?"

"Seems not."

"They have thousands of people going in there every day. A ton of kids. Surely their CCTV is better than that. Connie, can you get onto Security at Cadbury World. Find out if there's anything else they can give us. Maybe they stored the continuous feed somewhere else."

"On it." Connie grabbed her phone.

"Right," said Zoe. "So that's Mo at Cadbury World, Rhod looking into the parents, and Connie on CCTV. Surely Lesley can't complain now."

"What can't I complain about?"

Zoe turned to see Lesley standing in the open doorway.

"You made me jump, ma'am."

Lesley smiled. "Glad to see you've got your team in hand. Where are we?"

"Mo's gone back to Bournville, check on the search. Connie's seeing what else she can get from the CCTV and Rhodri's looking into the parents, see if there's anyone might bear a grudge against them."

"Good. What about the children themselves?"

"What about them?"

"What do we know about them? Any problems at school? We can't rule out an adult they came into contact with outside the home."

"We're still hoping they're hiding in the factory, ma'am."

Lesley checked her watch. "Seven hours, they've been gone. I doubt that, don't you?"

Zoe's heart slowly dropped in her chest. "I've been trying not to think about it."

"I can imagine. It's getting late."

"We can't afford to hang around."

"You had the overtime authorised?"

"Shit. Sorry, ma'am."

Lesley leaned on the doorframe. "Don't forget, next time. I know we can't waste time, that we have to find these kids quickly, But you can't afford to be slapdash."

"I'll do the paperwork now."

"It's done."

"Sorry?"

"I had it done it for you."

"Thank you. I appreci—"

"Shush. No need to thank me. Just find those bloody kids."

CHAPTER EIGHT

"SORRY TO BOTHER YOU AGAIN." Zoe smiled at Alison as the woman let her in the front door. "Where's PC Bright?"

"Right here, ma'am." Trish was in the kitchen, stirring soup in a pan. "I thought they could do with some food."

"I'm not hungry," said Alison.

"You don't have to eat it," said Trish. "But it's here if you change your mind."

"Have you got news?" Alison asked. Her complexion was greyer than it had been earlier. She'd changed into a cardigan whose sleeve had been chewed.

"Not at the moment, sorry. I came back to talk to you, to find out anything else that might be relevant. The more we know about your family, the easier it'll be to find Maddy and Ollie."

Alison nodded, her eyes lowered. "Come through."

The living room at the back of the house was dim, only one table lamp switched on. The grandmother had left and Ian wasn't here.

"Where's your husband?"

"He had to go out."

"Where to?"

"I think he was going back to Cadbury World."

"It's best for you both to stay here."

"I know." Alison shrugged, a shrug that spoke of many conversations in which Ian hadn't listened to her.

Zoe gave her a smile. "It's helpful for us to be able to chat alone. Has your mum gone home?"

"She had to feed her dog. She'll be back soon."

"Right." They didn't have much time. "Mind if we sit?"

Alison raised a limp hand in the direction of the settee and Zoe took a seat. Alison sat opposite her, in the chair Ian had used earlier. She was little more than a silhouette against the table lamp.

"You work as a teaching assistant, is that right?"

"Yes. The school's just half a mile away. Maddy's in her last year there, Ollie just started."

"Have you worked there long?"

"Five years. Five-and-a-half. I like it."

"Have there been any run-ins, with other staff or with parents? Anyone you think might bear a grudge against you?"

"You think one of the parents might have taken Maddy and Ollie?"

"Right now, we're still hoping they're hiding at Bournville. But I need to explore every possibility."

Alison wiped her face with the cardigan sleeve. She sniffed. "I can't think of anyone. There was a boy in my class who was suspended for two days last month. His mum got pretty het up. But she seems OK now."

"Can you give me her name?"

"It's confidential. I can't just—"

"I'm sure the school won't mind. I'll be speaking to them first thing. Unless we find your children before then."

"OK. Ruth Keele."

"Is that the child, or the mum?"

"Child. I'm not sure of the mum's name. We just call them Mum."

"I know." Zoe remembered how odd that had felt when Nicholas was at primary school. "That's the only thing you can think of? No problems with management? No members of staff you've fallen out with?"

"No. Sorry."

"What about Ian? How much d'you know about his work?"

"Not as much as you, I imagine."

"Does he work long hours?"

A nod. "His job's hard. Stressful. They put him under a lot of pressure."

"Has he been working long hours lately?"

"There's been a case, he won't say much about it. But it's made him irritable. I can't wait till it's over."

Zoe made a mental note to find out what cases Ian was currently assigned to.

"You and Ian have been married for three years, is that right?"

"Three years August just gone." A flicker of a smile crossed Alison's lips. "We got married in Yorkshire, where Ian's family live. Maddy was bridesmaid."

"She must have been a beautiful bridesmaid."

Alison's eyes filled with tears. "She was." She looked Zoe in the eye for the first time. "I'm scared for her. She'll think she has to look after Ollie. But what if someone's hurting her?"

"This is hard, I know. And I'm not going to lie to you. Maddy might just be hiding with Ollie, they might be lost. But if someone has taken them, we'll do everything we can to find them. As quickly as we can."

"Thank you." It was barely more than a whisper. "I was married before."

"Before Ian?"

"Yes. Benedict."

"You divorced."

Alison shook her head, as if horrified at the suggestion. "He died."

"I'm sorry to hear that. Was this when the children were young?"

"Maddy was seven. Ollie was... I was pregnant. It was a climbing accident."

"Your first husband was a rock climber?"

"Mountaineer. Went all over the world. It scared me, not knowing if he'd come back each time. And then he didn't."

"What was his full name?"

"Benedict Tomkin."

Zoe made a note of the name. "Thank you. So you must have met Ian quite soon after he died."

Alison stiffened. "Yes."

"That must have made it easier. Finding a man who would be a father to your children."

"Yes."

"Hello again."

Zoe turned to see Barbara hurrying in. She wore a purple anorak and cold air wafted off her. Trish followed behind, trying to slow her down.

"Are you bothering my daughter?"

"No, Mrs Wilson. I'm just trying to learn what I can

about the family, it might help us find Ollie and Maddy."

"You need to be out there, looking for them. Getting up a search party."

"We are. There's a search happening at the factory right now."

"You can leave Alison alone now. She needs to sleep."

It was nine pm. Alison would be shattered. Zoe looked at her. "Is there anything else you can tell me? Anything that might be relevant?"

Alison shook her head. She glanced at her mum. She'd drawn into herself, as if trying to disappear.

Zoe stood up. "Thanks for talking to me. I want you to know that my team are working on this right now. They'll do everything they can to find Maddy and Ollie. I know them – they won't stop till you get them back."

Alison nodded and folded her arms around herself. In the hours since Zoe had last seen her, she seemed to have become thinner. Her limp hair hung in front of her face, tangled in places.

"I'll show you out," said Barbara.

"No need," replied Zoe. She approached the older woman. "I'd be grateful if we could talk in the morning, at your home."

"I don't see why that's necessary."

"I need to know everything I can about the children, about the people they're in contact with. You might be able to remember something Alison doesn't."

"Very well. I don't think it'll do you much good though. This isn't that kind of family."

"Thank you."

Sometimes it was so hard being polite to people like Barbara Wilson. Zoe glanced back at Alison, staring out of the blank rear window. She made for the front of the house, where Trish was clattering around in the kitchen.

"What's the atmosphere like, when I'm not here?" asked Zoe.

"Like you'd expect," said Trish. "Tense."

"When did Ian leave?"

Trish grabbed her notebook. "Eight twenty-five."

With the traffic at this hour, he'd be at Cadbury World by now.

"You'll let me know if anything unusual happens, won't you?"

"'Course, ma'am."

"Arguments, any of them acting odd, hiding anything. People coming and going. Just keep a note of their movements."

"There's something I should tell you, ma'am."

"Yes?"

"I used to know Ian Osman. Worked with him in Coventry six years ago."

So Ian Osman was in the habit of moving departments.

"I didn't think you were old enough to be on the force six years ago."

"I'm twenty-nine, ma'am."

"I'm sorry. That came out wrong. I didn't mean to—"

"It's alright. I look young. I know."

"You want me to get another FLO assigned?"

"No. I don't think he remembers me. Not really. I was a PC, he was a new DC. He pretty much ignored me."

"Right. Well, if you feel uncomfortable about any of this, I'd rather have you moved to another job."

"It'll be fine." Trish slapped her pocket. "I'll keep an eye on them for you."

CHAPTER NINE

"WELL, THAT WASN'T EASY." Connie pushed away from her desk and leaned back, tired. The office was quiet, the only sound Rhodri tapping his mouse and occasionally grunting. Outside, the corridors were empty.

"You alright, Con?"

"Don't call me that. Please."

"Sorry." Rhodri flashed her a grin. He could be exasperating, but he meant well. "What's up?"

"Ta. Had to work through four different people, two of them at home, to get anywhere with this CCTV."

"But you got somewhere, right?"

"It'll be with us tomorrow. Not bloody soon enough."

"Yeah." Rhodri looked back at his screen and rubbed his eyes.

"This case gives me the willies," Connie said.

"First missing child case?"

"Yeah. Horrible, innit?"

"Too right. We just need to get our heads down and do what the boss says."

"You're right. How's it going with the social media stuff? Need a hand?"

He dragged a hand through his hair. "Yes please. You're better at this stuff than me."

She consider contradicting him but stopped herself. He was right. And she shouldn't talk herself down. Her mum had drummed that into her since she'd started at secondary school and made out she was some sort of thicko.

"Go on then." She pushed her chair over to his desk. He had Facebook up, the account of a woman called Barbara Wilson. "Who's that?"

"Alison's mum. You'd hate her."

"That's a bit unfair."

"You see the stuff she shares on here, and you'd take that back. The woman's a dinosaur."

Connie leaned in. Rhodri was right. Barbara Wilson was sharing posts from far-right pages. The kind of pages that hid their racism behind gung-ho patriotism. She grimaced.

"Yeah," she said. "Still, doesn't make her a suspect."

"No."

"Does her daughter share her politics?"

"Not as far as I can tell. Her feed's all stories about the kids, funny cat memes, books she's reading. Dull as hell."

"What about him?"

"I haven't managed to get into his yet. He's actually bothered to configure his security settings."

"Want me to have a go?"

"Yeah. You do that, and I'll check Instagram. There's a couple of Facebook posts that seem to have come from there."

"Right," said Connie. "Look at the people she's friends with, the people who follow her. See if any of them have posted anything dodgy. Anything having a go at her, or about Maddy and Ollie."

Rhodri turned to her. "It makes you a better copper, you know."

"Hmm?" She slid back to her desk and pulled up Facebook. "What does?"

"You care. I know it makes it harder, but it means you'll work harder. Like the boss."

Connie nodded. It didn't feel any better, being so anxious about those poor kiddies. She'd run away from home once herself, when she was eleven. Mum had been ragging her about her hair and her little brother Jaf had been pissing her off. She'd made it two miles and turned back home. She remembered the increasing emptiness as she got further away from home, the warmth she'd felt when she'd pushed through the front door and found them waiting for her. No raised voices, no recriminations. Just a hug from her mum that felt like it would never stop.

"Ouch," she said. "He isn't exactly tactful."

"You on Ian's feed?"

"Yup. He's got it in for one of his colleagues. A DI. He doesn't say his name, just 'the DI'. Wonder who it is."

"What's he say about him?"

"He's an imposter, according to Ian. Doesn't belong in the team, doesn't pull his weight. Pisses everyone off by disappearing when he should be working on cases."

"Someone new to the station?"

"That imposter comment would make you think that."

"I'll check if anyone new has started there."

"At DI level. Why does he put all this on Facebook? Surely he's got mates in the force who know who he's talking about?"

"You don't think this DI could have it in for him?" Rhodri was peering into his screen, looking through police records. "Damn."

"What?"

"I need HR files to find out about transfers. No way I can get that without the boss."

"So call her."

"It's alright. I'll ring Arjun."

"Who's Arjun?"

"My mate at Kings Norton. He's in Uniform but he'll know if there's a new DI."

"Right. There's more here. About Alison."

"Go on."

"Nothing much," she said. "Snidey comments, stuff about her not understanding him."

"Maybe she doesn't."

"He's commented on a friend's post about having a wife who understands what it's like to be on the force. Imagining what it would be like."

"Ouch."

"Yeah. Ugh, and there's an argument with some guy about police brutality."

"A troll?"

"Possibly. Hang on... the troll's in the US. Not a potential suspect then."

Rhodri started talking into his phone. Connie delved deeper into Ian Osman's online life.

"Damn." Rhodri slung his phone onto his desk.

"No help?"

"Voicemail." He checked the clock over the door to the DI's office. "It's half ten. No call from Cadbury World. Those kids have been snatched, Con. Haven't they?"

Connie pushed down the lump forming in her throat and continued flicking through screens, determined to help find Maddy and Ollie.

CHAPTER TEN

Zoe sat in her car on a quiet street near the city centre, peering up at a lit window. Jory Shand's bedroom window.

She shouldn't be here. If he spotted her, she'd be reported for police harassment. But she couldn't shake the frustration at his release. She didn't even know if he was up there. Maybe his wife was alone. Maybe she'd kicked him out after what he'd done. Or maybe she believed the bullshit the lawyers had peddled and thought her husband was innocent.

Zoe had to find another way to get him, and the others who'd got away. Men like Trevor Hamm, whose thugs had attacked Mo and Connie when they'd been working the Jackson murder case. Kyle Gatiss, who'd provided Shand and his sick mates with kids for them to abuse. Simon Adams, who'd broken bail and was God knew where.

Watching Shand's house like this wouldn't get her anywhere. It was paperwork that had brought her into the Canary case, and it would be paperwork that'd open it up again. Paperwork she had no legal access to, right now.

She had to either find a way of getting that access, or persuade herself to let it drop. At least for now, while she was trying to find Madison and Oliver.

Her phone rang: Mo.

"Hey."

"Hi, Zo."

She smiled, pleased he was still using the nickname despite her being his boss now. "What's up?"

"They've finished for the night at the factory. Searched every bit of Cadbury World too. They aren't here."

Her body sagged. "Yeah." It wasn't a surprise. "What's happening there now?"

"Inspector McManus has sent everyone home. There's just two PCs keeping an eye on the place. Just in case whoever took the kids comes back."

"They won't."

"Yeah."

She stared ahead, mulling over the events of the last few hours. Mo would be sitting in his car doing the same thing. Sitting together in companionable silence. They normally did this in her car, in the car park at Harborne police station where Force CID was based. Tonight they were on opposite sides of the city.

"You go home," she said. "Catriona'll be wondering where you are."

"She's on call. Had to go out. My mum's looking after the girls."

"Even more reason to get home, give your mum a break."

"Nothing else I can do?"

"Not tonight. Get some sleep. We'll start again in the morning, fresh heads and all that."

"Six am."

"Yeah."

She hung up and took a last look at the lit window. The light had gone out. Jory Shand, or maybe just his wife, was asleep. Bastard.

She turned the ignition and headed home.

CHAPTER ELEVEN

THE HOUSE WAS QUIET. Zoe went to the fridge, hoping Nicholas would have cooked and left her something. Of the two of them, he was the only one with culinary skills.

She rifled through the cans of Pepsi Max, bottles of beer and cartons of leftover takeaway. Nothing.

"Sorry, Mum." Nicholas came into the kitchen. "I was out with Jaf. His mum cooked."

"That's nice."

Jaf was Connie's younger brother and Nicholas's new boyfriend. Zoe had only met him once, but she'd used his knowledge of modern art in a previous case.

"It was. No sign of Connie though. You got her working overtime?"

"Shit." Zoe grabbed her phone. Voicemail. "Connie, it's Zoe. I don't know if you're still in the office, but this is me telling you to go home. I need you to get some rest, so we can carry on in the morning. Hope you get this."

"Oops." Nicholas opened the fridge and grabbed a bottle of beer. He handed her a can of Pepsi.

"Thanks."

"You left her there?"

"Hours ago. I had to go and interview... never mind. Hopefully her voicemail was on cos she's on the bus."

Her phone pinged. A text from Connie, who'd just got home. Zoe let out a relieved whistle. "I'm a crap boss."

"Connie thinks you're great."

"She does?"

"Sure. You just need to look after yourself better."

"Thanks, love. But it's my job to worry about you. Not the other way round."

"Yeah."

He headed out of the kitchen and upstairs, back to his room. He would be on Discord, chatting to Jaf. When the two of them weren't together, they were connected online. It was sweet, but maybe a little intense for two eighteen-year-olds.

There was a knock at the front door. She checked her watch: gone eleven. Who the hell...?

She heaved herself to the door.

"Carl?"

"We had a date."

"We what? Oh, shit. I'm sorry. But it wasn't a date."

He raised his eyebrows. "What happened? Lost your nerve?"

DI Carl Whaley was a former colleague, an undercover officer for Professional Standards. Tonight she was planning to finally tell him what she knew about her old boss David Randle.

"No," she said. "A case."

"Must be a big one."

"Come in. I'll make you a coffee. But I'm not talking about Randle, not with Nicholas upstairs."

He mock-saluted and followed her into the house. "Nice place."

She turned to him. "Yeah, right."

"It is."

"It's a shithole."

"A shithole you've brought your son up in."

"Please don't try to flatter me by making out I've got interior design skills or something. This place is home, yeah. I like living here. But that doesn't mean I can't see the damp patch on the ceiling."

"There is that." He flashed her a grin.

She flicked at his arm. "You're full of shit, you know that?"

"I do. Been told many times."

"Good. Well, sit yourself down in my beautifully appointed living room while I stick the kettle on."

She trudged into the kitchen. She was planning on getting into the office at five and needed her bed.

"You hungry?" Carl called from the living room.

Starving, she thought. "No, I'm fine."

"Shame. I would have taken you to that chippy."

She stood in the doorway, a mug in each hand. "To be honest Carl, I'd love fish and chips right now. But I'm knackered, and I've got to be up early in the morning."

"Get it. I'll drink this quickly." He picked up the mug she'd put on the coffee table. *Star Wars* this one, second choice after the *Dr Who* one she was holding.

"May the force be with you," he muttered as he sipped. "Good coffee."

"It's the only thing I know how to make." She slumped onto the settee next to him.

"You certainly do. So, what's the case?"

"Child abduction. Cadbury World."

"I thought they might give you that one."

"How d'you know?"

"I'm based at Kings Norton now, remember. Ian Osman works for me."

"So he does." She pulled her legs beneath her and turned to face him. "Tell me about him."

Carl took his time sipping his coffee. He placed it on the table and scratched his nose. "That's it. I can't."

"You can't, or you won't?"

"I can tell you what kind of man he is. Weaselly, in my opinion. One of those coppers who makes it look like he's really busy but is actually just coasting. But I can't tell you any more."

"Why not?"

He took a breath and turned to her. He surveyed her for a moment.

"What? What is it?" she snapped.

"I'm investigating him, Zoe. That's all I can tell you."

CHAPTER TWELVE

MADDY RUBBED HER EYES. She was cold, the duvet must have slipped off her bed in the night.

She sat and stretched her arms above her head. The Pokémon poster over her bed was coming loose in one corner. She reached up and smoothed it into place, pressing down on the blu-tac.

She lay back on the pillows, listening to the sounds of the house. Every morning she did this. Listening to her family, working out who was here and who'd gone out to work already. Normally it was Dad who'd gone. He was grumpy before work, and she liked to wait till he'd left.

The house was silent.

The room smelled wrong. There was a sharp smell, like...

She sat up, her heart racing.

In the corner under the window, a shape moved in the darkness. Maddy held her breath.

"Hello?"

Fear stabbed at her, making her eyes sting and her

stomach ache. She watched the movement, wishing she hadn't said anything.

The shape shifted and turned into a person.

It was OK. It was just Ollie.

"What you doing here?"

"Huh?" He crawled to her bed and looked up at her. "Mads?"

"It's OK, Ols. You must've been sleepwalking again." Maddy heaved her feet over the edge of the bed. "Come on, I'll take you back to your room."

She padded to the door, wondering where her slippers were. *Frozen* slippers, from her gran who thought she was still six. She grabbed the handle.

"Huh?"

She turned the handle again and tugged. It didn't budge. That was odd. It was a silver handle. Her room had a white doorknob.

She looked around. Everything was the same. Her pink and purple striped curtains, the Manga posters on the walls. Even the plushie she'd bought at Cadbury World the day before.

"I'm tired," said Ollie.

"Go back to sleep. Get on my bed." She pushed him onto the mattress. The bed was bigger than normal. It had the same purple spotty duvet, the same red pillows. But there was space either side of them. The mattress had grown.

She went back to the door and opened her mouth to call Mum.

"Mads? What's happening? I'm wet."

Ollie knelt on her bed, his face red. He was about to cry. His pyjamas were soaked through, the bottoms ruined.

"It's OK, Ols," she said. "Here, you can have my spare pair."

She should have called Mum but something inside her was telling her not to. That door handle, and the bigger mattress.

Her spare pyjamas lived in the drawer next to her bed. It was empty.

She pulled back against the wall and scanned the room. The clothes she'd been wearing yesterday, her favourite jeans and purple hoody, hung over the back of her yellow desk chair.

None of this made sense. Everything was the same, but different.

Ollie was crying. Maddy stroked his hair. "Shush. Here, have mine." She took off her pyjamas and helped him put them on. She slung the dirty ones to the floor. That was where the smell was coming from.

Hurrying to her desk, she pulled on her clothes, worried someone might come in. She didn't know what to expect on the other side of that door, that was hers and yet not hers.

The bed felt safer than the floor. She scooted back onto it and wrapped her arms around Ollie. He was shuddering, trying to stop the tears.

"Shush. It's alright."

He leaned into her. Maddy stared at the door, her mind racing.

CHAPTER THIRTEEN

ALISON STARED out of the window while the kettle boiled. A blackbird was hopping across the front lawn, stopping to peck at the grass. She watched it, her chest tight.

"Hey, love." Ian was behind her, his arm around her waist. She shrugged it off.

"Sorry," he said. "You OK?"

She continued staring, her mind foggy. She'd barely slept, starting at every sound in case it was Maddy and Olly coming home. The FSO had been relieved by another officer, a young man. He'd slept on the sofa in the living room. She couldn't decide if his presence made her feel better or worse.

"I'll go into the station, see what I can find out. What's going on."

Alison turned, her face close to her husband's. "No."

"I might be able to..."

"No. No work today. I need you here."

"Al, I'm no good here. It's not as if I can do anything."

"You don't give a shit about me, do you?"

He backed up. "Come on, love. You're tired,. You're stressed. Please, let's not—"

"Just go if you need to. Don't worry about me."

He frowned, surveying her. "You said you want me to stay."

The kettle clicked. She put out a hand, steam wafting over her fingers. She ignored the heat.

"Just go. I know it's not the same for you."

He put a hand on her shoulder. "Come on love, you know it's not like that."

She grabbed the hand. She squeezed. "No? What *is* it like? How can you know what I'm feeling?"

He pulled her to him. "They'll find them. I'm sure they will."

She buried her face in his shirt. He was wearing a tie. He'd been intending to go into work all along.

"What if they don't, Ian? Or what if they do but they've been hurt... or worse?"

"We have to hope for the best."

She lifted her face. Mascara stained his shirt.

"I can't," she sniffed. "What if it's those men?"

"What men?"

"The ones on TV... the men that got released. What if they've got them?"

Ian held her at arm's length. "They haven't. They won't have done that. It's impossible, so soon after release. And they wouldn't take that kind of risk."

"Did you work on that case? Canary?"

"No, love. I had nothing to do with it. So it's not as if they'd target me."

She pushed him away. "I don't know what to think. I..."

She slid to the floor, her back scraping down the front of the kitchen cupboard. There was a crash next to her.

"Shit." Ian pushed her to one side. She'd pulled the kettle off the counter, her mug with it. Her arm was splashed with boiling water.

"We need to get you to A&E." He grabbed her arm.

She yelped and yanked it away. "I'm not going anywhere. It's fine."

He bit his lip. His face was pale and damp. "You've scalded your wrist. You need to see a doctor."

"It doesn't hurt."

She was right. It didn't. She couldn't feel a thing. Not on the outside, at least.

He pushed the kettle back onto the worktop and gathered her into his arms. She felt a sob rip through her.

"I don't know what to do, Ian."

"I know, love. I know." He kissed the top of her head and she leaned into him, her body empty.

CHAPTER FOURTEEN

ZOE HAD BEEN in the office since five am. She and Connie were clicking through the social media accounts of the Osmans, searching for anything unusual.

There was nothing. Alison's account was as dull as Zoe had ever seen, and apart from his comments about the 'impostor', Ian hadn't been active much lately. Alison was active on Instagram, photos of the children filling her feed. Zoe stared at them, trying not to dwell on what those poor kids might be going through.

"Come on," she said. "Let's do the briefing."

Mo nodded at Rhodri and Connie in turn and they filed into the vacant DI's office. Rhodri stifled a yawn and Connie gave him a jab in the ribs. Leaning against a wall was a thin package wrapped in cardboard.

"What's that, boss?" asked Rhodri.

Zoe grabbed her car keys from her pocket and used one to tear into the cardboard.

"It's a board, Rhod." She leaned it against the wall. "Your

job later today is to get it put up on this wall. Speak to Sarita in admin, she'll sort it for you."

"Randle didn't like boards," said Mo. "Old-fashioned. Can't take them with you."

"You can't exactly take HOLMES with you," said Connie.

"Exactly," said Zoe. "And this is more visual. Staring at it sometimes helps the connections form in your brain. Connie, I want you to fill this out. Photos, maps, plans, notes. Anything we find goes on here. Now, let's update on progress. Mo, what's happening at Cadbury World?"

"They searched the whole place twice over, boss. Grid and quadrant. There's no one there that shouldn't be."

"OK. So they've gone somewhere else. We have to assume they were taken, not that they wandered off. Connie, CCTV?"

"The recording they've given me isn't much help. They show Alison with Maddy and Ollie before she went off to get the food. But I'm waiting on more. The original feeds, so I get both cameras in real time.'

"That's the most important thing. We can only hope the moment they were taken is on camera."

Connie nodded, her face tight. "I'll get on the phone straight away. You want me to go over there and fetch it in person?"

"You don't have transport."

"I do, boss," said Rhodri.

Zoe raised an eyebrow. "That's new."

Rhodri twisted his lips, trying not to smile. "Got meself a motor, boss."

"Good for you. A nice one?"

"Saab. Three years old."

Zoe didn't have Rhodri down as a Saab driver. "You and Connie head over there together. Then come back and carry on going through the social media stuff. And there'll be witnesses to interview, from Cadbury World."

"Uniform are already working through it," said Mo. "Any of interest, they'll let me know."

"You coordinated that with Jim?"

"I did. Not a problem, I hope?"

"Course not." Zoe didn't like working with Jim, but she'd have to put up with it. "OK. I want to talk to the grand-mother this morning."

Rhodri grimaced.

"You found her on the social media accounts?" Zoe asked.

"Yeah. Rabid right-winger."

"Well, that doesn't make her a suspect."

"It doesn't," said Connie. Her voice was tight.

"You don't think that's got anything to do with this, do you? Just how rabid?"

"Some dodgy Facebook pages," said Rhodri. "She prob-ably doesn't even know how nasty they are."

"Does she engage with them actively?"

"No," said Connie. "Shares the occasional post. Dog-whistle stuff. I don't think we need to worry about it."

"Right. Well, she made it clear what she thought of me last night. I'm not looking forward to interviewing her."

"You want company?" asked Mo.

"No. We've got enough to get through, and we need to act fast." She looked up. "Ma'am."

Lesley leaned on the door frame. "Good to see you using your office, Detective Inspector."

"We're using it as a briefing room," Zoe replied.

"Glad it's not being wasted. There are advantages to having a private space for a DI, you know."

Zoe nodded.

"I like the board, too. None of this modern PowerPoint nonsense."

Zoe hid a smile. David Randle had been an advocate of using digital resources for briefings, when he'd been their DCI. Lesley had sat in on his briefings, uncritical. "Yes, ma'am."

"Good. Well, I'm not going to keep you. Get on with it, yes?"

There was a chorus of *yes ma'am*s. Lesley pulled a banana from her pocket and peeled it as she left through the outer office.

"She going to be watching over us?" asked Rhodri.

"She might, constable," said Zoe. "So we need to make sure we don't give her any reason to criticise."

"Course."

"Good. What else?"

"There's the toys the kids bought at Cadbury World," said Mo.

"Toys?"

"Yes. Alison got each of them a souvenir from the gift shop."

"Not chocolate?"

"Not just chocolate. Ollie got a Freddo frog and Maddy a Caramel bunny. Soft toys."

"What happened to them?"

"Both gone. With the kids I assume."

"That doesn't help us much." Zoe tapped her front teeth with a pen, thinking. "We've been looking at the parents' social media, what about the kids?"

"They're a bit young," said Mo.

"Maddy's twelve. Connie, any sign of her online?"

"Apart from all Alison's Instagram posts, no. If she's on social media, she isn't friends with her parents."

"If she is on social media, she probably hasn't told them. Look for her. Start with WhatsApp. There might be a group for her class. She hasn't got a mobile phone of her own, but that doesn't mean she didn't borrow from her parents. We've got their phones, see if you can find anything."

"Yes." Connie grabbed a whiteboard marker from the desk and wrote on the board.

"We need to talk to the school as well," said Mo.

"I'll go there after the gran," said Zoe. "And we need to check out the history with the birth father."

"What birth father?" asked Mo.

"Alison was married before. Benedict Tomkin. He died in a climbing accident. Mo can you check it out, see what you can find out about him?"

"I'll do it," said Rhodri.

"OK. Any reason?"

"I'm into climbing myself." Rhodri blushed.

"OK. Where d'you suggest we start?"

"There are a couple of centres, one each side of the city. People there might have known him."

"Find out what you can from here first. You've got enough to do, and we don't know how relevant Benedict is. Ian's their dad now, he's more important to us." She thought back to her conversation with Carl.

"No problem." Rhodri nodded while Connie wrote Benedict's name on the board.

"Right," said Zoe. "Rhodri and Connie, get that CCTV

footage first, then you've got your tasks. Mo, can you walk with me?"

CHAPTER FIFTEEN

"You OK, Zo?" Mo matched pace with Zoe as they sped along the corridors. Her brain was racing and her body needed to follow suit.

"I need to talk to you. Not here."

"Right."

They turned a corner to see David Randle coming out of an office. Zoe skidded to a halt leaving Mo to almost crash into him.

Randle turned to them and smiled. "DI Finch. DS Uddin. How's things without me?"

Zoe pushed her shoulders back. "We're working on the Osman abduction, sir."

"Not necessarily an abduction."

"We have to assume the worst."

"Hmm. So, where are you heading?"

Mo pulled back, leaving Zoe closest to Randle.

"DS Uddin has witnesses to question, and I'm talking to the school."

"Why?"

"People from that school will know about the family's movements, their routine. There will be relationships going back years. There could be grudges, enmities."

"Enmities? That's a very grand word."

"We want to find out if anyone had a reason to hurt this family, sir."

"Of course. Well, it sounds like you have it all under control." He turned in the direction of the front entrance.

"I was disappointed to hear about Shand and Petersen's release, sir," Zoe said. Randle stiffened, his back to her. He turned and looked into her eyes.

"So was I, Inspector."

She held his gaze. "We'll get them, sir. Men like that won't be able to stay on the right side of the law for long. We'll get their associates, too."

Randle narrowed his eyes. Had she meant to threaten him, or had it just come out like that? Zoe couldn't be sure.

"Good for you, Zoe. Never give up." Randle turned and picked up pace. Zoe and Mo followed slowly. As they left the building, his Audi was leaving the car park.

"What was all that about?" asked Mo.

Zoe shook her head. Mo didn't know her suspicions about Randle, and he didn't know Carl had been investigating him along with ACC Jackson. She'd told Lesley, who'd insisted she needed more evidence.

Lesley was right. Lesley was often right.

"Nothing. Sit with me a minute."

She headed to her car and they both got in. She leaned back in her seat. She liked being in her Mini, it made her feel safe. Connected her to her dad, who'd built Minis at the Longbridge car plant.

"Go on," Mo said. "Why the cloak and dagger?"

She turned to him. "It's about Ian Osman."

"What about him?"

"This is confidential."

Mo mimed zipping his lips. "You know you can trust me, Zo."

"He's under investigation by PSD."

Mo's mouth fell open. "Professional Standards? Why?"

"I don't know."

"Who told you this? It's no help if we don't know why."

"I do know that."

"Sorry. Who told you? You have to get them to give you more information."

She swallowed. "I swore I wouldn't tell anyone. Sorry. You know what it's like when they're investigating someone..."

"I do." A sergeant they'd both known in local CID had been investigated for framing a suspect in a robbery case. Zoe and Mo had worked alongside him, as well as the undercover officer who'd been pretending to be part of the team. The whole thing had left a nasty taste in their mouths.

"You think it has a bearing on what's happened to the kids?" asked Mo.

"It might do. Depends what he's been up to."

"If he's been up to anything."

Mo put a hand on the dashboard. He pinched the plastic, his knuckles white. "We can't go barging in there asking Ian about this. It'll compromise PSD's investigation, get us into all sorts of trouble."

"But at the same time, we can't just ignore it if it's the reason Maddy and Ollie were taken," said Zoe.

"No." He withdrew his hand and punched himself lightly on the head with it three times. "This is messed up."

"I know."

"What d'you want to do?"

"I have to see what else I can find out."

"Be careful."

"I will," she replied.

"Good. Anyway, I need to get over to Bournville. And you've got a fascist granny to interview."

"I'm not sure she's a fascist."

"I was exaggerating. Good luck."

"I'll need it."

CHAPTER SIXTEEN

ALISON SAT in the chair by the back window, watching her coffee go cold. The FLO who'd been here yesterday was back. She was in the kitchen, emptying the dishwasher.

Alison wanted to do it. She wanted to keep busy. But Trish had insisted.

Ian rattled down the stairs and pushed through the door. "I won't be long."

She let out a long breath. No point arguing with him. This was his way of occupying his mind, of telling himself he was being useful.

She wondered if the DI would be back today, with more questions. She'd have to talk about Benedict's death again.

"Al?"

She looked up. "What?"

"Did you hear me? I said I won't be long."

"I know." She turned away, not wanting him to see the rings around her eyes.

He left the door open – he always did that, he forgot it caused drafts – and made for the front door.

"Oh. Hello again."

So he'd seen that Trish was back.

"Hello."

"Did they assign you deliberately?"

"Well, I don't think it was random."

"You know what I mean."

Alison frowned and pushed herself up. She crept towards the door.

"They assigned me because this is my job, sarge. They tell me I'm good at it."

"Spying on families when they're at their most vulnerable."

"That's a bit below the belt."

Alison stepped closer to the open doorway, careful to stay out of sight. Did this woman know her husband? How well?

"Sorry, Trish. I'm... well, you understand. People do weird things when this kind of thing happens to them."

"Yes."

"You probably see it all the time."

"Sometimes."

"Good."

Silence. What was Ian doing? Had he left?

"Well, I'll see you later."

He hadn't left. He was still talking to her. Alison should stop listening in like this. They were both police officers. Chances were, he'd know most of the people assigned to the case.

But still...

She held her breath, waiting for Trish to respond.

Instead, the door slammed.

CHAPTER SEVENTEEN

"Detective Inspector."

"Mrs Wilson. Thanks for agreeing to see me."

"Did I have a choice?"

"Not really."

"Well, then."

Barbara Wilson led Zoe through a sparse hallway into a living room that was anything but. The walls were lined with landscape paintings, all in ornate frames. Trinkets covered every surface and a bookshelf in the corner was crammed with plants. No books.

"Mind if I sit?"

"Do as you please."

"Thank you." Zoe chose a heavy armchair. It was upholstered in a textured floral fabric with an antimacassar draped over the back. Zoe hadn't seen an antimacassar in at least twenty years.

She pulled out her pad and pen.

"This won't take long."

"Good." Barbara lowered herself to the chair opposite,

one hand in the small of her back. She looked about sixty years old, with dyed blonde hair and shrill pink lipstick. She wore a crimson satin shirt over a pair of jeans that didn't fit.

"We're trying to find out everything we can about family and friends, in case there's someone who might have wanted to harm Maddy and Ollie. Anyone who might want to hurt their parents."

"Madison and Oliver, please."

"That's not what Alison calls them."

Barbara snorted. "It's what I call them. Poor loves."

"Can you tell me if there've been any problems for the family recently? Anyone they've fallen out with?"

"Apart from myself, you mean?"

"Sorry?"

"I'd have thought this was pretty obvious, if you were any good at your job. Ian and I don't exactly see eye to eye. He's not right for my daughter."

"I see. And you think her first husband was."

Barbara barked out a laugh. "Good God, no! He was a disgrace. Idle and useless, with his mountaineering and his inability to stay in one place for more than five minutes."

"He travelled a lot."

"He was never home. He neglected poor Madison. Alison was better off without him."

"Did she start seeing Ian soon after Benedict's death?"

"You're asking me if there was an overlap."

"Not necessarily," aid Zoe.

"There's no reason to be coy about it. She told me Ian was a friend. She met him through work, some sort of school police liaison thing. Supposed to benefit the kids, keep them out of trouble. Waste of bloody time. Kids with any sense know to keep out of trouble without having to have a couple of police officers come into their school and let them play in their car. At least, if the parents are any good, they do."

"So Ian and Alison were an item before Benedict died?"

"They were."

"And would you say they are happy together?"

"As these things go, I imagine. Happier than my late husband and I were. Happiness is much overrated, you know."

"Is Alison happy in her work?"

"Of course she is. Why else would she do it?"

"No problems with colleagues? No enemies?"

"Enemies? People don't make enemies. So melodramatic."

Zoe dug her fingernails into her palm. "What about Ian? Is there anyone apart from yourself he doesn't get along with?"

"I've no bloody idea. I don't talk to him about that kind of thing."

"What about Alison?"

Barbara flinched. "What about her?"

"Does she talk to you about Ian? I thought she might confide in her mum, if her husband's having problems."

"We don't have that kind of relationship." Barbara glanced at her watch. "Is that everything?"

"Just one more thing."

Babara stood up and brushed her hands down her jeans. They were pale denim, cut like regular trousers. "Go on."

"Alison was pregnant with Ollie when Benedict died. Could he be Ian's?"

"My daughter is many things, Inspector. But she isn't stupid. No, of course he isn't. Now, I have things to do. If you don't mind..."

CHAPTER EIGHTEEN

CONNIE WENT STRAIGHT to her desk when she and Rhodri returned from the Cadbury factory. She pulled her chair up without taking off her coat and slid the USB stick into its port.

She chewed her lip as she waited for the files to transfer onto her machine. Behind her, Rhodri hung his coat on the back of the office door and clapped his hands together.

"Coffee?"

"Tea, please." She kept her eyes on the screen.

At last the first file opened. There were four of them: two cameras, covering a two-hour time span. She opened the first one.

A time and date stamp was in the corner of the screen. Ollie and Maddy had gone missing at around twelve thirty. The time stamp said 12:01.

She fast forwarded to ten minutes before it had happened. She would go back and check the entire feed later, but first she wanted to see if the moment the kids had been taken was on camera. She held her breath, leaning forwards, as the footage shifted past in front of her eyes. She felt sick.

At 12:20, Alison was sitting at a table, her back to the camera. Ollie sat next to her, leaning over the table and staring at its surface. The boss had said something about him chasing a line of ants.

Alison turned to Ollie. The picture wasn't clear, but Connie assumed she was talking to him.

"Alright?" Rhodri put a mug on her desk. She grunted thanks but didn't take her eyes off the screen.

"Anything interesting?" He hovered behind her, blowing on his coffee. She pushed back irritation. "Not yet."

He bent over, his face close to her shoulder. She wanted to brush him away, but he was intrigued too. He'd taken her to get these files, the least she could do was let him watch.

Onscreen, Alison turned to her daughter. Madison sat sideways in her chair, her head propped up in her hand. She stared offscreen. Towards the play area, perhaps? Alison leaned towards her and she shrugged.

Connie swallowed. *Breathe.*

Alison stood up. 12:25. She would be going to the hot dog stand. She would be gone for ten minutes, fifteen at most. The videos would confirm that.

After two minutes and twenty-six seconds, Alison returned. Connie frowned.

Maddy looked up and said something to her mum. Alison put a hand on Ollie's shoulder, and he turned to her. Both children were giving her their full attention.

Alison's head turned from one to the other. They watched her as she spoke. Then she stood up, holding Ollie's hand. He looked up at her for a moment then stood too.

Madison looked at her brother and then her mum. She stood up. Alison still had her back to the camera.

"That makes no sense," Connie breathed.

"No," whispered Rhodri.

"She told us she went to the hot dog stand, that they weren't there when she came back."

"Maybe the time's wrong on the video."

"Yeah."

Connie waited while Alison and the children walked out of shot. The children flanked their mum, each of them holding her hand. Each carrying an object: the soft toys she'd bought them.

Connie sped the video up to double time. If the time was wrong, Alison would come back. Maybe she'd taken the kids somewhere before coming back for food. They'd return to the table, then she'd go out of shot, and the kids would be taken.

At 12:33, Alison reappeared. She rushed towards the table. She circled it twice then headed off towards the play area. She came back, another woman with her: the witness the boss had interviewed.

Connie stopped the video. 12:41. She turned to Rhodri. His eyes were wide.

"What the hell?" he said.

CHAPTER NINETEEN

ZOE PUT her phone on hands-free and dialled, then started her car up. She'd rather have done this face to face, but she didn't have time to drive all the way across the city to Kings Norton.

She turned out of Barbara Wilson's tree-lined street as the call was answered.

"Zoe."

"Morning, Carl."

"I thought you'd be in touch."

"Yeah."

"Go on then."

"Go on what?" She came to a roundabout and squinted. Connie had tracked down the headteacher at Alison's school and she lived nearby.

"You want me to tell you what I'm working on," he said.

"I know it's sensitive, but this is a live abduction case. If he's got anything to do with those kids going missing..." She chose the first exit and pulled into the traffic.

"You know the deal, Zoe."

She glanced in her rear-view mirror and cursed Carl under her breath. "This is too important to be playing games."

"So is Canary."

She gripped the steering wheel. "Is your investigation into Ian Osman connected with Canary?"

"You're not going to trick me like that."

"Worth a try."

She turned into the road where the headteacher lived. Heavy drops of rain fell from the slate-grey sky.

"You already promised me, Zoe. I can't see why it's so hard."

She pulled up outside the house. Suddenly more intense, rain beat against the windscreen, obscuring the buildings outside.

"Alright," she said. "I tell you about Randle, you tell me about Ian."

"Good. So what can you give me?"

"Not now."

"Shit Zoe, when?"

"I'll meet you later. Five pm, same place as last night."

"You didn't show up last night."

"I will this time."

"Good. See you later."

She hung up and stared out at the rain. She had no idea if there was a connection between the abductions and Carl's investigation, but it seemed plausible. If Ian was corrupt, someone might want to punish him, to teach him a lesson. What better way to do that than through his kids?

Step-kids, she reminded herself. Maybe they didn't mean enough to him to be used as leverage.

She took a deep breath and stepped onto the pavement. A car passed, showering her in water.

"Numpty!" Zoe called after it. She batted at her leather jacket. Water didn't agree with it.

She shook herself off and headed for the house. It was small but neat, with a brightly-painted blue door.

A tall blonde woman in high heels answered. She smiled, then caught herself and frowned. "You must be DI Finch."

"Thanks for seeing me."

"Deborah Maskin, head teacher. But you know that. Come in."

Zoe followed her into a bright study. Family photos linked the walls, along with children's drawings. Clay sculptures sat on a shelf to one side and piles of paperwork were scattered on the desk.

Deborah pulled the paperwork together. "Sorry about this, I'm not normally this messy." She flashed a smile. "I was just sorting out the gold stars for next week. Favourite part of the job."

"I won't keep you. I assume you know about Alison Osman's children disappearing?"

The smile flicked into a frown. "Of course. Poor Alison. How is she?"

"It's not easy for her."

"No."

"But I'm hoping you might be able to help."

"Of course." Deborah waved a hand in the direction of an pink armchair. "Take a seat."

Zoe sat down while Deborah took a place behind her desk.

"Did Alison have any enemies?"

A frown. "She's a teaching assistant, detective. You don't really pick up enemies."

"Not just among the parents. Are there any staff members she might have fallen out with? Has she had any problems that you've had to get involved in? Disciplinary, competence, that kind of thing?"

"You're wondering if I've got anything against her."

"I'm wondering if *anybody* has anything against her."

"I've been thinking about this. I'm glad you came."

"Go on." This would be nothing, but the woman had given up part of her Saturday.

"Two years ago." Deborah leaned over the desk, her hands clasped in front of her. "We had a staff member who had to be let go."

"What did this have to do with Alison?"

"It was a safeguarding issue. It was Alison who raised the initial concerns, but that was anonymous. There's no way Mr Grainger would have known it was her."

If a school was anything like a police station, news like that would travel fast. "What happened to this Mr Grainger?"

"The governors had to fire him. The local authority got involved, it was all we could do to keep it from the parents."

"Did he attack a child?"

"There was no evidence that he hurt any of the children. But he had photographs." Deborah's hand had moved to a file on her desk, sitting next to a pile of certificates.

"Photographs?" Zoe asked.

"From sports day. Inter school competitions, that kind of thing. Photos of some of the girls. From certain... angles."

"Was this reported to the police?"

"Yes. He received a suspended sentence, for keeping

obscene photographs. It was a really horrible incident for the school."

"was Madison one of the girls?"

'No. She was in Year Four then. It was the Year Six girls he targeted."

"Where is this Mr Grainger now?"

"I don't know. He moved away, I think."

"Do you know where to?"

"Sorry. I tried to put it all behind me."

"Is that his file?"

Deborah's fingers dragged on the file. "It is."

"Can I have it please?"

"This is a copy. It's yours."

CHAPTER TWENTY

Z OE DROVE THROUGH THE CITY, Mike Grainger's file on the passenger seat next to her. She hadn't stopped to examine it. She wanted to get back to the office, to check for a criminal record.

Her phone buzzed and she pressed the button on her steering wheel for hands-free. "DI Zoe Finch."

"It's Mo."

"I'm on my way back in. Where are you?"

"In the office. Connie's got something weird."

"So have I."

"Go on."

"There was a teacher at the school. He was sacked for keeping photos of the girls in their PE kit. Alison was the one who raised the alarm."

"What's his name? We'll check him on the system."

"Michael Grainger. Thirty-eight years old." She gave him Grainger's Birmingham address.

"Have you been round there?"

"He's moved away. No one knows where to."

"We'll find him."

"Thanks."

She sped up, anxious to be with her team. They had two leads now. Whatever Ian was up to, and this Mike Grainger. Zoe checked the clock on the dashboard: 2:45. Time to catch up with the team and get to her meeting with Carl. If she was late, he'd wait.

———

In the office, all three of them had heads bent over computers.

"What news?" Zoe said. "Come on, let's use the office."

She slapped Mike Grainger's file down on the desk and eyed the board. Connie had added photos of the entire Osman family, plus Benedict Tomkin, Barbara Wilson and Mike Grainger. The last photo was a mugshot. He was thin, with a greying beard and dull eyes that stared into the camera. A thin scar sat under his right eye.

"So he was arrested?" Zoe said.

"No charges were brought," said Mo. "CPS said it didn't meet the threshold."

"Shit. What does a pervert have to do to get himself sent down?"

She pulled the photo down and surveyed it. Grainger had a scruffy beard and messed-up hair. He stared into the camera, his eyes blank.

"Where is he?"

"Last known address is in Devon, ma'am," said Rhodri. "Exeter."

"Contact the local police force. Get them to knock on his

door, find out what his movements have been for the last few days."

"Right, boss."

"Is there any sign of him having had contact with Alison since he was fired?"

"None that we can find," said Mo. "We'll have to ask her."

"Another question to add to the list."

"Boss, we've got the CCTV," said Connie.

"Good. Anything useful?"

"Not so much useful as odd."

"Go on."

"Probably best if you watch it."

Connie switched on the computer on the desk and turned the monitor to face them. They all stood. Zoe would have to have chairs brought in here. The screen came to life and Connie bent over it. She stood back as an indistinct image of Alison came up.

"This is at Cadbury World," Connie said. "Twenty minutes before she says the children went missing."

Zoe raised an eyebrow. "She *says* they went missing?"

"Just watch it, boss."

Zoe folded her arms across her chest and watched. She was aware of the team's eyes flicking between her and the screen. They'd seen it already. They wanted her reaction.

Onscreen, Alison disappeared and then reappeared. She took Maddy and Ollie's hands and walked away. Then she came back, searching for them.

"She never said anything about going somewhere with them."

"No, boss. It makes no sense," said Mo. "The guy on the hot dog stand says there was a queue. She couldn't have got through it and bought the food in just a couple of minutes."

"Is there a camera on the hot dog stand?"

"No."

"Typical. OK, maybe she didn't buy anything at all. Maybe she changed her mind."

"She's got a tray. At 12:33," said Connie. She froze the screen on a shot of Alison side-on to the camera, a tray in her hand. Two parcels sat on it, and a cardboard coffee cup.

"Play it through again," said Zoe. "Slower this time, if you can."

"No problem."

Zoe stepped towards the screen. "Is that definitely her?"

"Looks like her," said Rhodri.

Zoe squinted, trying to see what she was missing. The woman onscreen wore a grey fleece and green scarf, the same clothes she'd been in at the house that night. She had thin dark hair. It was her in all the shots.

She looked up. "So why is she lying to us?"

"Lying?" asked Rhodri.

'She says those kids disappeared when she was off getting food. But she clearly takes them somewhere. Maybe to the loo, maybe to look at the menu. But then they're gone. And it all happened so fast."

Zoe leaned against a wall.

"What now, boss?" asked Connie.

"There was a security guard who says he saw her leave with them. Mo, I want you to find him. Let's get him in here, see what he saw. And we need to talk to Alison again. Not just about this, but about Grainger."

"You going to go over there?" Mo asked.

"Yes. Later."

"Not now?"

"I've got a meeting. Once that's done, I'll head over to the Osman's. And Rhodri, I want you to organise a base for us closer to their house. This is ridiculous, driving back and forth across the city. See if Erdington nick has a room we can borrow."

"Me, boss?"

"You've got mates everywhere, Rhod. I trust you."

CHAPTER TWENTY-ONE

IT WAS GETTING DARK. Madison huddled on the bed, her knees drawn up and her arms wrapped around them. Next to her, Ollie played with the two plushies. Her rabbit and his frog were going on an adventure. One that involved being alone together in the rabbit's room, then taking off in some kind of spaceship.

She'd dozed off earlier and woken to find a bowl of soup on her desk. Not her desk. It looked just like her desk. But it wasn't.

She still hadn't been brave enough to knock on the door or call out. Ollie thought this was a game, that they were playing a version of hide and seek. Mum or Dad would burst in any moment, surprising them. He'd spent half an hour searching the room for them, pulling out drawers, checking under the bed, opening the wardrobe doors.

The light behind the curtains was orange now, the glow of streetlamps. Her own room faced the garden and the curtains didn't glow like this. She could hear traffic through the window, and the occasional voice. She knew this wasn't her room, but didn't understand whose it was.

She'd given the soup to Ollie, after testing it first. She wondered if he'd seen the person who'd brought it, or if he'd been asleep too. He'd said nothing. She didn't want to scare him. She had to look after him.

She was hungry. Her stomach gurgled in a way that made Ollie giggle. Maddy felt tired and sticky, the chocolate film still on her skin despite having rubbed at it with her sleeve.

Then she remembered.

"Ols, give me your hoody."

"Mummy wants our hoody," he told the rabbit. She gritted her teeth: I'm not Mummy. Mummy would be along soon. She hoped.

"Why?" he asked. "I like my hoody."

"Only for a minute. Let me check the pockets."

"Ollie do it."

She gave him a tired smile and watched him pull the pockets of his hoody inside out. His eyes lit up as he found the Curly Wurly. The one they'd argued about.

"Wurly!" he cried.

She reached out. "Give it to me. We'll share it."

"'S yours." He handed it to her.

She wanted to hug him. How could he go from being such a pain to being so cute?

"It's OK, Ols. We'll both have some."

She twisted it until it broke in two and gave Ollie the bigger half. He grinned and stuffed it in his mouth, crumbs falling onto the sheets.

What it was to be four, and have no fear.

She watched the door as she nibbled at the Curly Wurly,

determined to make it last. The chocolate felt good on her dry lips, but the sugar made her feel sick. She forced it all down, knowing she needed to eat.

"Maddy wanna play with Bunbun?"

"Who's Bunbun?"

He held up her rabbit. A souvenir from Cadbury World, too young for her but secretly she loved it. She'd told Mum she didn't need it but Mum had given her that look, the sad one she had when Maddy acted her age.

"Yeah, Ols. Let's play."

CHAPTER TWENTY-TWO

ALISON STARED AT THE TV, the pictures dancing in front of her eyes and not reaching her brain.

Ian was in the armchair opposite her, home at last. He'd returned from work at three, with nothing to report. Why he'd bothered going in, she had no idea. To be away from her, no doubt. To escape the atmosphere in the house.

If she could escape the atmosphere, she would. But she carried it with her, and would until her children were returned.

The doorbell rang.

"Don't look at me," Ian said. "I don't know who it is any more than you do."

He heaved himself up from the chair. There was muttering as he passed the kitchen. The family liaison officer was in there, preparing food for them to eat tomorrow. Keeping out of their way, more like.

More voices, from the front door. A woman. The door to the living room opened and Ian returned, followed by DI Finch.

Alison stood up, her heart racing. "Have you found..."

The detective shook her head. "I'm so sorry. I just needed to ask you a few more questions. We've looked over the CCTV and it doesn't quite make sense."

Alison dropped to the sofa, her body numb. They had to stop doing this to her.

"I don't understand."

DI Finch sat across from her, her hands resting on her knees. Cold air streamed off her.

"Can I show it to you?"

Alison nodded. The detective bent to a laptop bag at her feet and took out a computer. She balanced it on her knee and pressed a few keys.

"Is there something I can rest it on?"

Ian fetched a dining chair and pulled it into the space between the sofa and the armchairs. The detective rested the laptop on it and turned it to face Alison.

"What's this?" Ian shuffled along next to Alison to get a better view.

"It's the CCTV from Cadbury World, from Friday lunchtime."

A lump was growing in Alison's throat. "I'm not sure I can..."

"Watching your children on the feed will be hard, I know. But it might help us find them. Would you rather I fetch the FLO, so she can support you?"

"I'm here."

Trish was behind Alison, standing at the dining table. The inspector glanced up at her.

Alison stared at the screen. There was no video feed on there yet, just a West Midlands police logo. "OK," she breathed.

"Thank you." DI Finch reached forward and started the video. She sat back. Alison was aware of the woman's eyes on her and Ian as they watched.

Alison fought an urge to close her eyes as she saw herself walk into the frame with Olly in front, followed by Maddy. Tears pricked her eyes as Ollie sat down next to her, his head bending to the ants on the table. She put the back of her hand up to her mouth to stifle a cry and felt Ian's arm snaking round her shoulders. She leaned into him.

Onscreen, the other Alison, the one who was still intact, spoke to Maddy who was staring off towards the play area. She'd been sulking over a chocolate bar. A Curly Wurly. Alison tensed. They'd still have that Curly Wurly, wherever they were. And the soft toys she'd bought. Maybe.

She walked out of shot, heading for the hot dog stand. Alison's heart picked up pace. This was it. She was about to see her children be taken by a stranger.

She watched herself walk back into the shot and sit down. Her shoulders slumped. That made no sense. How long had she been in the queue? Had she come back?

Yes, she'd come back. To check what they wanted to eat. To argue with them.

Dear God, her last words to them... what had they been? Oh, if she could do it again.

She watched herself take the children's hands and walk out of shot with them. Ian's arm tightened around her. He was trembling.

Onscreen, Alison reappeared after a pause, carrying the food. On the sofa, she shoved her fist into her mouth. The feeling when she'd found them gone. It had been like nothing she'd felt before.

She turned to the detective.

"I don't understand."

The detective's eyes were already on her. "Nor do I, Mrs Osman. I hope you can help."

CHAPTER TWENTY-THREE

THE MEETING PLACE was an anonymous pub in Kingstanding, miles away from where either of them worked but not too far from the Osmans. The place was half full, small post-work groups and lone men at the bar cradling their pints. Carl was already at a table for two in a far corner. Two glasses sat in front of him: mineral water and Diet Coke. And a bag of her favourite salt and vinegar crisps.

Zoe weaved through the tables, his eyes on her the whole way. He looked thoughtful, as if he was figuring out what to say.

"Carl."

"Zoe. Thanks for coming."

"Yeah."

She sat down and tore open the crisps. She hadn't had a chance to eat all day.

"Slow down." He smiled, his blue eyes flashing.

"I'm bloody ravenous. Didn't realise. Thanks."

"Case like the one you're working on, I know what it's like. Finding those kids is more important than eating."

"Yeah. So let's get on with it." She tipped the last of the crisps into her mouth. "What's up with Ian Osman?"

He leaned across the table. "I only tell you if you give me what you know about Randle."

"Of course."

"Go on then."

"Come on, Carl. Those kids aren't coming back any faster with you playing silly buggers."

"Has it occurred to you there might be a link with Canary?"

She ignored the lump in her stomach. "Yes," she breathed. "I'm hoping not."

"Tell me about Randle."

She pursed her lips. "Alright. He was having an affair with Margaret Jackson."

Margaret Jackson was the widow of the Assistant Chief Constable.

"Bryn Jackson's wife?" he said.

"The very same. Ended a while ago, but I think he was trying to start it up again, when we were investigating her husband's murder."

"Did Jackson know?"

"Not that I know of. There were letters, between the two of them. She kept them well hidden."

"Surely you've got more than that."

"Not much, really. Irina Hamm said her husband had his business card. I think Randle was Jackson's bag man, helping him with what he was up to with Hamm."

Trevor Hamm was a target of the Organised Crime division. The kind of man it was difficult to pin anything to, because he had other people carry out his dirty work. One of his thugs was wanted for attacking Mo and Connie, and Zoe was sure he'd had his wife Irina killed. She'd known about his involvement with the Canary paedophile ring, and Jackson's.

"So when Jackson died, Randle took over."

"Possibly." Zoe sipped at her Coke, wishing it wasn't diet. She needed the sugar.

"Tell me you've got more than that," said Carl.

Zoe sat back. "He was desperate to pin Jackson's murder on Margaret."

"Nice way to treat the woman you've been sleeping with."

"Mmm. I showed him the first letter we found, the one wishing Jackson dead. Randle thought it was ridiculous. But then he flipped."

"When?'

"In the interview. From that point on it was like he was twisting the evidence to make it point to her."

"Can you prove this?"

"Of course I can't. That's why Lesley gave me the brush-off."

Carl rubbed his chin. He had a thin layer of stubble. It suited him. "You talked to DCI Clarke?"

"I had to talk to someone. It was mainly about the letters, the affair. She told me I needed more evidence. And then it turned out Winona Jackson killed him anyway, so the letters became irrelevant."

"Do you still have a copy of them?"

"They're in the evidence store."

"Can you get me a copy?"

"I'm not going sniffing around there, if that's what you mean. That kind of thing can get you fired."

"And telling Professional Standards you think your boss is bent can't?"

She shrugged. "If you want the letters, you'll have to get them yourself. I'm sure PS can requisition them."

"We're trying not to draw attention to ourselves."

"I bet."

He picked up his phone and glanced at it then put it down again.

"Your turn," Zoe said. "Tell me about Ian."

Carl glanced around the pub, his expression grave. "We think he's linked to Hamm's network."

Zoe's heart lurched. "Shit. And that's why the kids were taken?"

"We don't know. But if he's done something to piss them off, they might have taken his kids to get him to toe the line. It could be a punishment."

"Those kind of people don't mess around."

"No."

She sat back in her chair and stared at him. If Ian Osman was tangled up with people like Trevor Hamm, then God only knew what was happening to those kids.

"Carl. You have to let me investigate this."

"No. It's part of something bigger."

"At Kings Norton?"

"There, but in a couple of other stations too. I can't tell you any more."

"What about Harborne?"

"Zoe, I told you I—"

"If there are bent coppers in the station I work at, I want to know."

He stared at her. "I'm not telling you, Zoe. It would compromise our investigation, and you know it. It was hard enough getting permission to talk to you about Ian Osman."

"This is official?"

"It is."

"Blimey. You couldn't have pulled me into Lloyd House?"

"How d'you think that would look?"

"Fair point." She downed her Coke. "Anything else I need to know about Ian? Anything I can use without getting you into trouble?"

"We're watching him, Zoe. If we see him make contact with anyone we think might have those children, I'll tell you."

"And meanwhile I sit on my arse and wait? No thanks." She stood up.

"Zoe, please—"

"Thanks for the drink, Carl." She hurried away.

CHAPTER TWENTY-FOUR

ZOE CLATTERED BACK into Harborne police station, examining faces, wondering who here might be under investigation. She hurried to the team office, her footsteps heavy in the narrow corridors. It was seven thirty. Maddy and Ollie had been gone for over thirty hours.

"I'm back," she announced.

"Boss," said Mo.

"What have you got for me?"

She sped into the briefing room, ignoring the wary looks her team were giving her. She plonked her jacket on the back of the chair and ignored it as it slid to the floor.

"I spoke to Exeter, boss," said Rhodri. He gestured at the photo of Grainger on the board. A map of Exeter had been added. "They went round to his house. No one in."

Zoe dragged a hand through her hair. "Have they spoken to his neighbours, contacts? Anyone know where he is?"

"He's on the register, boss," said Connie. "He reported to his local nick yesterday morning."

"What time?"

Connie grabbed here notepad. "Eight am."

"How long would it take for him to drive up to Birmingham?"

"Three hours, boss. And that's with good traffic. At that time of day..."

"What about public transport? Trains?"

"I'll check," said Connie.

"Please."

Mo stepped towards her. "Go easy on them."

She frowned at him. "I'm fine."

"You're stressed. We all are."

Zoe gave him an irritated look, then looked at Connie and Rhodri. They stared at her with open expressions, waiting.

"Sorry, guys. OK, so that's where we are with Grainger. We need to be certain he couldn't have got to Birmingham in the time between reporting to the police and Maddy and Ollie going missing. Until then, he's a suspect. We'll need CCTV from the motorways and train stations."

"You want me to do it now?" asked Connie. "I could..." she pointed at the computer on the desk.

"Yes."

Connie scurried to the desk and fired up the computer.

"What else?" asked Zoe

"Did you ask Alison about the CCTV?" asked Mo.

"She says she might have misremembered. Maybe she took them to the hot dog stand, they went off while she was waiting for the food."

"Understandable to forget stuff, given what happened," said Rhodri.

"Hmm. We still have to consider the possibility that the pair of them are faking the whole thing."

"Why would they do that?" asked Rhodri.

"Beats me. Attention seeking. For money. I don't know."

"How would they get money from their kids going missing?" asked Mo.

Zoe looked at him, aware she couldn't talk about Carl's investigation in front of the team. "I don't know. I'm fishing."

"You think they're both in on it, boss?" asked Rhodri.

"I don't know." Zoe slumped onto the desk, perching onto its edge. "I don't know."

"There's a train from Exeter St David's at 8:27," said Connie. "Gets into New Street at 10:55. Connection to Bournville arrives at 11:36."

"So he could have made it up here in time."

"By the skin of his teeth," said Mo.

"That's all he'd need. Rhodri, get onto Exeter again. Tell them we need to know where Grainger is. They keep knocking on his door until he turns up. Get them to ask his neighbours, find out if he's got any friends or family down there."

"Right, boss. What about the ex?"

Zoe looked at the photo of Benedict on the board. "What about him?"

"You wanted me to look into his death."

"Did you?"

"He went missing during an expedition on K2. A couple of other climbers went looking for him, apparently they thought they saw his head torch in the middle of the night. But there's only so much they could do without putting themselves at risk."

"Was there a body?"

"It's common for bodies not to be found, boss. George

Mallory wasn't found until 1999, and he went missing on Everest in 1924."

She didn't need to know about George Mallory. "Maybe he survived."

"No way. He was climbing at eight thousand metres, on one of the world's nastiest mountains. You'd die from exposure."

"Right. Find his parents. See if they have contact with the children, if they can tell us anything."

"No problem." Rhodri pointed at the photos. "She definitely has a type."

"Sorry?" said Zoe.

"Ian and Benedict. They look alike, don't they?"

Zoe leaned in. The two men were both short and skinny with hollow, colourless faces.

"I suppose so," she said. She pulled back. "Not that it makes any difference. Go on, Rhodri. You've got stuff to do."

Zoe watched Rhodri go to his desk in the outer office. She turned to Connie.

"Connie, can you give us a minute? Call transport police. We need CCTV from the M5 and Bournville station. And go back to Cadbury's, ask for footage from the car park."

"No problem, boss." Connie stood up and hurried after Rhodri. She looked relieved to have been let out.

Mo closed the door. "What's up? You disappeared."

Zoe slid off the desk and into a chair. "I told you Ian Osman's being investigated."

"Yes."

"They think he's in league with Hamm."

"Trevor Hamm?"

"The one and only."

Mo paled. "Oh, hell."

"Indeed."

"If those bastards have got the children..."

She closed her eyes, her bottom lip clamped between her teeth. "I know. And we can't investigate it. It's part of something bigger."

"That's ridiculous."

"Tell me about it."

"I'm sorry boss, but you can't let him do this."

She cocked her head. "Let who?"

"Carl. I know you're close to him, but if Hamm has got hold of those kids, it doesn't matter how secret or important his investigation is. We have to take it further."

"I'm not close to Carl. And we can't."

He leaned towards her. "Zo. We can. We do."

She met his gaze. He was right. Carl would be pissed off, and they could both lose their jobs. But Maddy and Ollie were more important.

CHAPTER TWENTY-FIVE

MAKING coffees for her team was the least Zoe could do. It was gone nine, and they were still at their desks. Rhodri and Connie were chasing the Mike Grainger lead, while Mo was trying to find out what he could about Ian Osman without blowing Carl's cover.

She stared out of the window as the kettle boiled. The kitchen looked out to a fire escape, a red brick wall opposite her. She liked to gaze at it and clear her mind when she was stuck on a case.

"Zoe."

Zoe jumped. "Ma'am."

"Enough for me?" Lesley indicated the kettle.

"I think so."

"Good." Lesley opened a wall cupboard and brought out a Pot Noodle.

"I didn't know you were still here, ma'am."

Lesley placed the Pot Noodle on the worktop and peeled the lid open. The smell of curry powder filled the tiny kitchen.

"No rest for the wicked. Drowning in paperwork."

"Rough."

"How's progress on the Osman case?"

Zoe thought back to her meeting in the pub with Carl. Official, he'd told her. So his high-ups knew about their chat. "It's suddenly got very complicated, ma'am. Can I talk to you?"

"Sure."

The kettle clicked and Lesley gestured to it, her eyebrows raised in question. Zoe poured water into the pot.

Lesley stood back, watching it settle. "How can I help you?"

"I'd rather we spoke in your office." Zoe poured four coffees, all strong. She trickled milk into two of them.

"No problem. You take your team their coffees and report to my office. Want one of these?" She stirred the noodles and brought them up to her face, sniffing.

"No, thanks."

"Sure? Have you eaten today?"

Zoe eyed the pot. Nicholas hated reconstituted food. He'd roll his eyes at her if she brought those things home. But she loved them. "Yes, please. I'm famished."

"Right you are. Five minutes, my office."

———

Five minutes later, Zoe pushed through the door to Lesley's office, coffee mug in hand. Two Pot Noodles sat on the desk, both curry flavour. Zoe allowed herself a smile.

Lesley grabbed hers and prodded at its contents. "What's up?"

"It's sensitive."

Lesley eyed Zoe over her pot. She forked a pile of noodles into her mouth. She inhaled sharply at the heat, then motioned for Zoe to continue.

"Ian Osman's under investigation by Professional Standards."

A spray of curry sauce flew out of Lesley's mouth. "Next time you're going to tell me something like that, warn me first. These stain."

"Sorry."

"Who told you?"

"I can't tell you that, ma'am."

"Can't, or won't?"

"I promised not to tell anyone."

"Hmm. What's he being investigated for?" Lesley held her fork halfway to her mouth. "Do I need to wait before I eat this?"

Zoe nodded. "He's involved with Trevor Hamm."

Lesley slammed the pot onto the desk. "Bloody Nora. Glad you stopped me." She pushed the pot away, her brow creased. "What's your plan?"

"I want to send teams to all the properties associated with the Canary case. To the houses of Robert Oulman, Howard Petersen and Jory Shand."

"Oulman won't be there."

"His family will be." Oulman was in prison. "And the other two..."

"Yeah. Those slippery buggers." Lesley sighed. "Look, I'll need a warrant to search their properties. Normally without more from your source, that would be tricky. But given the history of those men, and the nature of this case..."

"Trevor Hamm, too," said Zoe. "I want to search his flat,

his building sites." She hesitated. "And I'd like to speak to Detective Superintendent Randle."

"Why?"

"You know my concerns."

"You haven't given me any more evidence to back that up."

"No, ma'am. But two children are missing, and if there's any chance..."

"Are PS investigating Randle too?"

Zoe felt heat rise up her neck. "Yes."

"Shit. He's in charge of Force CID now. How am I supposed to look him in the eye, with all this going on?"

"I think Maddy and Ollie's safety is more important."

Lesley grabbed her pot. "You haven't eaten."

"I'm not hungry."

"Take it with you. Get those warrants. And leave me to talk to David. I know him better than you do."

"Are you sure that's a good idea?"

Lesley shovelled noodles into her mouth and gave Zoe a warning look.

"Right, ma'am. I'll get onto it."

CHAPTER TWENTY-SIX

CONNIE RUBBED her eyes as her computer booted up. She'd never been first in before. The corridors had been empty when she'd arrived and she'd set off the motion-sensor lights as she'd walked to the office.

Sergeant Jenner had been on the front desk. He'd thrown her a friendly nod as she'd passed, too shy to make small talk.

She brought up her web browser. She was monitoring the parents' emails and social media feeds. They'd been inundated with messages. Well-wishers mainly, the occasional troll. Connie could only hope that Alison and Ian weren't looking at these themselves.

She had their phones, and Alison's iPad. She was confident they wouldn't be on the internet.

She scrolled through the posts in Ian's Facebook feed. Not much. One from a colleague, wishing him the best. One from an old school friend, who struggled to find the right words. Alison's feed was different. It was full of messages, questions and outpourings from other mums. Women who were seeing Alison's plight as an excuse to voice their own fears about losing their kids.

There were three messages in Alison's inbox. One from a colleague at the school, one from a neighbour, another from a friend. All three had been in touch yesterday as well. They were checking in, offering support. Alison was lucky to have this network. It made Connie think of her own mum and the women she surrounded herself with: aunts, cousins, neighbours. All of them clucking around Connie and Jaf when they'd been growing up. All of them women she knew she could trust with her life.

She went back to Ian's account, planning to switch over to Twitter. She liked to keep Alison in one browser window, and Ian in another. A message had arrived in his inbox.

She read it, a cold chill creeping over her.

She read it again.

She felt sick.

The door opened. Sergeant Jenner, offering her a coffee. Connie shook her head, mute, staring at the screen.

She picked up the phone.

CHAPTER TWENTY-SEVEN

"STRAP IN."

"Don't worry, Mum. I know how you drive."

"Oi."

Zoe reached across the car and mock-slapped Nicholas. He pulled back, pretending to be hurt.

"That's child abuse, that is."

"Don't joke about that sort of thing."

"Sorry."

She hit the gas and made for the Bristol Road, cutting in front of a white van as she turned onto the main road. Lights flashed behind her and she gave a wave.

"Numpty," she muttered.

"Calm down, Mum. There's no hurry."

"I need to get into work."

"Better a few minutes late than not at all."

"Hmm." She forced herself to slow down a little, falling into the pace of the Sunday morning traffic. It was busying up already, shoppers and parents ferrying kids to weekend activities. People like her who had to work.

"Where d'you want me to drop you?"

"Bottom of Edgbaston Park Road. I'll get the bus into town."

"Where are you meeting Jaf?"

"Bullring. We're gonna sit in the cafe at the top of Debenhams, he said he'd help me with my uni application."

"I can do that."

"It's fine."

"OK. Debenhams? Very rock n' roll."

"'S got a good view."

She smiled. She loved the idea of him making the city his own, finding his own haunts. When she was a sixth-former it had been the cafe at the top of Rackhams. She and her mates could make a pot of tea and a slice of chocolate cake last all morning.

"What time will you be home?"

"What's this, the Spanish Inquisition?"

"Just a mum wanting to know her son will be safe."

"Long before you, I imagine."

She pulled over before Edgbaston Park Road. "I'm sorry, love."

"It's OK. It's important, what you're doing. I'll bring Jaf home. We'll get a pizza."

"You, pizza?"

"A good one, from the Italian. None of your Pizza Hut crap."

"I like Pizza Hut," she said.

"You would."

A car behind honked its horn and Zoe stuck out her tongue in the mirror. Her phone buzzed in the console between them. Nicholas grabbed it.

"Hey," she told him.

"You're driving. Anyway, it's Gran."

Zoe slumped in her seat. The last time she'd seen her mum was after they'd caught Bryn Jackson's killer. Something about a man being murdered by his daughter had prompted her to find out if she could forgive Annette for the years of neglect.

It hadn't worked.

"I'll call her later," she said. Nicholas didn't know about Annette's past. Sure, he knew she had a drink problem, but not the extent of it. Zoe tried to shield him from its excesses. "Have a good day."

"Will do." He slammed the door and sprinted to the bus stop just as the bus pulled in in front of her.

She waited, watching him get on. He climbed to the top deck, his head shadowy in the rear window. Eighteen years old, and still sitting in the back seat of the bus. She smiled.

Her phone buzzed again. She slammed it into the holder and hit the button on her steering wheel.

"DI Zoe Finch." She pulled out into the traffic and indicated to turn towards Harborne.

"Boss, it's Connie."

"You're in early."

"Yeah. There's been a development."

"What kind of development?"

"A really bad one."

CHAPTER TWENTY-EIGHT

ZOE HALF-RAN from her car to the doors of the station. Two men blocked her way, coming out. She tried to push through them.

"Excuse me," she muttered.

The men laughed. She glared at them. They weren't CID. Civilians. She flashed them her most fake smile. "Please."

One of them stood back with a flourish. "After you, madam."

She clenched her fist, digging into her palm, and walked past them. It was all she could do not to run.

"Morning, ma'am." Sergeant Jenner was at the front desk. "Working on a Sunday?"

"Sorry, Tim. In a hurry."

"Yes, ma'am." He hit a button and the interior doors opened.

She hurried along the corridors, glad of the relative quiet. Lesley would be in her office today, but not this early. Zoe wondered who else out of her team had made it in, apart from Connie.

"Talk to me." Zoe let the office door slam behind her. Connie was here, and Rhodri.

"Where's Mo?"

Rhodri shrugged. "Not here yet."

"Right." She checked her watch. Seven thirty. She was impressed Rhodri had made it in this early. Either he'd quit the cheap lager while they worked this case, or his stomach was made of cast iron.

She strode to Connie's desk. "Show me."

"This message on Facebook, boss," said Connie.

Rhodri was looking at his own screen, his face drawn. He opened his mouth to speak then thought better of it.

Zoe bent to the screen. On it was a Facebook message.

I have your children. You can have one back. You have three days. Choose.

She felt like she'd been punched in the ribs. "When did you find this?"

"A couple of minutes before I rang you. It was in Ian's Facebook account."

"A message?"

"Private message, ma'am. It's been sent to Alison as well."

"Shit. Do they have access?"

"We've got their phones, and the iPad. I don't think so."

Zoe stared at the screen. Both kids were coming home. She was going to find them both. She didn't want Alison or Ian freaked out by this.

What kind of bastard made a parent choose between their kids?

"Right," she said. "We don't tell the Osmans about this yet. Not till we know more. D'you know who it's from?"

"That's the thing, ma'am."

"Yes?"

"It's from PC Trish Bright."

CHAPTER TWENTY-NINE

ALISON SAT on her bed in her dressing gown. She knew she had to get dressed, but couldn't face it. She'd refused the meal Trish had put in front of her last night, her stomach full of worry.

That video made no sense. She'd left the kids and come back to ask them what they wanted. But she hadn't walked away with them. She was sure of it.

Was her mind playing tricks on her?

Ian had been off with her all night. He'd looked at her like she had something to hide. Like she'd taken Maddy and Ollie herself.

What kind of mum would do that?

One with a mental illness. She leaned over to her bedside drawer, checking her medicine box.

When Benedict had gone missing, she'd needed help. Six months pregnant, with a seven-year-old to care for and no idea if her husband was alive or dead. She'd disintegrated. Once Ollie was born her GP had prescribed antidepressants, and a course of cognitive behavioural therapy.

She'd got better, not so much thanks to the treatment as to her relationship with Ian. Once he'd convinced her to accept that Benedict wasn't coming back, there'd been relief that she didn't have to hide her feelings anymore. They'd married within a year.

She'd kept the pills, or what was left of them. Occasionally, when she felt low, she took one. It gave her a pick-me-up, a boost when she couldn't deal with Ian's neglect or with the demands of two young children.

She'd taken one on Friday morning, after a row with Ian. A row about his plan to head into the office when they were supposed to be going out as a family.

She knew she shouldn't. She had care of Maddy and Ollie, and she was driving. But she'd done it before, and she knew her limits.

Had the pill messed with her memory?

Had she left the playground with her children, then lost sight of them and come back looking for them?

And if so, where were they?

She plunged her face into her hands, too weak to cry. She'd lain awake, silent tears dripping into the pillow. Images of Maddy and Ollie being hurt by a faceless stranger filling her vision every time she closed her eyes. She wasn't sure when she'd last slept.

"Alison! Are you home?"

Alison wiped her eyes and stood up. She felt wobbly. "Mum?"

"Are you in bed?"

"No."

Alison pulled the dressing gown tighter around herself and trudged down the stairs. Her mum was at the bottom, by the front door. She looked out of breath, and her hair was dishevelled.

"Alison. Why aren't you dressed?"

"I couldn't..."

"Never mind. Have you been on Facebook this morning?"

"No. They took my iPad. And the phones. We can't..."

"Oh my dear God." Barbara pulled Alison to her, burying her daughter's face in her chest. Alison shook herself off.

"What is it? What's going on?"

"I think you should sit down."

CHAPTER THIRTY

ZOE RUSHED OUT of the building, car keys in hand. Mo was parking his car.

"I got your call, boss. Where to?"

"Trish Bright's. It's her day off, hopefully she'll be at home."

"You think she's got them?"

"I don't know what to think. But we need to question her, before she goes back to the Osmans'."

"Right."

They jumped into her car and sped out of the station car park. Mo gripped the dashboard.

"Where does she live?" he asked.

"Hall Green somewhere. Connie's going to call it through."

"Right. Just don't kill us on the way, huh?"

"Sorry." She slowed down, pushing out a couple of long breaths to force calm into her body.

"What happened?" asked Mo.

"Check your texts. I've forwarded the Facebook message to you."

There was silence as Mo checked his phone. The lights at Harborne Road changed to green and Zoe hit the accelerator, cursing when the car in front braked suddenly.

"Zo..."

"Yeah. Sorry. I don't want her going anywhere."

"Can't we send Uniform round? What's her nearest station?"

"Balsall Heath or Kings Norton. She's a copper, though. I can't just call a station and get them to raid her house."

"What about PS?"

"Let's hope it doesn't come to that."

The car in front turned off and Zoe blinked, clearing her vision. Trish Bright was a long-standing member of the Harborne team. She'd been FLO in countless cases. How had she got herself mixed up in this?

"Whoah," said Mo.

"You've read it?"

"Yeah," said Mo. "Have the Osmans got this?"

"I don't think so. We've got their phones."

"What are we going to tell them?"

"Nothing, for now. I want to talk to Trish first. Connie's checking her Facebook, see if we can find anything else."

"Right."

As they crossed the Bristol Road, Zoe's phone rang. Mo picked it up.

"It's the DCI."

"Shit." Zoe pressed the answer button.

"DI Finch." She stopped at the lights by the cricket ground, drumming her fingertips on the steering wheel.

"It's DCI Clarke."

Zoe exchanged a look with Mo. The tone of Lesley's voice...

"Ma'am."

"What the fuck is going on?"

"Sorry, ma'am?"

"You know what I'm talking about. I've just had Barbara Wilson on the phone kicking up shit about PC Bright."

Zoe gripped the wheel. *Damn.* "How did they find out?"

"That's not the issue, DI Finch. You need to get round there, right now."

"We're on our way to interview PC Bright."

"I'll send Uniform round. We'll need to get PS involved."

Zoe's heart sank. "Yes."

"You need to reassure those parents that we're going to bring their kids home. Both of them. Make sure they don't do anything rash."

Zoe glanced in the rear-view mirror. The car behind flashed its lights. She muttered under her breath and accelerated out of the lights.

"I don't think they'll do it," she said. "Choose."

"You don't know that. Get round there, right now."

"Yes, ma'am."

CHAPTER THIRTY-ONE

ZOE PULLED up outside the house. The scaffolding had grown and a van was parked in the driveway. A man walked to it, his expression thunderous.

"We're police. Who are you?"

"Why d'you wanna know?"

"Tell me who you are, please."

'Name's Rob. I'm s'posed to be doin' their roof."

"That'll have to wait."

"Yeah. So she tells me. Mardy old bat."

He slung a toolbox into the back of the van and threw himself into the driver's seat. He drove off, almost clipping Zoe's Mini as he did.

Zoe watched the van drive away. *Reynolds Contracting*. She frowned.

She knocked on the door, smoothing down her shirt. Barbara Wilson answered, her face hard.

"You."

Zoe pulled on a smile. "Mrs Wilson. Are your daughter and son-in-law in?"

"She is. God only knows where *he* is."

Barbara held the door open and Zoe and Mo stepped inside. A radio played in the kitchen, loud. The house had been silent every other time they'd been here.

She pushed the living room door open. "Alison?"

Alison was at the dining table, an iPad in her hands. Zoe felt her chest hollow out. She took a seat across from the woman, watching her face.

Alison stared at the screen, her face pale.

"It won't come to this," said Zoe. "You are not going to have to choose between your children."

Alison looked up at her. Her eyes were red and her cheeks tear-tracked. She stared into Zoe's eyes, silent.

Zoe swallowed. Mo was behind her, talking to the grandmother.

"This helps us," she said, her voice low. "We'll be interviewing PC Bright today. We'll find out what she knows. Who she's working with, if she is. We'll find them."

"They say three days."

"We'll find them. We'll work night and day, and we'll find them for you."

Zoe hated making promises like this. She knew that she and her team would do everything in their power to find those children. But she was scared it might not be enough.

Still, her fear was nothing compared to Alison's. If she didn't reassure her, the woman might do something stupid.

"I can't choose."

Zoe put a hand on Alison's arm. "You don't have to. We'll find both of your children for you. Maddy and Ollie are going to come home."

Alison sniffed. "She was here, in the house. She was watching us."

Zoe lowered her gaze. "I know. I'm sorry. I can't tell you anything about what PC Bright has been doing, but we will get to the bottom of it. It helps us, it's a lead."

Alison nodded. Zoe felt the tension ebb a little.

"Where's your husband?"

"I don't know."

"Did he go to work?"

"No idea."

Zoe looked back at Mo, still trying to calm Barbara Wilson. If Ian had seen the message, and gone to Trish's...

"Can you give me a moment please, Alison? I just need to talk to my colleague."

Alison slumped over the table, the iPad loose in her hands. Zoe took it from her, gently. She placed it on the table, face down.

She went to Mo. Barbara pushed past her, heading for Alison.

"She's making things worse," he whispered.

"I know. But she's her mum. Not much we can do."

"Hmm."

"Can you keep an eye on things here? I need to talk to the DCI."

"Sure." He headed for the table.

She went through the hall and into the front garden where she took her phone out.

"DCI Clarke."

"Ma'am. I'm at the Osman house. I've managed to calm Alison down. But Ian Osman isn't here."

"Where is he?"

"Alison doesn't know. If he got the message, he could have gone to Trish's. Is a team there yet?"

"Yes."

"Thanks, ma'am. I'm sorry."

"You're alright, Zoe. This wasn't your fault. But tell me when something like this happens again, right? Getting that call from Barbara Wilson wasn't the best start to a Sunday morning."

"Yes, ma'am."

She went back inside. Mo was in the kitchen, making coffee.

"Doing the FLO's job?"

"Mrs Wilson kicked me out."

"Ouch."

"She's toxic. We have to keep her away from Alison."

"How?"

He shrugged.

She went into the living room. Alison and her mother huddled together at the dining table.

"Alison?"

Alison pulled away from her mum and looked up.

"I need to ask you a few questions about your husband's relationship with PC Bright."

"What relationship?" asked Barbara. "Were they having an affair?"

"That's not what I mean. But they used to work together. I need to know if they were close."

"He didn't say anything," Alison said. "He was... a bit funny... when he saw her here. But they hardly spoke."

"Do you think Ian is involved in taking the children?" Barbara asked.

Zoe looked from her to Alison. *Shut up, woman.*

"I'm not in a position to—"

"Oh you police, you're full of it, aren't you? Not at liberty to tell us anything. Well, it's only my grandchildren we're talking about here!"

She approached Zoe, who held her ground.

"From where I'm standing, you're doing a godawful job, DI Finch. You need to pull your finger out and find those poor children. Before we have to do it for you."

CHAPTER THIRTY-TWO

MADDY SHRANK BACK as the door opened. She held Ollie to her, his head buried in her chest. *Don't look, Ols.*

She held her breath, not sure whether to look or not. The room was dim, grey light filtering through the curtains. It smelled bad. She'd found a plastic bucket in the corner and they'd both been using it. The stench made her feel sick.

A dark figure slid into the room. A person, wearing a grey hoody and loose-fitting jeans. He shuffled sideways into the room, his face hidden.

She watched him walk to the desk by the window. Ollie shivered against her, his pyjamas wet again.

The man put a tray on the desk and placed its contents on the surface. He hadn't looked at her. Maybe he thought she was asleep.

He picked up the soup bowl from yesterday and put it on the tray. Maddy closed her eyes, her chest tight. She could hear him moving again, going back to the door. There was a squeak and a rustle.

She waited. Now she'd closed her eyes, she couldn't open

them again. Her body felt numb and fizzy at the same time, like her insides wanted to crawl out of her skin. She imagined the man standing next to her, looking down at her and Ollie.

Don't look, Ols.

Ollie shuddered. She felt his fingers on her face. She opened her eyes, just a crack, making sure she was facing her brother. He was looking into her face, his eyes wide.

"Who was that, Mads?"

"Shush. Just Mum, bringing us some food."

"Why didn't she say anything?"

"It's a game. Hide and seek. She was listening for us. But you were quiet. Well done."

"I don't like this game anymore."

"It'll be over soon."

She shifted her gaze to the door, slowly. The room was empty again, the door closed. She let herself breathe.

"I'm hungry."

"I know."

She slid off the bed and shuffled to the desk. The bucket was gone. A new, clean one was there instead. The smell was still there but it wasn't as sharp.

"What did she bring us?"

"It's good, Ols. All your favourites."

"Iced buns?"

"Yes." She stared down at the food. Two iced buns, two jam doughnuts. A plate of chicken drumsticks. Prawn cocktail crisps. Cans of Fanta and bottles of Fruit Shoot .

How did this person know all their favourite foods?

She turned back to Ollie, forcing a smile. "Good news, Ols."

CHAPTER THIRTY-THREE

"Carl."

"Zoe. We've got Trish Bright. I thought you might want to watch the interview."

"Watch? This is my case."

"She's police. You know the drill."

"Carl..."

"I'll set up a video feed for you."

"Look," said Zoe. "Let's do the interview together. I know you have to talk to her about the corruption angle, but I need to know where those kids are being held."

"I'm not even supposed to let you watch."

Zoe glanced at Mo. They were driving back to Harborne police station. When they got there, she'd push Rhodri to get a shift on with that base in the north of the city. Connie would be examining Trish's Facebook account, seeing if she'd been hacked. But they all knew access could be revoked by PS at any moment.

"Do you know where Ian Osman is, Carl?" she asked. "He's gone AWOL. Was he at Trish's?"

"No sign of him."

Where the hell was he?

"OK. Please, I'm asking you as a personal favour. Let me sit in on this interview. I'll sit at the back, keep my mouth shut."

"You might as well watch the feed."

"I want to be in the room with her. I want to see her body language up close. This is about more than Trish Bright's career. More than protocol. It's about the lives of two kids."

A sigh. "I'll see what I can do."

"Thanks. We're heading your way."

She came out of the Queensway tunnel and turned off in the direction of Lloyd House.

"Did you notice that van?" asked Mo. "Outside the Osmans'."

"The Reynolds one."

"Yeah."

"Same guy who worked on the Jackson house," she said.

"Maybe Ian's being paid the same way Jackson was."

Zoe took a breath. "Looks like it."

They came to the entrance to Lloyd House car park and Zoe showed her warrant card. They found a spot easily and made for the lift.

Carl was waiting when the lift doors opened.

"Just you. DS Uddin will have to watch the video feed. And you sit tight, say nothing. Otherwise my boss'll have my balls on a plate. Got it?"

"Got it. Thanks, Carl."

Carl led them along a corridor and into a windowless room with a line of computers against a wall. Only one of them was active, showing an image of an empty interview room.

"You stay in here," he said to Mo. "There's an officer outside the door. If you need anything, ask her."

Mo nodded. The officer outside the door wasn't there to make Mo a cup of tea. Her job would be to keep him from exploring the building. Neither of them had ventured inside the Professional Standards offices before, and it was an unnerving experience.

"See you in a bit," she said. Mo gave her a nod.

She followed Carl to the interview room. A tall man with a neat beard had arrived. He held out a hand.

"DI Finch. You understand the restrictions on your being here?"

"Yes, sir." She knew who the man was. Detective Superintendent Malcolm Rogers, Head of Professional Standards.

"Sit there." He pointed to a chair against the wall. She did as she was told.

Rogers left and a woman came in. She shook Zoe's hand, saying nothing. She gave Carl a look that spoke volumes about how happy she was to have an observer. Carl ignored it.

Zoe sat down as PC Bright entered with a man in a suit: her Federation rep. She frowned as she spotted Zoe, and opened her mouth then closed it again.

"Sit down please, PC Bright," said Carl.

They arranged themselves around the table. Zoe leaned to one side to get a better view.

"For the tape, I'm DI Carl Whaley, this is DS Layla Kaur."

"PS Roger Lake, Federation rep," said the man in the suit. "And my client, PC Trish Bright."

"Observing is DI Zoe Finch from Force CID."

Sergeant Lake stared at Zoe for a moment then turned back to Carl.

"PC Bright," said Carl. "We have a Facebook message sent by you to Ian and Alison Osman at 05:30 this morning. You also forwarded it to Barbara Wilson, Alison Osman's mother, at 7am. This is a copy of it."

"I didn't send that," said Trish. The rep nodded, leaning back in his chair.

"Can you prove that?" asked Carl.

"I was asleep at 5:30. You can ask my boyfriend."

"We will. But you do know that Facebook messages can be scheduled?"

"You have to believe me. I know nothing about this message. My account must have been hacked."

"Have you been able to access it this morning?"

Trish's neck flushed. "Yes."

"Did you check your messages, after sending this one?"

"I already told you, I didn't send it."

"Did you check your messages?"

"No. I logged in when I was having breakfast. I had a lie-in, it's my day off. Jake brought me a cup of tea in bed. I keep my phone downstairs, so I didn't look at it till about nine. I checked if I had any notifications, and that was all."

"What is the nature of your relationship with Ian Osman?" DS Kaur asked.

"We worked together for eighteen months, in Coventry. Six years ago. We didn't know each other very well."

"But you're friends on Facebook?"

"He sent me a friend request when I first joined the team. Just being friendly, I guess. But we never interacted. I'd forgotten we were still friends."

"Did you deliberately get yourself assigned as FLO in the Osman case?"

"My sergeant gave me the assignment. I didn't even know it was Ian till I got there."

"And when you did get there, did you acknowledge that you knew him? That you were friends?"

"I told DI Finch."

Carl looked across at Zoe. She nodded.

"What did you tell DI Finch?"

"What I've just told you. She asked if I wanted to be reassigned. I said no. Ian barely remembered me."

"Did you remain friends, after he left Coventry?"

"We aren't friends. I already told you." Trish was keeping her voice low but there was a quiver.

Carl turned a page. "We have a photo of you and Ian together in a bar. You look like very good friends to me."

Zoe wished she could see the evidence. She lifted herself in her seat, trying to get a view.

"That was Zahid's leaving do. We were all pretty drunk."

"Ian has his arm around you."

Another blush. "He had a bit of a crush on me, at the time. At least, he seemed to."

"But he doesn't remember you."

"It was a long time ago."

Zoe leaned forward. "Trish, where is Ian now? Does he have Maddy and Ollie?"

Trish turned to her, her eyes full of panic.

"DI Finch, please let us ask the questions." Carl glared at her.

"Did you plot this together," she continued, "so Ian could get Maddy out of the way?"

Carl clenched his fists. "DI Finch, please."

Zoe twisted her lips and sat back. Trish's face was clear: she had no idea what Zoe was talking about.

"PC Bright, we are checking your phone, laptop and Facebook account. If you have been hacked, as you claim, we'll find out. If you haven't been hacked, this will be very serious for you."

"I must have been hacked," Trish said. "I never touched those kids. I haven't spoken to Ian in six years. I have no idea where they are." Her voice shook. "You have to believe me."

As PC Bright was led away, Carl grabbed Zoe by the sleeve of her jacket and pulled her back into the interview room.

"What the hell was that?"

"Ian Osman has gone AWOL. Finding him will help us find Maddy and Ollie."

"And what was that about getting his daughter out of the way?"

"She's not his daughter. Alison was married before. She says Ollie was her first husband's, but I believe Ian thinks he's his. He has one child, and he wants to get rid of the other one."

"Why on earth would he do that?"

"Why does anyone do anything? It could be related to his involvement with Hamm. I can't see a connection right now, but there has to be one. We need to find him."

"I know." Carl relaxed his grip on her jacket. She shook herself off. They were inches apart. She could smell his after-shave, mixed with sweat.

"What about Trish?" she asked. "You think she's involved?"

"My gut says no. But that Facebook post... We'll keep her here for a bit, make her sweat. Hopefully she'll tell us more."

"I don't think she's got anything to tell you."

"If you're so sure it was Ian," Carl said, "then haven't you considered that he and Trish might have done this together?"

"If they have, then why would she send a message to him on Facebook?"

"Cover his tracks."

"I'm not so sure. I need to get back to my team."

"Right. Remind me not to let you twist my arm in future. If the super finds out what you did in there..."

She brushed his arm with her fingertips. His eyes flashed. "Sorry," she said. "Wouldn't want to get you into trouble."

CHAPTER THIRTY-FOUR

IAN OSMAN PULLED up outside the industrial estate, his hands shaking on the steering wheel. He turned off the ignition and stared at the building, his mind racing.

He'd only been here once before, and it had been made clear to him that he wasn't to return. But the phone numbers he'd been given had stopped working and he was desperate.

His own phone was with Force CID. But he had two burner phones they didn't know about. Both were basic models, designed for making calls and sending texts. No email, no internet. Both were hidden in the boot of his car, tucked under the spare wheel.

He licked his lips. His throat was dry and his hands clammy. He gave the steering wheel a squeeze, closed his eyes and got out of the car.

There was no sign of life in the unit. Ian approached it, his eyes roaming the windows, his police senses kicking in. There was no movement behind the glass, no shadows shifting. He wasn't being watched.

At least, not by human eyes. On the wall above the door

was a camera. He looked up at it, determined not to show his fear.

He put a hand on the door and pushed. To his surprise, it opened.

He eased himself inside, expecting someone to jump out at him. He found himself in a small reception area with a tidy desk and a door at the back that led through to the workshop. A man stood behind the desk, wiping a hammer with a dirty cloth. Ian glanced at it, his heart thudding in his ears.

"I told you not to come here."

"I tried the phone numbers you gave me."

"Maybe I turned them off deliberately."

"I need to talk to you."

"You've got police crawling all over your house. I don't want you anywhere near me. And my guys aren't going to be finishing that roof till your place is clean. I don't care how much it leaks."

Ian clenched his toes inside his shoes. "Let's make this brief, then."

A smile flickered at the man's lips. "You think I've got your kids."

"I was hoping you knew where they were."

The man chuckled. "So polite, Sergeant Osman." He gave the hammer a wipe and placed it on the desk between them. Ian eyed it.

"No. I don't know where your kids are. And nor do my associates. You're barking up the wrong tree."

"Are you sure?"

"Ooh, let me think..." he put a hand to his chin and raised his eyes to the ceiling. "Nah. Definitely no kids out the back. Wanna check?"

"OK."

"You can't."

Ian looked at the door to the back.

"You think I'd keep them here if I had them? I'm not that stupid."

Ian looked back at him, saying nothing.

"Good. Now run along like a nice piggy and get back to your wife. I'm sure she needs you more than I do."

"If you've got my kids..."

The man took a step forward. "Then what, Ian? What will you do?"

"I'm a police officer."

"A bent one."

Ian stared back at him. He shouldn't have come here. "Don't hurt them."

"I can't hurt them if I don't have them. Now fuck off."

Ian glanced at the hammer again then backed out of the door. His chest felt like lead and his ears were ringing. If Maddy and Ollie were in this building somewhere...

He looked up at the windows again. There was movement in one of them. He squinted, raising his hand above his eyes. Nothing.

He returned to his car, passing the *Reynolds Contracting* van. He gave it a brush with his fingertips as he went, longing to take his car key to it.

CHAPTER THIRTY-FIVE

"WHERE ARE we with the Facebook account?"

Zoe's team were in the briefing room. Trish Bright's photo had been added to the board, along with a printout of the Facebook message. Zoe was glad that board was hidden away in here, not in the outer office.

"Her account was hacked, boss." Connie placed a sheet of paper on the desk between them. "I've traced it through seven IP addresses so far. Whoever did this knows their stuff."

"You sure about that?"

"Yes. She needs to shut it down."

"OK."

Zoe slid into the chair. She rubbed the back of her neck. "It could be someone who knows her. Someone who's friends with her on Facebook."

"It wasn't that kind of hack, boss. I guess this person knew she had history with Ian. They might have known she's the FLO. But there's no reason it would be someone connected to her online, any more than it could be a random stranger."

"It's not a random stranger."

"No," said Connie.

"So who, then? Has Mike Grainger turned up yet? What about Ian Osman?"

"The new FLO reported in," said Rhodri. "Ian called Alison twenty minutes ago. He was at Cadbury World, chasing them."

"Why?"

"Maybe he wanted to feel useful," said Mo.

"Are any officers there still?"

"No," said Mo.

"We checked with Cadbury's though, and it squares up," said Rhodri. "He was there."

"He was gone for hours," said Zoe.

"You think we should check traffic cameras?" asked Mo.

"I think we should ask him first."

Zoe considered. "He's already being watched."

"Who by?" asked Connie.

Zoe looked at Mo then back at Connie. "This goes no further." She turned to Rhodri. "Both of you."

"Scout's honour, boss," said Rhodri. Connie nodded, her expression grave.

"He's being investigated," Zoe said. "He's suspected of involvement with Trevor Hamm. You all know what that means."

Rhodri whistled. Connie muttered something unintelligible.

"Exactly what I thought. Professional Standards are watching him, or they will be when he shows up again. We have to liaise with them."

"But it's our case," said Rhodri. "They can't just butt in."

"They can," said Zoe. "I have to play the politics. What about Mike Grainger? Any news?"

"Nothing," said Connie. "He's still not at home."

"That's suspicious in itself."

"He might have just gone on holiday," said Mo.

"Hell of a coincidence. No, we have to find him. Rhod, see if you can get his phone records."

"Will do."

Zoe gazed at the board. She felt stuck.

"Any suggestions? Anything else come in?"

"Sorry, boss," said Rhodri. Connie pursed her lips and shook her head.

"Right. Connie, keep on at that Facebook hack. Tell me as soon as you can trace it."

"I'm not holding out much hope."

"Speak to Digital Forensics. See if they can help."

"Yes, boss."

"Mo, can you intercept Ian before he gets home? I want him talking to us before he speaks to Alison. He doesn't know about the message yet."

"Just me?"

"Just you. I need to think."

"Right, boss."

They had so many leads, but none took them anywhere. She needed twenty minutes of quiet time, to clear her head and unpick all the threads.

"Have we got any paperwork on the Osmans? Family records, finances, that kind of thing?"

"Over there." Mo pointed at a box in the corner, decorated with a floral pattern.

"What's that?"

"Alison's filing system."

"That's all they've got?"

"That's what she told us."

"Right. Come on everyone, you've got things to do."

She pulled the box onto the desk. Even if there was nothing here, the process of sifting through paperwork would help her think.

CHAPTER THIRTY-SIX

THE OFFICE WAS QUIET. Connie bent over her computer while Rhodri muttered on the phone. Mo had gone to find Ian Osman.

Zoe lifted the files out of the box, unsure where this would get her. Documentary evidence was her thing. It had given her a way in to the Canary case, and to Bryn Jackson's murder. Maybe it would help again.

If nothing else, this would calm her mind. There were connections here, and she couldn't see them. She needed to do better than this.

There wasn't much. Medical records, a few guarantees for household appliances, payslips from Alison's school. Zoe ploughed through them, scanning each one as she went, trying to let her subconscious join the dots.

At the back of the box was a file of family documents. Large documents, folded carefully. She spread them out on the desk.

Alison's birth certificate. She was thirty-six years old,

born in Manchester. Maddy's and Ollie's. Benedict was listed as the father in both cases.

Behind them were two adoption certificates. Ian had adopted Maddy in 2017 and Ollie in 2018. She checked them again, puzzled by the dates. If he was going to adopt both children, then why not at the same time?

At the back were two wedding certificates, and a death certificate. The first wedding certificate, dated 2005, was from London. Alison and Benedict. The second was for Alison and Ian, from Birmingham. The death certificate was dated 2016. Benedict Tomkin, unascertained cause of death. A year after he disappeared.

She went back to the second wedding certificate. It was dated before the death certificate. So Alison had still been married. What did that mean, legally?

She sat back in the chair, slapping her thigh with a ruler. *Think.*

Why hadn't Ian adopted Ollie at the same time as Maddy? Did he believe Ollie was his child? Surely he'd adopt the boy anyway.

She let her eyes roam over the board. Maddy and Olly were at the top, with Ian and Alison immediately below them. To one side were Benedict, Grainger, Trish and Barbara.

Her gaze stopped. There was one last thing to check out. She grabbed her jacket and opened the door to the main office.

"Rhod," she said. "Come with me."

CHAPTER THIRTY-SEVEN

THE CLIMBING CENTRE was busy at this time on a Sunday afternoon. Zoe squeezed past the queue to the front desk, Rhodri trailing behind her.

She smiled at the man behind the desk. He wore a t-shirt with a silhouette of a mountain range, and a woollen beanie. He was lean with arm muscles he must have worked hard for.

"Can I speak to the manager, please?"

"Rick's on his break."

She widened her smile. No need to get her warrant card out, not yet.

Rhodri stepped in. "We want to book a climbing party. For our daughter."

The man looked between Zoe and Rhodri. Zoe clamped her lips between her teeth, trying not to imagine her and Rhodri as parents.

"Alright then. One minute."

A woman in the queue behind them muttered under her breath. Rhodri turned to her. "Good place, this?"

"Normally."

"What d'you mean, normally?"

"There's a good vibe. Friendly. We don't normally get people in suits pushing in."

"Sorry. Not my idea." He glanced at Zoe who flashed the woman a reluctant smile.

The beanie-clad man returned with an older man with more hair on his chin than his head. "You want to book a party?"

"Yes please."

"Can we see the party room?" asked Rhodri.

"Sure. Come with me."

They followed the man up a flight of stairs. Zoe leaned in towards Rhodri. "How do you know this stuff?"

"Used to come here a lot, when I was in Uniform. Seen plenty of kids' parties. Makes them lots of money."

"Nice one."

At the top of the stairs, the man held a door open for them. He looked Zoe up and down as she passed.

They followed him along a corridor to a scruffy room with a long table in the centre and a mountains mural on the wall.

"This is it," he said. "How many kids are you thinking of? You want catering?"

Zoe showed him her warrant card. "Sorry. We don't want a party."

"Shit." The man scratched his head. "Why all the cloak and dagger?"

"I don't think your customers would be all that keen on CID showing up."

"You're not wrong there. If it's about the lights-out party last week, I got a permit..."

"Nothing like that." Zoe sat on one of the low chairs surrounding the table. The man followed suit, as did Rhodri.

"What's your name?"

"Rick Kent. How can I help you?"

"Did you have a regular here called Benedict Tomkin, four years ago?"

Rick sucked his teeth. "We did. Bloody shame."

"Did you know him well?"

"No. He learned to climb here, but I was assistant manager at our other centre then. In Stafford."

"I know this might sound like an odd question, but could he have survived?"

"He was climbing K2. Do you know anything about K2?"

"Nothing."

Rhodri went to speak but Zoe raised a hand to shush him.

"Everest is the famous one," Rick said. "The one they go on about. But although it's the highest, it's not the toughest."

"And K2 is."

"Don't get me wrong, Everest isn't a walk in the park. All this bollocks about people being dragged up, if you'll excuse my language. Well, it's bollocks. But K2... K2 is different."

"So you don't think he could have survived."

"Ten percent of people who climb K2 don't come back."

"Ninety per cent do though."

"No one has ever gone missing on K2 and come back alive. Everest, yeah. You heard of Beck Weathers?"

"No."

Rhodri shifted in his chair. "Lucky bastard. Should have died."

"He climbed K2?" Zoe asked.

"No, boss. Everest. '96. Year of the disaster. Left for dead

three times but got down alive. Lost half his face, though."
He shivered.

"That kind of thing wouldn't happen on K2," Rick said.
"It's a more technical climb, much riskier. Fall, you're dead."

Zoe nodded. "Did he have any friends here?"

"He might have had a climbing partner, he could have
been in one of our clubs. Like I say, I wasn't working here
then. I can ask around for you."

"Thanks."

"Can I ask why?"

They hadn't spoken to the press. Zoe was beginning to
wonder if that needed to change, but wasn't about to break
the story here, with this man. "I can't tell you, I"m afraid."

"You think he was murdered."

"Nothing like that. Like I say..."

"He wasn't murdered. Climbers look out for each other. I
promise you his death would have been an accident."

CHAPTER THIRTY-EIGHT

"THANKS." The two detectives trailed down the stairs after Rick and made for the door. Brian watched them, his chest tight.

Rick approached the desk. "You signed in the youth group?"

"All here except Paul."

"Paul never turns up."

"Yup. They're having their safety briefing. The main wall's filling up."

"Good. I might as well come back now, finish my break."

Brian shuffled out from behind the desk and let his boss take over.

"What did they want?"

Rick opened a drawer beneath the till, searching for safety forms. "Who?"

"Those two coppers."

Rick stood up. "Who said they were coppers?"

"They had it written all over them, mate. Everything alright?"

"Why, you done something I should know about?" Rick smiled.

Brian felt his skin bristle. "Course not. Not good for business, though."

"Well, they were pretty discreet. I wouldn't be surprised if the bloke came back. Keep an eye out for him, eh?"

"You want me to roll out the red carpet?"

"I just want to know if he comes back."

Brian looked towards the climbing wall. There were police officers who climbed here. They gave a ten percent discount to emergency services. He'd spoken to most of them, and they were all PCs. No CID.

"Right, boss."

Brian headed for the bouldering room, committing the male detective's face to memory.

CHAPTER THIRTY-NINE

MADDY WAITED for the door to be opened again. Olly had eaten most of the food that had been left out for them earlier and was playing with the plushies. Most of the time he was content, absorbed in his game. But every now and then he would stiffen, stare at her, and start crying.

Maddy did her best to console him, but she wasn't his mum. She had no idea how to do this. At home they spent most of their time arguing. It felt weird to want to care for him.

At last the door opened. She lowered her face and pulled Ollie to her. She looked up through her eyelashes, determined to see.

The figure slunk in, pausing to look at her and Ollie then heading for the desk. The door was open.

Maddy pulled in a quick breath and grabbed Ollie. She lifted him off the bed. He cried out but she ignored him.

The figure turned to face them. "Stop!"

Maddy ignored him and jumped off the bed. She ran for the door, Ollie in her arms. He was heavier than she expected. Mum carried him around all the time, she made it look easy.

She yanked the door wide and threw herself through it. They were in a narrow hallway, nothing like the landing outside her door at home. She hesitated, the unfamiliarity jarring her.

At the other end was what looked like a front door. She ran towards it, heaving Ollie up over her shoulder.

"Stop it!" Ollie cried. "That hurts."

"Shush, Ols. It's OK. This is part of the game. We have to beat Mum in a race."

"Where's Mum? That isn't Mum."

He'd shifted his weight and was looking behind them, at their kidnapper.

"Don't look, Ols."

"That's not Mum!"

Maddy landed against the door, gritting her teeth. She grabbed the latch and turned.

It didn't budge.

She gave it a twist. Nothing happened.

She looked down. There was another lock, one with no key.

She felt her body hollow out.

She leaned against the door, hammering. "Help! Someone help us!"

Footsteps approached from behind. Ollie was crying. "Stop it. I'm scared."

Maddy pulled him over her shoulder so he was in her arms. She cradled him. She bent into him, sliding to the floor. Her tears mingled with his.

Stop it, she told herself. *Be brave.*

But she couldn't.

The man's hand landed on her shoulder. Every muscle in her body tensed.

"Come on, Maddy. Ollie."

Don't talk to us like that. Maddy retched.

Ollie clung to Maddy, convulsing. His cries were more like screams now.

"Ollie, sweetheart, be quiet now," their captor said. "It's all going to be OK. We'll take good care of you."

CHAPTER FORTY

TRAFFIC WAS heavy in the tunnels under the city centre.

"Where are you with sorting us an office closer to the Osmans?" Zoe asked Rhodri.

"Erdington are being difficult, boss."

"Difficult? Why?"

"They won't say. But they're on Birmingham North's territory."

"Oh, for God's sake."

Birmingham had two branches of Force CID. Their own in Harborne, and Birmingham North, in Aston. Which lay between them and the Osmans.

"What do they want, an in on the case?"

"Like I say, it's just a hunch boss."

"OK. I'll talk to Lesley. Her oppo'll help us."

"Let's hope so."

Zoe's phone rang and she pressed the hands-free button.

"DI Finch."

"Boss, it's Mo. Where are you?"

"Stuck in traffic in the city centre. Rhod's here with me."

"How did it go at the centre?"

"Dead end. No way Benedict would have got back alive. What about Ian Osman?"

"Still waiting for him."

"He hasn't turned up yet?"

"'Fraid not."

"Maybe he's heading into work."

"I've asked the front desk at Kings Norton to tell me if he comes in."

"Well, he has to come home at some point. Sit tight."

"Will do. I've got something that'll cheer you up."

"Go on." Zoe glanced at Rhodri. He gave her a sheepish grin.

"Connie's tracked down Mike Grainger. He's visiting his mum. Guess where?"

"I don't know, Timbuktu?"

"Castle Bromwich."

Castle Bromwich was in north Birmingham, not far from the Jaguar factory at Castle Vale. Not far from the Osmans. Much closer than Exeter.

"Great news. We'll head over there."

"You want me to join you?"

She glanced at Rhodri. "You stay where you are. Rhodri can take up the mantle."

"Good."

"How's Connie getting on with the Facebook thing?"

"Still working on it."

"Let me know if anything changes."

"Will do."

"Right." She pulled into the outside lane and did a U-turn at the next lights.

"Boss, that was left turn only."

"I'm not sitting in that all day. If Mike Grainger took those kids, we need to get there fast."

CHAPTER FORTY-ONE

A CAR DROVE past Mo and pulled into the Osmans' drive. Mo watched in the mirror as Ian got out. He carried a laptop bag and looked haunted.

Mo slid out of the car and approached him.

"Sergeant Osman, I'm DS Uddin. I work with DI Finch. I need to talk to you, if you don't mind."

"Don't imagine I have any choice."

"Thanks. Can we sit in my car?"

Ian gestured towards his front door. "I'd rather go inside."

"I don't think we want to involve your wife in this conversation."

Ian paled. "Do I need a lawyer?"

"Not as far as I'm concerned."

"Right. OK, then. Let's get on with it. She'll be waiting for me."

They got into Mo's car. Mo twisted in his seat to face Ian.

"Has your wife been in contact with you today?"

"I went out before she was awake. She needed her sleep."

"I can imagine."

"So are you any closer to finding my children?"

"We've got a number of leads we're following up. One of which is a Facebook message sent to you early this morning."

"Sorry?" Ian patted his jacket pocket then sighed, remembering he didn't have his phone.

"It came from PC Trish Bright. Do you have a relationship with her?"

"A what?" Ian drew back. "No. I used to work with her, that's all."

"We believe someone hacked her Facebook account to contact you."

"What's this message? What aren't you telling me?"

Mo took a breath. "Before I tell you this, you have to know it makes no difference to our investigation. We're doing everything we can to find your children and bring them home. Both of them."

"What do you mean, both of them? What aren't you telling me?"

"The message was an instruction to you and your wife." Mo pulled a printout from his pocket. "Best if you read it yourself."

Ian scanned the sheet, his fingers trembling. He glared at Mo. "What the fuck is this? Why didn't you tell me this morning?" His eyes flashed.

"We've been looking for you all day. Where have you been?"

"Driving around. I went to Cadbury World, just in case."

"Like I say, this doesn't change our investigation. We don't expect you to take any action on this."

"What sort of action could I take? I'm not exactly going to tell Trish which of my kids I want her to kill, am I?"

"It does give us another lead. We're checking where it came from, tracing the hack."

"You've got Digital Forensics working on it."

"And a member of our team."

"I expect you to give this to the experts."

"We know what we're doing, Mr Osman."

"So why can't you tell me this inside? Aren't you telling her?"

Mo glanced in the mirror. The house was still, as was the rest of the street.

"I wanted to ask if you might know of anyone who might want to hurt you."

"Hurt me? It's not me who's been taken."

Mo tugged at his tie. "Someone might want to hurt you, through your children."

"I get that. Who?"

"That's what I'm asking you."

Ian turned to face forwards in his seat, avoiding eye contact. "Can't think of anyone."

"You've been a DS for ten years. I'd be surprised if you didn't have someone that holds a grudge against you."

"Nope."

Mo eyed Ian. He sat stiffly in the passenger seat, his eyes on the road in front of them.

"Think about it, Sergeant Osman. Someone you arrested who's been released. Someone who's in jail but had friends on the outside. Any criminals you've had to do deals with."

Ian's head shot round. "What d'you mean, do deals with?"

"Informers. Anything. Organised crime."

"I have no idea what you're talking about." Ian's eyes were on Mo now, his face hard.

"I'd appreciate it if you could give this some thought. If there's anyone you can think of who might have taken your children, I'm sure you'll want to tell us."

"Of course."

"Thank you."

"Now I think it's time I went to my wife."

Mo nodded. Ian got out of the car and hurried to his house, his footsteps echoing in the empty street. Mo watched him, wondering if a word of truth had passed his lips.

CHAPTER FORTY-TWO

MIKE GRAINGER's mum lived in a low block of council flats in Castle Bromwich. The street was scruffy, litter piling up against the curb and a car on bricks in the driveway opposite.

"You want me to go round the back, boss?" Rhodri asked.

Zoe looked up at the building. "Not sure there'll be a back door. But yeah. Just in case."

They made their way to the building. Two teenage boys stood at a bus stop a couple of hundred yards down. They gave Zoe a look of hostility.

She walked up the building's front path as Rhodri disappeared round the side. The tarmac was cracked, weeds sprouting through potholes. She wondered how old Mike Grainger's mother was, how mobile.

She looked up at the windows. Grainger's mum lived on the second floor. The curtains were drawn, no sign of movement.

Rhodri reappeared. "Fencing all the way along the back, boss. No sign of a door, though."

She nodded. There was a bank of buzzers next to the

front door. She pressed the one for trade and put a hand on the door. It didn't give.

"They only work in the morning," said Rhodri.

"Huh?"

"My aunty lives in one of these blocks. The trade button stops working at midday."

"Right." Zoe eyed the buzzers, considering. She didn't want to give Grainger any warning. She pressed the two for the top floor.

A voice came from the speaker. "What?"

"Hiya, I've just moved in to flat one and I've lost my keys. Can you buzz us in please?"

"Whatever."

The door buzzed and she pushed it open. Rhodri stepped in before her.

The hallway was dark and dingy. There was a smell of vegetables cooking.

The stairs were off to one side. Rhodri went ahead to check there wasn't a back door and Zoe started up them. At the second floor, Rhodri joined her.

"What now, boss? You think he's got them?" Rhodri whispered.

"I think we need to talk to him."

She didn't have enough evidence to seriously expect Mike Grainger had taken Maddy and Ollie. But he could have made it up here in time. He had form, and a reason to hate Alison. And there was something about this building that gave her the creeps.

"Let's be cautious, OK?" she said.

"Shall I call it in?"

"Tell Connie where we are."

He grabbed his phone. "Con, listen. We're at Grainger's

mum's place. If you haven't heard from us in twenty minutes, raise the alarm. Ta."

They were keeping away from Mrs Grainger's door, out of view of any potential spy hole. Zoe moved to it in a swift motion and banged hard on the wood.

They waited. No answer.

Zoe tried again. She leaned into the door. "Mike Grainger, are you in there?"

Nothing.

Rhodri squatted on his heels and pushed the letterbox open. "No sign of life. Maybe we should call Uniform, get them to open it by force."

"We'd need a warrant for that."

"What d'you want?"

Zoe span round to see a young woman with thin curly hair standing in the doorway opposite. She raised her warrant card.

"We're looking for Mike Grainger. His mum lives here."

"What d'you want him for?"

"Does he come to visit much?"

The woman shrugged. "Don't ask me. She's lovely, though. I help her with her shopping, she makes my little girl a cake."

Zoe allowed herself a smile. She pressed her card into the woman's hand. "If he comes here, call me please. We need to speak to him urgently."

"He might be at the hospital."

"Sorry?"

"There was paramedics here, earlier. She collapsed, fell or something. If he's here, I guess he'd have gone with her."

Zoe and Rhodri exchanged glances.

"What time?" she asked the woman.

"About eleven? You'd have to ask the paramedics."

"Which hospital did they take her to?"

"Don't ask me."

"Thanks for your help."

"No problem." The woman blew a stray hair out of her eyes and closed the door.

Zoe turned to Rhodri.

"You think he went with her?" he asked.

"One of two things. Either he went with her, or he's taking advantage of the fact her flat's empty."

He eyed the door. "Right. Shit."

She bent down to flip the letterbox open. There was no movement, no sound. She squinted and held a hand up for Rhodri to be quiet, her mind focusing. There was a clock ticking somewhere, one of those loud ones old people had.

Surely if two children were in this flat, she'd hear them?

Not if they were scared. Not if they were keeping quiet.

"Right," she said. "Rhodri, you stay here. Make sure no one comes in or out. I'll send a squad car to back you up. I'm heading for the hospital."

CHAPTER FORTY-THREE

"Connie, I need you to check A&E admissions this morning. Castle Bromwich, picked up around eleven o'clock."

"The kids?"

"No. Mike Grainger's mum. Find out where she is. I'm going to head to Heartlands now, it's the closest."

"Leave it with me."

Zoe stopped at an island, tapping her foot on the accelerator while she waited for the cars in front to move. The M6 was off to the right, beyond it Spitfire Island. She'd encountered her first body there as a detective. Spring 2003. Before Nicholas was born, before she'd got to know Mo properly. It seemed like a lifetime ago.

Her phone rang. "Connie?"

"She's at Heartlands. She had a mini stroke a week ago, seems to have had a recurrence. And her full name's Emma Grainger."

"Thanks. Find out which ward I need to go to."

"OK."

Ten minutes later Zoe pulled into the car park at Heartlands hospital. She raced to the main entrance, cursing the layout of these places. It was as if hospitals were designed to stop you getting where you needed to be.

Her phone buzzed. "She's in the stroke unit, boss. Ward 23."

"Thanks, Connie." Zoe headed to the reception desk. "Where will I find Ward 23?"

The woman curled her lip. "I've got a queue here."

"I'd be grateful if you could tell me, please." She showed her warrant card. "It's an emergency."

"Oh. Sorry. First floor. That way. Take the first right and follow the signs."

"Thanks."

Zoe sped along corridors, weaving between people. This place was vast and sprawling, walkways connecting buildings and ramps that made it hard to know which level you were on. At last she made it to Ward 23.

A nurse was at the front desk.

"DI Finch. I need to know if you've admitted an Emma Grainger."

"She had a stroke, Inspector. I don't see why you need to—"

"It's her son. I need to speak to him urgently, in relation to a current investigation."

"Her son?"

"Michael Grainger. Did he come in with her? Has he been to see her?"

"We don't keep records of that kind of thing. It's enough to keep on top of the patients, not relatives too..."

"OK. Could he be with her now?"

"Visiting finished over an hour ago."

Of course it did. "Can I at least take a look at her?"

"I'm not letting you in there, if that's what you mean. Mrs Grainger has been through a lot—"

"Through the window. I want to see if there's any sign he's been here with her."

The nurse pursed her lips. "Very well."

"Thank you."

The nurse muttered to a colleague behind her before leading Zoe along a wide corridor to a set of double doors. She pushed through them and Zoe followed. They were in a narrower corridor now, with windows and doors leading into wards on both sides. Zoe scanned them for someone who might be Emma Grainger.

"She's in there," the nurse whispered. She pointed through a window on the left. Beyond it were six women in six beds.

"Which one?"

"Nearest to us."

A grey-haired woman sat in the bed closest to Zoe. Her skin colour wasn't much less grey than her hair and her face was lined. She stared ahead of her, focusing on nothing.

"Can I speak to her?"

"I've already told you no."

"What time is visiting tomorrow?"

"Two pm."

"I'll send someone back, to speak to her son. If he visits."

"Please, don't be too obvious about it. Patients on this ward don't need the stress of police hanging around."

"We won't be hanging around. And yes, we'll be discreet."

The nurse nodded, her eyes cold. She led Zoe back to the front desk. Zoe took one last look back at the double doors and turned away. She had to be patient. She had to hope

Grainger would go back to his mum's flat, that Rhodri would stop him.

She didn't have time. Three days, the message had said. Now they were nearing the end of day one.

She checked the map again. All those ramps, she'd got confused. She stood in front of the lift, her limbs heavy. It felt like she was chasing shadows, with nothing concrete.

The lift door pointed open and a man got out, holding a cup of coffee. He was tall and thin, with a grey beard and a scar beneath his right eye.

She stepped forward and put a hand on his arm. He flinched.

"Mike Grainger," she said.

The lift door closed behind him. "What? Is it my mum? Where have you taken her?"

"It's not your mum."

"Where is she? How is she? Are you her doctor? I'm sorry I didn't get here earlier. I..."

The lift door opened again and two nurses came out. Zoe stepped to one side.

"I'm not a doctor. My name is Detective Inspector Finch. West Midlands Police."

Grainger's eyes widened. He took a step back.

"I need to talk to you about—"

"No."

A woman came out of the lift, holding a toddler by the hand. Grainger slid behind them, making it impossible for Zoe to reach him. His eyes flicked to the lift controls as Zoe tried to edge forwards. Grainger held her stare, jabbing at buttons as the lift doors closed between them.

CHAPTER FORTY-FOUR

ZOE STARED at the lift doors in front of her. *Shit*. She looked up at the display. The light for the ground floor came on.

There was another lift next to it, but that was going up.

A man in scrubs passed her.

"Where's the stairs?" she barked at him.

"What? Over there. That door."

"Thanks."

She ran to the door and clattered down. Only one flight, but he had a head start.

At the bottom, Grainger was nowhere to be seen. A set of automatic doors was gliding shut a few metres away. Zoe ran through it.

It was dark now and the cold air blasted her face. In front of her was a set of wide steps and a ramp. She ran down the steps, eyes roaming the space ahead. There was a patch of grass, a couple of benches, a road, and then a car park. Dark figures moved between the cars. One of them might be Grainger. Or maybe not.

She ran out to the centre of the grass, hoping to get a

better view. She caught movement off to her left, around the side of the building. Someone running?

She ran after them. She rounded the corner of the building and almost crashed into two paramedics coming the other way.

"Watch out." One of them held his hands up in front of him.

'Sorry. Did you see a man come this way? Tall, with a grey beard and a scar right here?" She pointed to the spot on her own face.

"Sorry."

She ran past them. The car park was almost empty now, visiting hours over and no outpatients on a Sunday evening.

She ran to the middle of it and stopped, turning in a circle. Scanning.

He could have gone the other way. He might be the other side of the building, hiding.

Or he could have made for the road.

She ran to the entrance to the car park, watching for signs of him. A bus stop was immediately outside. A bus pulled up.

She sprinted to it, slamming into the side of the shelter.

"Careful," muttered an elderly man sitting on one of the bus stop's plastic seats. The bus pulled away.

She ran after it, waving to the driver, but he was oblivious. She returned to the bus stop.

"You alright, bab? I think you missed it."

"Yeah." She panted. "Did you see anyone get on that bus?"

"Couple of people. You missed your mate?"

"Something like that. Was one of them a man, tall, with a beard?"

"Not sure, bab. Mighta bin. There was a couple of blokes but I can't be sure."

She grabbed her phone. Somewhere on here was a photo of Grainger. She showed it to the man. "Did you see this man?"

The man squinted. "My eyesight's not so good these days. Didn't put me glasses on this morning. Too vain!" He laughed.

"OK. Thank you."

She headed back to the hospital. At least this gave them a reason to search Emma Grainger's flat. And she would put someone from Uniform at the hospital, in case he came back.

She leaned against the side of her car and dialled Lesley.

CHAPTER FORTY-FIVE

ZOE PULLED up outside Emma Grainger's building. Rhodri got out of a squad car in front of her.

"Alright, boss?"

"I saw him."

"Grainger?"

"At Heartlands. When I told him I was police, he ran."

Rhodri's eyes widened. "Shit."

"Too right. Anyway, there's a unit on its way. We've got authorisation to break into that flat."

Rhodri rubbed his hands together. "Good."

"This isn't something to get excited about, you know."

"Sorry boss." He dropped his hands to his sides.

A crowd had gathered in the street, kids and adults watching them. Two PCs held them back, refusing to field questions.

Another squad car pulled up and a man got out. "Sergeant Ford, Force Response. Who's in charge?"

"Me. DI Zoe Finch."

"Which property is it?"

Zoe pointed. "Second floor flat, left hand side. We've looked through the letterbox and can't see any movement, but there might be two frightened or injured children inside."

"We'll go carefully, then."

He turned to his team and briefed them. Zoe shifted from foot to foot, willing him to hurry. At last he turned to her and nodded. "You stay here, ma'am."

"I want to come with you. Those kids..."

"Alright. But stay behind us."

The outer door to the building was open, one of the neighbours having placed a brick against it while they came outside to watch. The crew hurried in, signalling to each other as they went. Sergeant Ford gestured to Zoe and then to the stairs, his eyebrows raised. She nodded.

She followed him up. He went slowly, not making a sound. Anyone in that flat could have seen them from the window. But the curtains had stayed closed the whole time.

They reached the door.

"Police!" Sergeant Ford called. He waited a moment then stood back to let two of his team to come through with the enforcer. Zoe stood back.

The door splintered and Ford's team went in. Zoe followed, watching them split up to cover each of the flat's rooms.

The flat was brighter than she'd expected. Framed photographs lined the walls of the hallway, and a bowl of pot-pourri sat on a narrow table.

"Clear!"

Zoe squeezed past the uniformed officers into the living room. A heavy armchair sat to one side, facing a bulky TV set. Ornaments and trinkets covered the surfaces. She thought of Barbara Wilson's house.

She went back into the hallway. There were just three other doors: a kitchen, bathroom and bedroom. The kitchen was tiny, rammed with food packets and chipped teacups. She pushed open the door to the bedroom. A uniformed constable stood inside.

"It's clear, ma'am."

Zoe nodded, her stomach heavy. The room was empty. The bed dominated, barely enough space around it to walk. The space was neat and tidy, the pink bedspread pulled smooth.

She went downstairs. Rhodri was leaning on her car. He leapt away from it like he'd been caught keying it.

"Well, boss?"

"Nothing," she sighed. "They're not here."

CHAPTER FORTY-SIX

"CONNIE. Sorry we left you on your own all day."

"It's alright, boss. I'm working on the Facebook hack."

"Good." At least someone was doing something useful. Zoe slumped into her chair, her limbs aching. She rubbed her calf.

"You alright, boss?"

"Grainger's out there somewhere. Running like that... it makes him our number one suspect."

"You want me to change up the board?"

"Carry on with what you're doing. Got a source yet?"

"No. But it's not just Trish's Facebook that was hacked. Her Twitter too."

"Go on."

"I've managed to close it down. But there's a photo."

Zoe felt a weight plunge inside her. "Show me."

Connie brought up an image on her screen. Two children: a boy and a girl. Maddy and Ollie. Asleep, huddled together on a bed with a blue sheet.

"Can we trace this?"

"Not so far. I called Adi Hanson in Forensics, hope that's OK. Yala in his team is helping me."

"Good. She knows her stuff."

"This is beyond me, boss."

"Don't talk yourself down. You've closed the Twitter account?"

"And deleted the tweet. Luckily Trish doesn't have many followers. I guess anyone who saw it would have thought it's her own kids."

"I don't know if she's got any."

"They're a bit younger, boss. But she's got a boy and a girl. Like the Osmans."

Zoe sat back in her chair, remembering Trish Bright's look of fear in the interview. Had that only been this morning?

The door to the office opened. Rhodri slumped into his chair, sighing heavily.

"Thanks for your help back there, Rhodri."

"No problem, boss. What now?"

"We need to track him down. God knows how."

"I'll get on to Exeter. See if they can help."

"Get his reg. We can check CCTV."

"There's no car registered to him."

"Then he definitely got the train up. OK." She clasped her hands behind her neck, leaning back. "At the hospital, he got on a bus."

"Which one, boss?" asked Rhodri.

"I didn't see. Find out what bus routes go from outside Heartlands. Where they lead. It's a long shot, but it's something."

"Right."

Connie leaned back, gazing at her screen. The image of

the two children filled it. They looked peaceful. Zoe felt a stab in her gut.

Mo walked in and hung his suit jacket over his chair. "What's up? Where did that come from?"

"It's Maddy and Ollie," Zoe said. "Taken by their kidnapper. Who we think is Mike Grainger."

"How so?"

She filled him in the events of the evening.

"We can use that, to find them," Mo said.

"A blue sheet doesn't give us much to go on."

"No."

"The number 28, boss," said Rhodri. Last one was at 7.45, goes to Small Heath." He rounded the desk to see Connie's screen. He made a small noise, like a squeak.

"What is it?" Zoe asked.

"They *are* asleep, aren't they?" he said. "Not... dead?"

The photo was dim and unsaturated, but the children's faces had colour in them. "Not dead, Rhodri," said Zoe. *Not yet*, she thought, but didn't say.

"They're just asleep," said Mo.

"When was the tweet sent?" Zoe asked Connie.

"An hour ago. Sorry, I should have..."

"You were busy getting it taken down. It's OK."

"Thanks. I'm sorry."

She turned to Mo. "Any joy with Ian?"

"He's saying nothing. Seems to care more about protecting his own hide than getting his kids back."

"Maybe it's because they're not his kids," said Rhodri.

"He adopted them," said Zoe. "And he's brought them up. There's still the possibility that Ollie is his."

"Should we check that out?" asked Mo. "Get a DNA test?"

"I don't see what good that would do."

"Ian may have done it himself."

Zoe thought back to the adoption certificates. "If he did, I reckon he found out that Ollie isn't his."

"How so?"

"He adopted Maddy in 2017 but Olly in 2018. I reckon the gap was for him to find out about Ollie's parentage."

"It wouldn't have made any difference," said Mo.

"No?"

"If he's not on the birth certificate, he's not his dad. Not legally. Doesn't matter if they share DNA. The certificate is what matters."

Both birth certificates had had Benedict's name. Zoe wondered what it would be like not to know if your child was really yours. If you would love them the same.

"Right," she said. "I want you all to get home. It's gone nine, and there's a lot to do tomorrow. Yala Cook's working on the hack, and we're not going to find Mike Grainger tonight. Go home, all of you. Back early in the morning."

CHAPTER FORTY-SEVEN

ZOE LEANED into the bathroom mirror. Her eyes were blood-shot and her skin dull. It was five am. She'd been awake since four, staring at the ceiling and turning the case over in her head.

Mike Grainger had run from her. He'd had time to get up to Birmingham after checking in at his local station in Exeter. And he probably had a grudge against Alison.

Ian – there was plenty Ian wasn't telling them. Where had he been all day yesterday? Going to Cadbury World didn't take as long as he'd told Mo. Did he know who'd taken Maddy and Ollie and was trying to get them back himself?

Then there was PC Bright, and her social media hack. Zoe couldn't rule out Trish's involvement. If her relationship with Ian had been closer than the two of them claimed... Could they both be working with Hamm?

She shuddered. Trish Bright had been there all through the Jackson case. She'd had access to ACC Jackson's house, his private belongings... If she was corrupt, then who knows what she might have found. Or hidden.

Zoe spat out her toothpaste and rinsed the sink. Trish had looked terrified in the interview. She'd done nothing suspicious when she'd been FLO at the Jackson house. And her accounts had been hacked. Chances were she was an innocent victim of all this, just as much as Alison.

Zoe wiped her face on a flannel, trying to drag the blood back into her cheeks. None of this would solve itself. She needed to go back to the office. First priority was to find Mike Grainger.

Her phone was buzzing on the bedside table.

"DI Finch."

"Boss, it's Mo."

"You in the office already?"

"No, I've got to get the girls ready for school. Cat's on an early. But I've had a call from Connie."

"Go on."

"She's found the source of the hack."

Zoe gripped the phone. "And?"

"It's local."

Zoe chest tightened. She knew it. "Where?" She half expected it to be Kings Norton police station. If not that, one of Hamm's offices.

"It's an accountancy firm in the city centre."

"I'll be right there."

Connie was at her computer, searching through the Companies House website.

"How long you been here, Connie?"

"Not that long."

"Long enough to crack this hack."

"Oh, it wasn't me, boss."

"No?"

"Yala. She ran a trace overnight, called me on my mobile."

"Well done anyway."

Connie shrugged.

"So," said Zoe. "What we got?" She pulled a chair over to Connie's desk.

"It pings through ten IP addresses in all. Scattered all over the world. But the originating one is right here in Brum."

"Where?"

"Hatton and Bannerjee. Accountancy firm, in Colmore Row."

"Who are the partners?"

Connie brought the firm's website up on her screen. She clicked through to the 'team' page. "Two senior partners. Sheila Hatton and Ashok Banerjee."

"Never heard of them." Zoe made a mental note to get those names checked against the Canary files. "Can you find out who their clients are?"

"Not without a warrant."

"OK. We'll go round there. I don't suppose they're open yet?"

"They open at six."

"Good."

Rhodri entered. He looked glum.

"We'll find him, Rhod," Zoe said. "That's your focus for today. The priority is to monitor his mum's flat, and see if we can trace his movements around the city over the last few days. He could go back to the hospital, too. Uniform have got someone on both locations."

"You really think he'll go back, boss?"

She leaned on the desk. "It's got to be worth a shot. You OK to liaise with Uniform?"

"Yeah. I'll see what CCTV I can get too. That bus."

"Good thinking."

Connie sat back, intent on her screen. Zoe looked over her shoulder. Mugshots of the accountancy firm's partners stared back at them: the two senior partners and a gaggle of juniors. Trying their best to make themselves look businesslike but approachable.

"OK," she said. "Let's go."

"Can I help?" Mo hung his suit jacket on the back of the door.

"Mo. I'd like you to keep an eye on Ian. Watch him, check if he goes anywhere unexpected. I've got a feeling he's trying to work this case himself."

CHAPTER FORTY-EIGHT

HATTON AND BANNERJEE was in a Victorian building that had been refurbished to within an inch of its life. Zoe and Connie waited at the front desk, taking in the leather sofas, bold artwork and plush carpets.

"Nice work if you can get it," said Connie.

"Too right."

A man Zoe didn't remember from the company website approached them, hand outstretched. "Eldon Coots, Public Relations Manager," he said.

"We asked to speak to the senior partners."

"They're in a meeting right now. You'll have to make do with me."

Zoe made a mental note to get the partners' home addresses. They could be in a meeting, or they could be hiding.

They followed the man to a vast office overlooking Pigeon Park. Connie paused to take in the view of the cathedral and gave Zoe a wide-eyed look. Zoe shrugged and took a seat opposite Coots.

"How can I help you?" He clasped his hands together and placed them on the table. He'd arranged his face into a picture of calm. Gentle smile and steady gaze. But sweat beaded on his forehead.

"We believe a police officer's social media accounts were hacked by someone in this building on Saturday night," said Zoe.

Coots shifted his face into a grave expression. "That's a very serious accusation."

"Which is why I asked to speak to one of the partners."

Coots leaned back. "I understand that, Inspector. But as I explained, the partners are indisposed. They're in a conference call with our Boston office."

"Your website says nothing about an international operation."

"It's brand new." He smiled. "I guess IT need to catch up."

"Maybe they're the people I need to be talking to. Who's your head of IT?"

"I can assure you that this firm uses all the latest digital security protocols. A hack couldn't have originated from this building."

"Our investigation says that it did."

Coots sighed. He pulled a phone from his pocket. "Shaun, can you get down here? Meeting room ten." A pause. "Yeah, I know. Sorry, mate."

"Is Shaun your head of IT?"

"Shaun Rice. He'll reassure you."

Zoe leaned back as the three of them waited in silence for the IT head to arrive. When he did, she was surprised to see him as smartly dressed as his colleague. A brightly patterned tie was the man's only concession to the fact that he wasn't an accountant or a PR bod.

"Mr Rice, my name is Detective Inspector Finch. This is DC Williams."

Coots turned to his colleague. "They reckon someone hacked our systems."

Rice shook his head. "There's no way this building's cyber security could be breached."

Connie leaned forward. She had her notepad open on the smooth table. "Does your system use Imprion?"

"I can't tell you that."

Zoe rolled her eyes. "You're talking to the police, Mr Coots, not a competitor."

He gritted his teeth, avoiding Zoe's gaze. "We do."

"Did you know that system's being updated by its developers because of a known bug?" asked Connie.

Rice scoffed. "They overreacted. The minivik bug makes no difference. Imprion is the most robust system out there."

"Mr Rice, you work for a mid-sized accountancy firm, is that right?" asked Zoe.

"I wouldn't say mid-sized," interrupted Coots. "We're expanding into the States, we..."

Zoe held up a hand. "You aren't one of the big four."

Coots looked as if she'd slapped him. "No. We aren't."

"Right. So why d'you feel the need to use the most robust cyber security systems on the market? They don't come cheap, I imagine."

"Starting price for a bespoke installation is fifty grand," said Connie.

Zoe whistled. "That must equate to a lot of audits."

"Our client's data is important to us," said Coots. "We

know that if it was to be compromised, we would lose all credibility as a firm."

"Is there anyone in particular you don't want accessing your data?"

Rice grunted. "Look, Inspector, I don't know what you're getting at, but there's no law against securing your business."

"No." Zoe turned to Coots. "Is there anyone you don't want accessing your clients' data? Organised crime, for example, or the police?"

"I have no idea what you're talking about."

Zoe sat back, watching the two men's reactions. There was no shiftiness there, no sense that they were lying. Coots's job was to protect his company's public reputation, and Rice's was to protect its data. To find out more she'd have to speak to the partners.

"OK," she said. "This hack. Connie. What time was that Facebook message sent?"

"Five am Sunday morning, boss."

Zoe nodded. "Many people in this office at that time? I know firms like yours keep punishing hours, and if you've got multiple time zones to keep up with..."

"The east coast of the US is five hours behind us. That would be midnight their time," said Coots.

"Like I say, long hours."

"So you think someone in this building used our systems to hack the Facebook account of one of your officers. Why?"

"Twitter, too," said Connie.

Coots gave her an exasperated look. "But why?"

"That's not the point," said Zoe. "We need to find out who did this." She leaned in. "There are lives depending on it."

Coots held her gaze, not flinching. He was one of those

men who thought his good looks gave him permission to be thoroughly unlikeable, she thought. "Terrorism?"

"No. That's all I can tell you."

"It'll be those kids," said Rice. "The ones from Cadbury World."

Connie made an involuntary sound. Zoe clenched her fist in her lap. They'd asked witnesses not to tell anyone they'd been interviewed. So far, they seemed to have complied.

"Just tell me were the hack came from," Zoe asked. "That's all I want to know."

"Very well," said Rice. "I've got kids of my own." He looked at Connie. "You got an IP address, data trail?"

"Yes." She pulled a laptop out and placed it on the desk. Rice rounded the table to sit next to her and they leaned into the screen together.

"Any sign of the partners?" Zoe asked Coots while they worked.

"Not yet." He stared back at her. They didn't need him here, not now the geeks had their work to do. But she got the impression his job was less to help her than to guard her.

"Hang on a minute." Rice left the room and came back with his own laptop. It was sleeker than Connie's police-issue one. He opened it up and returned to his spot next to Connie.

After a few more moments, Connie looked up. "Bad news, boss."

"What?" Zoe stood behind her chair and looked at the screen.

"We've tracked it to a workstation. The woman who uses it is on honeymoon in the Maldives. And the entry systems show no one was here at 5am on Sunday."

"Are you sure?" Zoe asked.

Rice span round in his chair. "Sorry. On a weekday, yeah. There'd be people here. But even we have lives."

"It had to come from somewhere."

"The building was empty."

"Security guards?"

"I've checked the job logs and the camera system. They were downstairs, in the basement. Security office."

"Could it have been a laptop that was taken home?"

"The IP address would be different, boss," said Connie. "Sorry."

CHAPTER FORTY-NINE

ZOE PULLED out from the Five Ways roundabout, wishing she could put her foot down and release some of this tension.

"Sorry, boss," said Connie.

"Not your fault. I still want to speak to the partners, though."

"Home addresses will be registered with Companies House."

"Good. Did you believe those two?"

"Rice knew what he was doing. Coots... well, Coots was a PR guy. Who knows whether you can believe them?"

Zoe allowed herself a smile. She curled her toes inside her shoes, willing the traffic to clear. At last they reached the station.

Rhodri stood outside, shivering against the cold. The sky was leaden, and Zoe was grateful she wore a heavy shirt under her leather jacket.

"Not a fag break I hope, Rhodri?"

He blushed. Rhodri hadn't smoked for eighteen months, and it had been a struggle for him.

"No, boss. Uniform have brought Mike Grainger in."

She exchanged glances with Connie. "Excellent. Where from?"

"The hospital. He tried to get in another entrance."

"Right." Zoe walked into the station, feeling optimistic for the first time in over twenty-four hours. "Let's interview him."

The two DCs were behind her. She sensed a tension between them. Who would be chosen to accompany her?

She turned to them. "Is Mo around?"

Rhodri's shoulders dropped. "No, boss. He's gone to Erdington."

"Don't worry, Rhod. I was winding you up. Come with me. Connie, you check out Hatton and Banerjee, will you? I want to know everything about them. If they've so much as misfiled a receipt for a latte, I want to know about it."

"On it."

She smiled at Rhodri. "Have you seen Grainger, since they brought him in? Were you there?"

"I was at the house. But it's only ten minutes away. Fifteen, on a Monday morning. I got there just as the van left with him in it."

"And he's just got here."

"Yep."

"Good. Let's not give him a chance to compose himself. Solicitor here?"

"Duty solicitor."

She wondered which of the two regulars it was. Hopefully Frank Goad, who out of the two solicitors was less of a fan of the *no comment* interview.

Grainger was waiting with Goad in interview room three, the one that smelt of damp no matter how many times they cleaned it or brought in a portable heater. Zoe rubbed her arms for warmth and sat down.

"Michael Grainger, I'm DI Finch. We next yesterday at the hospital. This is DC Hughes."

"You have to let me see my mum. She's ill."

"I know that, Mike, but I also know that when I spoke to you yesterday at the hospital, you ran from me."

He shifted in his seat.

"Why did you do that?" she asked.

He shared a look with his solicitor, who nodded.

"No comment."

Zoe sighed. *Not this.*

"Mike, this really doesn't look good for you. Most people don't run away when they're approached by a police officer."

He shrugged.

"Do you know Alison Osman?"

Grainger looked up. He blinked a few times then looked down at his hands, clasped in his lap.

"You and she worked together, before you moved to Exeter."

Another shrug.

"Mike, we really need to clear this up. Just tell me if you knew her. We have already spoken to the school, you know."

"Yes. I knew her."

"And what kind of relationship did you have?"

"We didn't have any kind of relationship. What's this about? I thought it was just cos I'd left Exeter."

"Sorry?"

"I'm not supposed to leave the city. You know that, surely. That's why you came after me." He put his fingers to his forehead and scraped at the skin. "I'm sorry. But Mum could be dying. I feel bad enough that I wasn't here when she had the first mini stroke. If she…"

Zoe glanced at Rhodri then turned back to Grainger. "Hang on. You think I stopped you in the hospital because you broke the conditions of your court order?"

"Well, yeah. Why else?"

"You still haven't told us about your relationship with Alison," said Rhodri.

Grainger looked at him, frowning. "I hardly knew her. She was a TA in the infants, I taught Year Six. I don't see what she's got to do with anything."

Zoe pursed her lips. The head teacher had said it was all anonymous. It seemed that Grainger hadn't found out who'd reported him.

"Mr Grainger, do you have any reason to want to hurt Alison Osman? Did you have any misunderstanding during your time at the school? Did you argue?"

"I barely spoke to the woman. What's this about? I'll go back to Exeter, I promise. I'm sorry. I just had to see Mum."

He pulled back in his chair, his mouth widening. "Hang on. It was her, wasn't it? The one that reported me?"

Zoe pointed at the file in front of Rhodri. He cleared his throat. "When did you travel to Birmingham?"

Grainger stared off to one side. "*Bitch*." He looked at the file. "Dunno. Friday lunchtime. I got the train."

"Which train?" Rhodri asked.

"It was just a bloody train." He scratched his cheek. "I came to see my mum. She had a stroke."

"Which train, Mike?" Zoe asked.

He blew out through pursed lips. "Um. The twelve thirty. From Exeter St David's. Around that time anyway."

"The twelve twenty-eight?" asked Rhodri.

"Sounds about right. Got into New Street at about half two."

"Did you go straight to your mum's?" asked Zoe.

"Yeah. Course I did."

"Can you prove that?"

"You can ask my mum." His face fell. "Except you can't." He looked up. "Please, let me see her. She's all alone."

"Where were you yesterday afternoon?" asked Zoe.

Grainger flushed. "At the Villa. It's not often I get to see a game. I wish I hadn't gone."

"So, your mum was seriously ill. You came up to see her, despite the restrictions on your movements. And then you go out to a football match?"

"Makes me look like a right bastard, I know. But she seemed OK. They'd discharged her on Tuesday. I didn't know she was going to have another one, did I?"

Rhodri flicked through the file. "Can you prove you were on the twelve twenty-eight train?"

"No. It was an e-ticket. Open." He patted his pockets. "Hang on. Yes, I can. I bought a coffee, on the train. I kept the receipt. Your custody sergeant has got it, with my other stuff."

"DC Hughes," said Zoe.

"Yes, boss."

Rhodri left the interview room. Zoe eyed Grainger across the table. He returned her gaze, his eyes flicking from her to the camera behind her. He was nervous.

He'd broken the terms of his court order. He was right to be nervous.

"I'll have to tell Exeter police that you're here."

"I know. I had to see her."

She didn't respond. Her own mum had been hospitalised

with a stroke just a few months earlier. Hers had been caused by too much drinking. Zoe had been to see her when she was asleep, but not visited in daylight hours. They didn't have that kind of relationship.

Rhodri returned with a brown envelope, wearing forensic gloves. He tipped the contents of the envelope out. House keys, a paperback book, some cash, a pile of receipts. He thumbed through them.

"Here it is. Espresso and a muffin. Twelve forty-five from the onboard shop." He looked at Zoe. "He was on the train, boss."

CHAPTER FIFTY

"MA'AM."

Lesley beckoned Zoe into her office. "How's it going?"

"Not good."

"How so?"

"We had a lead, a guy Alison reported under Safeguarding a couple of years ago. He's got an alibi. We're following up on Trish Bright's social media hack, but there was no one in the building it came from. And we're watching Ian Osman. But there's nothing concrete."

"How can I help?"

Zoe pointed to the chair. "May I?"

"You don't have to ask."

She lowered herself into the chair, her breathing unsteady.

"I think we'll have to do an appeal, ma'am."

Lesley closed her laptop. "You resisted that, before."

"We had plenty of leads. One of them had to go somewhere. But we've got two days. We need everything we can get."

"It'll take more than two days to sift through the crap an appeal will generate."

"We'll work round the clock."

"There are better things for you to be doing than dealing with the results of a phone-in."

"With respect, ma'am. Someone might have seen something, maybe a car leaving Cadbury World."

"We've interviewed everyone who was there."

"Yes, and word's starting to get out."

"Bugger. Had to happen sooner or later. Who?"

"Someone at the firm where the hack come from knew about it."

Lesley sipped her coffee. "I know you're desperate, but I don't think this is the right way to go."

"We have to do—"

"Whoever's got those kids wants to be found. They wouldn't have sent that message if they didn't."

"I don't agree. They want to spook the Osmans. That's not the same thing as wanting to be found."

"I think there'll be another message."

"What makes you so sure?" Zoe asked.

"Feel it in my water," Lesley replied. "When you get to my age, you get a hunch for these things."

Did Lesley see herself as old? She didn't look more than five years older than Zoe. Perhaps she was ageing well.

"Have you run cases like this before?" Zoe asked.

Lesley nodded, her face grave. "Twice."

"And?"

"The first one, I was a DS. Victim was a girl, aged seven. She came back unharmed, it turned out to be her biological father. We'd been watching the stepdad all along, the SIO got a right bollocking. But she was OK, that's the important thing."

"And the second one?"

"I prefer not to talk about the second one."

"Sorry."

"Don't be. You're just trying to find an angle. I've got confidence in you. And your team. You'll find something. But if we run an appeal right now, we bring everything to a juddering halt. We'll be bogged down in horseshit and we'll never find them."

Zoe surveyed her boss. She was right. Zoe was clutching at straws, giving up too easily.

"Now," said Lesley. "You've got three lines of enquiry. I suggest you follow them."

CHAPTER FIFTY-ONE

IT WAS GETTING dark when Mo spotted movement in the house. The front door opened and two figures stood silhouetted in it. One of them was Ian. The other wasn't Alison. The new FLO, maybe.

He wondered what vetting process they'd gone through to replace Trish, and where she was now. Getting your social media hacked, that was bad news for a copper. Mo was bloody glad he never went near that kind of thing.

Ian scanned the street as he walked to his car. Mo shrank down in his seat. He'd borrowed Rhodri's car, a Saab that had seen better days. But Ian wouldn't recognise it.

Ian drove past him and Mo turned the ignition. It took a few tries but then roared into life. He chuckled, imagining Rhodri picking out this thing.

He followed Ian at a distance, reaching a roundabout where Ian turned left, towards the city centre. Traffic wasn't heavy, nor was it light. Perfect tailing conditions.

He wanted to call in to Zoe, let her know what he was

doing. But Rhodri's car didn't have a hands-free facility. He wondered if it had anything more advanced than a radio.

Ian stopped at a set of traffic lights. Mo waited for a car to put itself between them then pulled up.

The Saab went quiet.

Damn.

Mo turned the key in the ignition, muttering at it. It spluttered a few times, then stopped.

The lights changed and Ian drove off. Mo twisted the key again and pressed the accelerator, knowing he was flooding the engine.

He watched as Ian's tail lights disappeared into the distance.

CHAPTER FIFTY-TWO

CONNIE WAS FLICKING through websites when Zoe got back to the office, her breathing heavy.

"You alright, Connie?"

The DC turned, her eyes alight. "I had a thought."

"Yes?"

"Five am on a Sunday. No one from the firm was in the building. No one with a pass."

"At least that's what Shaun Rice told us."

"Yeah. But what about the cleaners? They might have been in. They might have seen something."

"Or it could be one of them who did it."

"I doubt it, boss. The security they've got on those work-stations is pretty intense."

"OK. But what if the cleaners let someone in? By a back door?"

Connie nodded. "It's possible, boss."

"What are you looking for?" Zoe nodded towards Connie's screen.

"Trying to find out which cleaning company they use."

"There's an easier way to do that."

Zoe dialled the main number for the accountancy firm. It was answered on the third ring.

"Hatton and Banerjee, how can I help you?"

"Oh, hi. Who's that?"

"It's Shona, on reception. Can I put you through to someone?"

"It's Mandy, from the cleaning company," said Zoe. Connie's eyes widened. She stopped scrolling through screens on her computer and watched Zoe.

"We've got a problem with our van," Zoe continued. "We'll be a bit late tonight."

"Er, OK. I'll tell admin."

"Thanks. And tell them we'll be in a different van. I know what your bosses are like about security."

"No problem. Will it still be a Cleanways van?"

"Cleanways. Different reg."

"Right. Thanks for letting us know."

Zoe hung up. "Cleanways. Find them."

Connie turned to her screen. She brought up the cleaning firm's website. "They're in Hockley, boss. Industrial estate."

"Right. I'll get over there. Find out who they send to those offices."

"Er, boss?"

Connie had a screen open with information about the cleaning company's employees. At the top was the employee of the month. The woman had pale skin, and long dark hair.

Zoe stared at the photo. "Since when did Alison Osman work as a cleaner?"

CHAPTER FIFTY-THREE

Brian watched the Focus pull away, followed by the Saab. The Saab had been sitting at the kerb since he'd arrived. He wondered why Ian was being watched and followed.

The house was in darkness. From time to time a light at the front would come on, but there were blinds at the window so he couldn't see if she was there. Or if she was alone.

He had to be sure she was alone.

He shifted position next to the tree he'd been sheltering under. His back hurt, and the damp seeped though his trousers. These things were supposed to be waterproof, but he'd bought them in the sale at the climbing centre and they were probably past their best.

The door opened again. Two people stood inside. He raised himself up to get a better view. One of them was in uniform. He hadn't seen a police car arrive. Was the Saab police? Was the sainted Ian Osman in trouble?

His phone buzzed in his back pocket. He answered it, his eyes on the two women in Alison's front door. It was a neat house, dull but he could see why she liked it. A far cry from the places she'd lived in in the past.

"Brian, where are you?"

He pressed the volume control button, convinced his girlfriend's voice could be heard despite him having the phone pressed so far up to his ear it hurt.

"Just on my way back from work," he whispered. "On the bus."

"I've bought a takeaway. I need to go back to mine tonight, got some stuff to do and an early start tomorrow. Shall I wait?"

Brian checked his watch. Eight pm. Across the road, the policewoman left the house and walked away. He watched her, wondering if a car would arrive to pick her up.

"Sorry, love," he said. "Don't let it go cold. Will I see you tomorrow?"

"Of course you will."

"Good. Love you." He blew a kiss into the phone.

Alison closed the door and went back inside. He stood up, eyes on the house. Ian could be back at any time, tail or no tail. He needed to act.

CHAPTER FIFTY-FOUR

Zoe stood outside the cleaning company's offices. She'd had half a mind to go straight round to the Osmans' and find out why Alison hadn't told her she had a second job. But she wanted to speak to the cleaning company first.

It was dark and no lights were on. She leaned on the glazed door, trying to see inside. There was a small entrance hall and a door beyond. No sign of life.

She hammered on the door again and stood back to look up at the building. Behind her, two cars were parked. They could be for this building, or for one of the neighbours.

She'd have to come back in the morning.

Sunday morning was over twenty-four hours after Maddy and Ollie had disappeared. Alison had been distraught. Zoe had seen her reaction. No one would go into work in those circumstances.

Or had her grief been for show, and she'd sent the message via Trish's account? Why?

But then...

There was the CCTV footage. Alison leaving with her children, then returning. Was she faking the whole thing?

Were they working together? Did Alison know Ian was involved with Hamm and Reynolds? Had they planned the whole thing, right up to Ian not showing at Cadbury World?

Damn. There'd been that Reynolds Contracting van outside the house last time she'd been there. She hadn't followed that up.

Her phone rang.

"Mo. Everything OK?"

"Not exactly."

'What's up?" She walked to her car. "What's Ian done?"

"He left the house about an hour ago. I started following him, but then the car broke down."

"His car?"

"No, Rhodri's."

"Rhodri with you?"

"I borrowed his car. I figured Ian would recognise mine. Only thing is, I can't get hold of Rhodri so I've had to call the AA out."

"Where are you? I'll come and get you."

"No need. They're almost done. Rhodri needs a better car."

"I can imagine. Any idea where Ian was going?"

"Sorry, Zo. He was headed towards the city centre, but we only got as far as Gravelly Hill. He could have gone anywhere, M6 even."

"Yeah."

"You still at the station?"

"No," she said. "There's been a development."

"Yes?"

"Turns out Alison Osman has a second job," she told

him. "Working for the firm that cleans the offices where Trish Bright's hack originated."

"Say that again."

"Connie tracked down the hack. It's an office in Colmore Row. Alison works for their cleaning company. Given that the message was sent at 5am, there's a chance it was her."

"Or someone else from the company."

"You think one of her colleagues might have the kids?" Zoe asked.

"Who knows?"

"Right. I need to talk to Alison." If someone from the cleaning company had a grudge against Alison, and had Maddy and Ollie...

"I'm closer," said Mo.

"I'll pick you up on the way. What's happening with Rhodri's car?"

"Hang on." There was a pause and muffled speech. "They're done," said Mo. "I'll get round there and wait for you. I'll keep an eye out for Ian."

"Be careful."

"Will do."

CHAPTER FIFTY-FIVE

Mo was waiting in Rhodri's car when Zoe arrived.

"Nice car," she said in a mock American accent.

Mo grumbled. "Bloody thing. Still no sign of Ian."

"Maybe that's for the best. Get her on her own."

A man crossed the street as they approached the house. He seemed to be approaching the house too. As he saw them, he hesitated then swerved away from them.

"Seen him before?" Zoe asked.

"Never."

"Hmm. Are we that obviously police?"

"I'm not. Maybe you..."

Zoe punched Mo's arm. "Oi."

He smiled at her. "You're doing a better job than you think, you know."

"We're no closer to finding those kids. And we have less than two days."

"Hopefully it'll all be resolved in a few moments."

"Hopefully."

She rang the doorbell, resisting the habitual police knock, and waited.

"Oh." Alison had been crying. Her eyes brightened. "Any news?"

"Sorry, no," said Zoe. "We need to ask you a few more questions, if you don't mind."

Alison's expression reverted to dejection. "Of course." She stood back to let them through.

"The house was silent. "Have you been assigned a new liaison officer?" asked Zoe.

"PC Lark. Yes." Alison didn't look happy. "She just left."

"Is your husband in?" asked Mo.

"He went out a few hours ago, had to go into the station."

Zoe exchanged glances with Mo.

They followed Alison into the living room, where she turned on the overhead light. Their reflections stared back at them from the long windows.

"Sorry," said Alison. She drew the curtains. "Do you want a drink?"

Zoe smiled at her. "You don't have to look after us. This won't take long."

"Oh, right." Alison stood in front of them, tugging at the sleeves of her cardigan. The hems were threadbare.

"It might be best if we sit down," said Mo.

"Of course." Alison gestured towards the settee. Zoe and Mo sat next to each other while Alison took the armchair. "How can I help?"

"You work as a teaching assistant at Pennfield school, is that right?" asked Zoe.

"You've been there. Deborah told me. Is everything alright?"

"Do you have another job, a second job?"

Alison frowned.

"I understand you might not have declared it. We're not worried about that, you won't get into trouble. But do you also work for Cleanways as a cleaner?"

Alison stared at them. "No."

"Are you sure?" asked Mo. "Two jobs can help make ends meet."

"Ian earns good money as a sergeant. And my TA salary is OK. I don't need a second job."

"It's just, we've seen a photo of you on the company website for this firm," said Zoe.

"That's impossible." Alison tugged harder at her sleeve. "Which firm?"

"Cleanways," said Zoe. She took out her phone and found the website. She held out the page with Alison's photo.

"That's not me."

"Are you sure?' Zoe peered at it. The photo was small on her screen. "It looks like you."

Alison looked up at Zoe. Her pupils were dilated, her expression hard. "It's not me."

CHAPTER FIFTY-SIX

OLLY WAS asleep on the bed. Maddy had plucked up the courage to tweak the curtains, just slightly, and was standing in the window.

The room looked over an alleyway, then a fence and a car park. Nothing like her own room, with its view of the garden. A high streetlamp was right outside, making the alleyway orange. A man walked along it, carrying a heavy bag. She wondered if he was from this flat, or just someone walking past.

She looked past the car park, trying to work out where this was. It wasn't familiar. There were no shops she recognised, no street signs. She could be anywhere.

She heard a sound behind her and turned to see the bedroom door being opened. Their captor was back, face obscured by the hoody.

Maddy shrank back into the window, her gaze darting to Ollie on the bed.

"Don't hurt him."

The man lowered his hood. The room was dark and Maddy couldn't make out his features.

"I won't hurt him as long as you stay there."

Maddy tensed. That was a woman's voice. She stared at Ollie, suddenly cold. On the one hand, the woman might hurt Ollie if she moved. On the other, she needed to protect him.

She took a step forward.

"I told you don't move."

The woman's voice was calm. Not angry, but firm. Maddy didn't want to make her angry.

"Do it to me," she said.

"Do what to you?"

"Whatever you're going to do to Ollie. Do it to me instead."

The woman sighed. "I'm not going to do anything to him. Or to you. You're too valuable."

Maddy frowned.

The woman went to the bed and watched Ollie sleeping. Maddy followed her gaze, her heart thumping in her ears. She heard herself make a small sound, a cry.

The woman turned. "Shush."

Maddy swallowed the lump in her throat. "Don't hurt him."

The woman bent over and gathered Ollie up. Maddy gasped. She ran forward. The woman held out a hand, stopping her in her tracks.

"You stay there, and he won't get hurt."

Maddy fought back tears. She had to be strong.

"Good girl. He'll be impressed."

"Olly will?"

"You'll see."

Olly stirred in the woman's arms. Maddy held her breath, waiting for him to scream. The woman slid to the door and let herself out. Ollie opened his eyes and looked up at her.

"Ols," said Maddy. The woman raised a finger to her lips again and closed the door behind her.

Maddy ran to the door and yanked on the handle. It was locked. On the other side, Ollie screamed.

Ollie's cries grew fainter as the woman took him away.

CHAPTER FIFTY-SEVEN

ZOE COULDN'T SETTLE. She'd gone home from the Osmans' and tried to watch TV, but her head was too full of the case. Nicholas was out again, seeing a film with Zaf.

Eventually she'd given up and driven to Mo's house.

She knocked on the door, scratching the skin on her palm.

It opened and a tall blonde woman stood silhouetted in warm light.

"Zoe."

"Hi, Catriona. Mo in?"

"He's upstairs, tucking the girls in. Something up?"

"I've caught you at a bad time.'

"No. It's fine. Come in."

Catriona let Zoe pass and closed the door behind her. She shivered. "Freezing out there."

"Yeah," Zoe replied. She hadn't noticed.

"Come through to the kitchen."

Zoe followed Mo's wife into a modern kitchen. A dishwasher rumbled in the corner. The worktops were clean and tidy, the door fronts sparkling. So different from her own kitchen.

"Coffee?" Catriona reached into a cupboard and brought down a bag.

"Please. You sure I'm not disturbing you?"

Catriona poured coffee into the filter machine and turned to Zoe. "You two have been thick as thieves for the last fifteen years. I'm used to it."

Zoe smiled. "Thanks. How are the girls?"

"Fine. Fiona's been having a bit of trouble with bullying at school, but we're working on it."

"I bet." Zoe wouldn't like to be the teacher who had to face up to Dr Catriona Denney. Twelve years a GP, she was the most efficient woman Zoe knew.

"Zo." Mo was at the door, rolling his shirt sleeves down. "I didn't hear the door."

"I'll leave you two to it." Catriona left the room.

"What's happened?" asked Mo. "Is it Alison?"

Zoe shook her head. "I just needed to think."

"And you think best in my kitchen."

"I think best when I've got you to bounce my thoughts off."

"OK. Bounce away."

"That coffee'll really help my brain work."

"Oh. Of course." He went to the machine and poured out two mugs. Zoe raised an eyebrow. He didn't normally touch caffeine in the evening. He gave her a dismissive look and put her mug down in front of her.

"So Grainger is a dead end," she said. "His alibi's tight as Rhodri's trousers."

"We've still got the cleaning company."

"Alison swears blind she doesn't work for them."

"She could be lying."

"She could. But I had my eyes on her face the whole time, when we went round there. She looked shocked."

"She could be good at pretending."

Zoe leaned over the worktop, blowing on her mug. "She could. But I don't think she was. I can feel it in my fingernails, she's a nervous wreck."

"Someone lying to the police about their kids being snatched would be a nervous wreck."

Zoe eyed her friend. "You really are very cynical sometimes."

He shrugged. "I'm a copper. Comes with the job."

She picked up her coffee and sipped. "This is good."

"Cat keeps it in, special for when you come round."

"She does?"

He nodded.

"You're drinking it too," she said.

"I'm keeping you company."

"Am I someone you need to mollycoddle now?"

He straightened. "I'm not mollycoddling you, boss."

"Don't call me that. You know I don't like it."

"Sorry. Zo. You're pissed off. You're frustrated. Don't take it out on me."

"Yeah. Sorry." She took a long drink of the coffee. It really was very good.

"So if it wasn't Grainger," she said, "and the cleaning company thing is a busted flush, then what?"

"Not a busted flush."

"Not entirely, no. We'll go round there, in the morning. I'll take Connie."

Mo placed his mug on the counter, very carefully. "We have to consider the alternative."

"Which is?"

He hesitated. "Canary. Shand and Petersen."

She felt her heart skip a beat. "I thought about that." She clasped her hand tighter around the mug. "But Ollie's too young. The age range they went for was pre-teen to sixteen."

"Maddy's twelve."

"You think they'd take both of them, to get to her?"

He shrugged.

"We have no evidence that any of them were involved. Not Petersen, or Shand."

"Or Hamm," Mo said, his voice low.

"No."

"No," he repeated.

"So what do we do?"

Mo looked up. "You're the SIO."

"All the kids they took were in care. The kind of kids no one would miss, or that if they did, they'd assume had run away. Ollie and Maddy come from a loving family. A family with a police officer in it, for God's sake."

"A police officer under investigation." Mo put his mug down, grimacing. "I don't know how you drink this stuff."

She grabbed his mug and tipped its contents into her own. "Thanks."

"Maybe we're imagining things, boss."

She raised an eyebrow. He pulled a face.

"I bloody hope so," she said. "There's no solid reason to think the Canary lot have got anything to do with this. Just timing, is all."

"And Reynolds."

She shivered. The Reynolds Contracting van. Had Ian

been paid the same way ACC Jackson had, Hamm hiring Stuart Reynolds to work on his house?

"Yeah. But the cleaning company, that's our strongest lead right now."

"Let's hope so," Mo said.

Zoe nodded, her coffee suddenly undrinkable.

CHAPTER FIFTY-EIGHT

CONNIE SLID INTO THE OFFICE. Mo was already here, no one else.

"Morning, Connie."

"Morning, sarge."

"I think the boss wants you to go with her to the cleaning company this morning. She'll be in soon."

"No problem. I just need to check the social media feeds."

"Of course."

He went into the inner office, closing the door. Through the glass partition, she saw him sit at the desk and pick up the phone.

Connie had to get through all the Osmans' social media accounts and emails before the boss got in. She settled into her chair and switched on her PC.

She scrolled through the social media feeds. More messages from concerned friends, a bunch of ads. Nothing had been posted to messages.

She switched to email. Ian's was unremarkable, something about a new credit card, confirmation of an Amazon order and a whole load of spam. She always wondered why people didn't strengthen their spam filters.

She switched to Alison's email and opened the first one. It was from an address she didn't recognise. There was an attachment. Checking the file type, Connie clicked on it.

It was a photo.

Connie stood up. Her eyes stayed glued to the screen.

"Guv!"

Mo was engrossed in his call.

She banged the door to the office. "Guv!"

He looked up, his hand over the phone. "What?"

She beckoned him out, her movements wild.

"You have to see this."

He hurried to her desk. She watched his face as he reacted to what was onscreen.

"Oh my God," he breathed.

CHAPTER FIFTY-NINE

ZOE LEFT THE HOUSE EARLY. She had time for a detour, and Reynolds's unit wasn't far away.

She turned her car in the direction of the light industrial estate he worked from, trying to convince herself it was just a coincidence his van had been at the Osmans' house. Surely the man had to do some legit work.

But Ian was police, and under investigation. This was no coincidence.

She pulled up at the end of the road leading into the estate, eyeing Reynolds's unit. A van was parked outside, identical to the one she'd seen at the Osmans'.

As she got out of her car, her phone rang.

"Boss, it's Mo."

"Mo, I've been going over what we talked about last night. I'm outside Reynolds's unit. I want to find out why he's working for the Osmans. You're not waiting for me at the cafe, are you?"

"I'm in the office. Drop what you're doing and get in here now."

Mo was getting more comfortable with her promotion, but he hadn't gone so far as to give orders before.

She slid back into her car, turning the key in the ignition. "Why?"

"It's Ollie Osman, boss. We think he's been released."

CHAPTER SIXTY

"SHOW ME," Zoe barked as she ran into the office. All three of her team had the same photo on their monitors.

It showed a small boy, hunched on the ground inside a phone box.

"Is that definitely him?"

"Blond hair, about the right height," said Connie.

The boy's face was obscured.

"When was it sent?"

"An hour ago."

It was seven-twenty now. Birmingham's streets would be busying up. Ollie might have moved from that phone box. Or the kidnapper might have moved him.

"We need to identify that phone box," said Zoe.

"We're already working on it," said Connie.

Zoe leaned into Mo's screen and zoomed in on the photo. It was a glass-sided phone box, on a street corner. Behind it the street was quiet, just one car parked on the other side.

"That car," she said. "We need to identify it."

"It might just be parked there," said Mo.

"But it might not." Zoe looked up. "Rhodri, get the plates off that car if you can, and find out who it's registered to."

Behind the car was a row of shops. A post office, a SPAR and another one with an indistinct red sign.

"Anyone know where that is?" asked Zoe.

"Sorry, boss," said Mo.

She bit down on her thumb, staring at the image. "Where do we start?"

"I'm on Google Streetview," said Connie. "And the post office website."

"Good. Meanwhile, let's get everyone in here and see if anyone identifies it."

"It could be anywhere in the city," said Mo. "I suggest we send it to all the local CIDs, see if anyone knows it."

Zoe didn't like the idea of sending a photo of this vulnerable child around all the police stations in the city, especially given Ian Osman's situation. She clenched her thumb between her teeth.

"Do it," she said. "But Kings Norton..."

"Don't worry," said Mo. "We'll handle that one sensitively."

Zoe nodded, her head light. Thoughts crowded in. *Was* that Ollie? Why had the kidnapper let him go? Was it a trap?

And if Ollie had been released, what did that mean for Maddy?

She watched, helpless, as her team made calls and searched websites. She squinted into the screen.

The red sign on the third shop looked familiar.

"Wait," she said. She pointed at the screen. "That's a bookie's. Google it. Binghams."

"Got it, boss," said Connie. She leaned forward in her chair, focused on her monitor.

Zoe rounded the desk to stand by her side as the search results came up. Connie gave out a yelp of triumph.

"Got it!" She looked up and noticed Zoe next to her. "Sorry. Binghams bookmakers, just off Ladypool Road."

Zoe ran for the door. "Mo, call Uniform. We'll need backup. Rhodri, how fast can you run?"

CHAPTER SIXTY-ONE

ALISON OPENED THE DOOR, expectant.

"Oh."

"Sorry, love. Husband in?"

"He's in bed."

"Get him up, will yer? I want to talk to him."

"Is it about the roof?"

"Yeah. Kinda."

She nodded. "Come in."

"It's alright, love. I'll wait here."

"I know the police said to stop work. I'm sorry if that's messed you around. But—"

He blinked at her. "Get yer husband please."

"OK. Sorry."

She put the door on the latch. Stuart Reynolds had been in her house plenty of times. He'd had one of his lads do the plumbing for the new bathroom, and he'd sat with her and Ian at the dining table when he'd priced up the roof work. But he'd never spoken to her like that.

She shook Ian awake.

"Ian love, someone to see you."

Ian grunted. "Wha?"

"Sorry. He won't put up with me."

"Shit. I'm knackered."

So am I, she thought. She'd slept no more than three hours in the last three days. But here she was, getting up first, waiting for the liaison officer, fielding visits from CID while he disappeared God knew where.

"Just talk to him. He probably just wants to sort out what's happening with the roof."

Ian sat up in bed. "What?"

"They made us stop his team working."

"Is it Reynolds?"

"Yes."

"Shit." He jumped out of bed and dragged on a pair of jeans. He thundered down the stairs, almost falling in his haste.

"Careful," she said. He raised a hand to shush her.

At the bottom of the stairs, Ian paused. He took a moment to check himself in the mirror then pulled the chain and opened the door.

"What d'you want?"

She couldn't make out what Reynolds was saying.

"Alright," said Ian.

Ian slid through the front door and closed it behind him.

Alison lowered herself to the bottom step, staring at the door. What was going on?

CHAPTER SIXTY-TWO

Two squad cars arrived at the same time as Zoe and Rhodri. They parked at an angle in the road and jumped out.

Zoe looked up and down the road. "What? There's no phone box."

Four officers piled out of the squad cars. A sergeant approached her.

"Ma'am. What are we looking for?"

"A small boy, in a phone box. Opposite that bookies."

She ran over to the bookies. It was the same one alright, Binghams. But there was no SPAR next to it, no post office.

She turned back to Rhodri. "Call the office. Find out if there are two of them."

He put his phone to his ear.

Zoe turned to the sergeant. "Do you know this area?"

'Worked here five years, ma'am."

"Is there another bookie's like this one? Next to a SPAR and a post office."

He frowned and gazed along the street. "There used to be."

"Used to be?"

"It moved. We closed it down last year, drugs being sold out the back. It shut down for a while, then reopened here. Been clean so far. Is that what this is about?"

"No. Where's the old location?"

"About quarter of a mile that way."

Zoe grabbed Rhodri by the arm. "It's moved. We need to hurry."

She nodded at the sergeant who jumped back in his car.

"Your car again, boss?" Rhodri asked.

"Jump in."

They sped after the two squad cars. Rhodri was still on the phone, explaining to Connie what was happening.

"Put Mo on," Zoe said.

Mo's voice came thorough the speaker. "You found him yet?"

"Not yet. Stay on the line. We'll need to tell his parents as soon as we've got him."

"I'll be right here."

She slammed on the brakes, almost hitting the squad car that had stopped suddenly in front of her. This was the street in the photo. It was unmistakeable.

The SPAR, the bookies, the post office... the phone box.

She ran to it. Two constables ran with her, one calling for her to keep away.

It was empty.

She felt like the wind had been knocked out of her.

She looked up and down the street, searching for signs of him.

"He could have run," she said. "He could be hiding somewhere."

The sergeant nodded and issued instructions to his team.

They fanned out, knocking on doors and searching gaps between buildings. One of them pulled lids off rubbish bins.

Rhodri arrived next to her. He stared at the uniformed officers. "I'll join them, boss."

She nodded. Tears pricked her eyes. If he'd been left here, and then got lost, or worse...

The sergeant approached her, his face tight. "No sign, ma'am."

She turned back to her car, wanting to scream.

CHAPTER SIXTY-THREE

"What was that about?" Alison asked Ian when he came back inside.

He flinched. "Just the roof. He wants to know when he can start work again."

"Don't you think we've got more important things to worry about?"

"That's what I told him." He passed her, heading into the kitchen. "Don't give me a hard time please, Al. It's not my fault."

She slumped against the doorframe. He was right. She needed a focus for her feelings, which changed from moment to moment. Ian was the closest target.

"Sorry."

He took her in his arms. She bent her head to lean against his chest. "They're doing everything they can, love," he said.

"It's been three days."

"I know."

She pulled away from him. "Are we going to have to do it?"

His eyes narrowed. "Do what?"

"What they said. In that message."

He grabbed her wrists. "No, Alison. No. We are not going to choose between them."

She nodded, her throat tight. "What if both of them die, because we weren't strong enough?"

He lifted her hands up, placing them on his face. "You *are* being strong. They won't die."

"How can you say that?"

"I know how Force CID work. They're good. You think I haven't checked up on that DI?"

"What have you found out about her?"

"She worked on the Canary case. Helped crack it. The ACC's murder. She's good."

"Canary. You don't think...?"

He closed his eyes. "We can't think like that, Al."

"I can't stop. I lie awake at night. And all I can think about is what might be happening to them."

He opened his eyes. "I know. I do too."

There was a bang at the front door. Ian reddened. "Bloody Reynolds. If he's back for..." He strode to the front door and hauled it open. He gasped.

"What is it?" Alison asked. "Reynolds?"

"No love. Oh my God!"

"What?" She felt her insides turn inside out. She was scared.

He turned to her. He was crying. Smiling. She frowned.

"It's Ollie," he said.

CHAPTER SIXTY-FOUR

ZOE THREW herself into the front seat of the car. Rhodri slid into the passenger seat.

"What now, boss?"

"I don't know."

"There has to be something."

"You're right, Rhodri. There has to. But I'm buggered if I know what it is."

The two squad cars were still here, and they'd been joined by two more. Uniformed officers had cordoned off the street and were mounting a systematic search of the area. She needed to get out there, help direct it.

She gazed at the officers. "Either he's run away from that phone box, or they've taken him somewhere else. We have to find him."

"Someone else might have him, boss."

"What do you mean?"

"He was left on his own in the middle of the street. Maybe someone's looking after him."

She clenched and unclenched her fists, digging her fingernails into her palms.

"Or worse," said Rhodri. Zoe gave him a look.

"God help me, there can't be two people abducting little boys," said Zoe. "We have to assume that either he's hiding somewhere, or this was a setup."

"If he's near here, they'll find him."

"Let's hope so."

Her phone rang.

"DI Finch." She closed her eyes.

"Zoe, it's DCI Clarke. Where are you?"

"Outside a phone box in Sparkbrook, ma'am. We thought Ollie Osman had been left here."

"He's not there."

"No. Have Uniform told you?"

"He's at home."

Zoe sat upright. "What?"

"We've had a call from the Osmans. Ollie has turned up back at home."

CHAPTER SIXTY-FIVE

IAN OSMAN LET ZOE IN, a tight smile on his face. Zoe nodded at him. Her first instinct was to congratulate him on Ollie's return. But Maddy was still missing.

"What happened?" she asked as they reached the living room. Ollie was bundled up in a blanket on the sofa, Alison's arms wrapped around him. She gave Zoe and Rhodri a nod.

"Let's go in the kitchen," said Ian.

"Of course." Zoe lowered her voice. "Had he been hurt? Does he need medical attention?"

"Physically, there's not a scratch on him." Ian closed the door to the living room and led them into the kitchen. "Mentally, who knows..."

Zoe nodded. "Your GP will be able to help with that. We'll set up a case management group, make sure he gets all the support the needs."

Ian stared at her. "What about Maddy?"

Zoe had been waiting for this question. "We're still looking for her. Do you think Ollie's up to talking to us? It's the best chance we've got."

"He hasn't spoken a word since he got back."

"No." Hardly a surprise. The boy was four years old and had been through an ordeal no one would wish on an adult, let alone a small child.

"Where did you find him?" she asked.

Ian looked out of the window. "He was sitting on the pavement, leaning on the front wall. Crying."

"Alone?"

A nod.

"Did you see any cars pull up, anyone coming or going?"

A flicker passed across Ian's face. He shook his head, gazing out of the window.

"Did anyone come to the house?"

He turned to her. "There was a bang on the door. Just one, and it didn't sound like a regular knock. More like something had been thrown at it."

Zoe nodded to Rhodri who left the room. She heard him open and close the front door.

"Are you sure you didn't see anything?" she asked.

Ian stared at her, his face pale. She waited. Finally, he slumped against the worktop and rubbed his forehead.

"Stuart Reynolds came round, a bit earlier on."

"He's your building contractor."

"Yes." Ian didn't meet her eye.

"How did you find him?"

He shrugged. "I dunno. Yellow Pages, maybe."

No one found tradesmen through the Yellow Pages anymore. "Are you sure?"

"I can't remember. He did our bathroom, last year."

"Was he recommended to you by another officer?"

A blush spread up Ian's neck. "No. Why would you think that?"

"Most people find roofers and that by word of mouth."

He shrugged. "I didn't."

"OK. What time was he here, and how long was that before Ollie appeared?"

"It was just before eight when he got here. I know because Alison had to wake me up. And I checked the alarm clock." He sniffed and looked at the floor.

Rhodri reappeared, holding a half brick inside an evidence bag. "Reckon it was this, boss. They must have slung it at the door. And it had a note wrapped around it."

Zoe took it from him. She unfolded the note, inside a second bag.

I chose for you.

Zoe felt her stomach dip. Why? Kidnappers normally asked for money. Either that, or you never heard from them again. Why did the kidnapper only want one child?

She turned to Ian. "Where were you when this hit the door?"

"What's that?"

She sighed and handed Ian the evidence bag. He turned grey.

"Maddy."

Zoe pushed out a breath. "Where were you, Ian?" She reached out and took it back from him.

He stared at the note in her hands. "In here. Talking to Alison."

"Did you see anything out of the window? Anyone passing, coming up the path?"

"We weren't looking out the window."

"And when you went to answer it, was there anyone there?"

"No one."

"Stuart Reynolds had left?"

"There was no sign of his van."

She sighed. Stuart Reynolds was definitely getting a visit.

"I know it's hard, but if Ollie can talk to us... I can get someone from the child welfare team, we'll do it here with you and his mum. We won't put pressure on him."

"I told you, he's not talking."

"Let me know if that changes, please."

"What about Maddy?"

"We're still looking for her. We've cordoned off the phone box, it's being examined. And we'll do the same outside the front of your house."

"What phone box?"

She realised the Osmans had no idea. "Sorry. We believed he'd been left at a phone box, this morning. When we got there, he was gone."

"What are you talking about? What didn't you tell us?"

"My DCI rang me to tell me he'd come home while we were still there."

Ian glanced towards the living room. "So they dumped him in a phone box, then grabbed him again and brought him home. Why would you do that?"

"I don't know."

"Well, bloody well find out."

"We will, Sergeant Osman. We will."

CHAPTER SIXTY-SIX

BRIAN HEARD the front door to his flat slam.

"Vic?"

"Only me!" she called.

There was clattering from the kitchen, the sound of her putting the kettle on. She appeared at his bedroom door.

"I thought you had an early start?" he said.

"I did. That's why I'm here, and not lying around in bed like you are."

"I thought you meant at work."

"Nah. What is this, twenty questions?"

He smiled and sat up, reaching for her. He pulled her down onto the bed. She smelled good.

"Where were you last night?" she asked. "Your curry's in the fridge."

"I know. I wasn't hungry when I got back."

"Where were you?"

"I went climbing."

"I thought you were sick of that place."

"I'm sick of running lessons for noobs. Getting a bit of climbing in myself is a whole different ballgame."

She nodded and leaned back into him. "Have you thought about what you want to do for your birthday?"

He pulled her long hair to one side and kissed her ear. Her skin was pale and smooth with a single mole right on the tip of her ear. He brushed the top of his own ear with his fingers, the spot where frostbite had eaten away at it.

"That's two days away."

She turned sharply. "I know." Her eyes gleamed.

"Vic..."

"What?"

"What you were saying the other night, about us having kids."

She leaned back, her eyes lowered. She said nothing.

"Maybe we can adopt," he said.

She shrugged, avoiding his eye.

"Just cos the treatment didn't work, doesn't mean we can't have kids."

"Maybe," she replied.

"We wouldn't get a baby," he said. "But we're sensible enough to look after an older child, aren't we?"

She looked into his eyes. "You think so?"

"Yes."

"Even a troubled child?" she asked.

He sighed. All the kids available for adoption would be troubled. "I've had plenty of troubles of my own. I think that would equip me."

She stroked the tip of his ear. He stiffened but didn't push her away like he had the first year of their relationship. He always wore a beanie at work, but was getting used to her looking at his injuries, to her touching them even.

"Sounds like you'd be perfect," she said.

He smiled. "Good. I'm glad we feel the same way."

CHAPTER SIXTY-SEVEN

ALISON WALKED behind Ian as he carried their boy upstairs. Ollie lay limp in Ian's arms, like a doll.

She couldn't take her eyes off him. He was like a feast, a feast she thought she'd never be able to enjoy again. Every now and then she would feel a stab of joy, followed by a twinge of pain at the thought of Maddy still being out there.

She passed Ian, Ollie still in his arms, and went into the bathroom. She ran the taps and poured half a bottle of Ollie's favourite bubble bath into it. She smiled at him, swirling her hand in the water and singing in a low voice.

When the bath was full she kissed the top of Ollie's head and took him from her husband. She peeled the boy's clothes off, watching his face for signs of distress, and sang as she went. He wore a pair of clean pyjamas. The police had asked for the clothes he'd been wearing when he came back. She'd watched them place the clothes into bags and take them away, a lump in her throat.

She stroked Ollie's hair out of his eyes. It needed cutting. She smiled into his face.

"Time for a lovely bath now, sweetheart. Lots of bubbles." His lips twitched but he didn't smile.

She dipped her hand in the water and brought it out, stroking his shoulders. He flinched. She bit her lip, fighting back tears.

She had to get him to talk, but had no idea how. The last thing she wanted to do was ask him what he'd been through, but suppressing it could be just as dangerous. It could scar him for life.

"Ready?" She gave him a cheery look and lifted him into the bath. Normally he would be either diving in or stiffening, not in the mood. Today he was limp, allowing her to lower him without a word.

Once in the bath, he leaned against her, not sitting up or kicking his legs like he normally would. She grabbed a sponge and washed him gently, her eyes roaming his body for signs of abuse. His skin was clear, if grubby. He didn't flinch or squirm when she touched him.

Ian stood in the doorway, watching. Silent tears traced his cheeks. Alison looked up at him, unable to smile.

She had to try. She had to show her son how happy she was to have him back. But with the terror of what he'd gone through and the dread that his sister might never come back, she felt like she was falling into a black hole.

Ian stepped forward. He grabbed a bath toy, a set of cups with holes in the bottom. He started playing a noisy game, filling them up and tipping them out, acting like everything was OK.

Ollie watched, his eyes dull. He blinked up at Alison. It was all she could do not to cry.

CHAPTER SIXTY-EIGHT

ZOE DROPPED Rhodri at the office and told him to work with Mo on the forensics from the phone box and the Osmans' front garden. Connie was already outside the main entrance, waiting.

"How was he?" she asked as she got in and fastened her seatbelt.

"Not talking," Zoe said.

"Poor darling. He must be traumatised."

Zoe nodded and pulled out of the car park. They drove in silence to the cleaning firm's offices, each one engrossed in her own thoughts.

Inside, the reception area wasn't as clean as Zoe would have hoped from a cleaning company. There was an empty desk and a bell. Zoe jabbed it.

A man came out of a door, wiping his hands on a paper towel. "Oh. Can I help? We don't get many walk-ins."

"I'm Detective Inspector Finch, this is Detective Constable Williams. We'd like to speak to the manager."

The man stiffened. He took a moment to finish wiping his hands then threw the towel at a bin, missing.

"He's not here."

Connie brought out her mobile. "Is your name Colin Clayton?"

"What makes you think that?"

'Because this is your photo, on your company website."

"Oh. Yes. Yes, it is me."

"In which case," said Zoe. "You're the manager."

Clayton blushed. "I thought you meant the duty manager. We have a roster of girls working the front desk. I'm strictly back of house."

Connie cleared her throat as she returned her phone to her pocket. Zoe smiled at Clayton. "So would you like to talk here, or inside?"

"Inside. Please." He ushered them through the door he'd come from, his breathing laboured. They walked along a narrow corridor and came to a pockmarked blue door. He fished keys out of his pocket and unlocked it.

"Come in. Please excuse the mess."

"Looks like you need to employ the services of your own company," said Zoe.

"Like I say, excuse the mess. It's not normally like this."

Mess was an understatement. The room was piled with paperwork. Mugs covered the surfaces, some with mould growing over the top, and there was a smell of stale milk. Zoe decided not to sit down.

"Do you clean for Hatton and Banerjee in Colmore Row?" asked Zoe.

"I'm afraid that's confidential."

Zoe gritted her teeth. "We're working on a major investigation, sir. Please answer my questions."

"I just don't have that sort of information to hand. Sorry."

"Find it then."

"Hmm." He started sifting through the paperwork on his desk, dumping files onto the floor as he went. When he turned back to them, the office was even messier.

"Sorry," he said. "Can't find the paperwork."

"What about that laptop?" said Connie. She pointed to a decrepit looking machine on top of a filing cabinet.

"Oh. That. That's not mine." He glanced at it then turned back to them, looking uncomfortable.

"OK," said Zoe. "Let me lay it on the line for you. We have reason to believe one of your employees might be involved in a serious crime. If you don't cooperate with our investigation, you could be arrested."

"I don't think so."

"Sorry?"

"I know my rights, DI... Finch, was it? You'd need a warrant."

"Very well."

His face brightened, a look of triumph appearing. Zoe wondered how his rights would be affected if she punched him.

"Very well," she said. "We'll be back."

CHAPTER SIXTY-NINE

DAVID RANDLE LEFT his office in Lloyd House, heading for the basement car park. He missed Harborne, the buzz of managing investigations. Heading up Force CID was a step up alright, but the politics was beginning to wear on him. Especially when he had to balance it with his other commitments.

His phone rang.

"Detective Superintendent Randle."

"It's me."

"How did you get this number?"

Trevor Hamm spat out a laugh. "Don't be a twat, Randle. Changing your number isn't going to get you off the hook."

"Wait a moment."

Randle hurried down the stairs, returning greetings from colleagues with brief nods, and dived into his Audi.

"Go on," he said.

"Your DI, that Finch woman."

Randle clutched the phone. "What about her?"

"Call her off, will you? She's sniffing around again."

"I'm not her boss anymore."

"Yes you bloody well are. You're top of the tree. You tell them to jump, they jump."

"Has she visited you?"

"Not me. One of my associates."

"Who?"

"It's the Osman case, she's barking up the wrong tree. Tell her to climb down."

"That's a bit vague."

"You suddenly go slippy, now you're a Superintendent?"

Two men walked past the car, glancing in. Randle watched them, wondering if they were from Professional Standards. "Just be more specific," he said. "Then maybe I can help."

"Tell her she needs to stay away from industrial units. Nothing to see there. And while you're at it, have a word with whoever's following Ian Osman."

"I have no idea if anyone's following Ian Osman."

"Well make it your business to know, and get it sorted. Alright?"

Hamm hung up before Randle had the chance to answer. Randle threw his phone into the glove locker, his head pounding.

CHAPTER SEVENTY

"MA'AM."

Lesley sat in the inner office, staring at Zoe's board. Mo and the rest of the team were outside, trying not to make it too obvious that they were looking in.

Lesley looked round. "I like your board."

"Thanks."

"I used to spend hours staring at those things, when I was a DS. Still useful. The subconscious latches onto it. Makes connections without you even knowing." She lifted her feet off the desk and span round in the chair. "How are the Osmans?"

"As you'd expect. They want to be happy to have Ollie back, but can't let themselves because they're scared Maddy won't come home."

"Why d'you think he let the boy out early? We were supposed to have another day."

"I'm hoping it doesn't mean there's no hope for Maddy. We've still got a day."

"How d'you intend to find her?"

"We're following up a lead on the Facebook message. The cleaning company at the accountancy firm. We thought Alison was working there but she denies it."

"She's got another job?"

"She told us she didn't. Said the woman in the photo wasn't her."

Lesley fished in her pocket and brought out a tube of mints. She held them out to Zoe who took one.

"What photo?"

"The cleaning company website." Zoe crunched down on her mint. "The employee of the month. I'm sure it's Alison. She's lying to us."

"So you reckon the whole thing is some sort of setup."

Zoe leaned against the wall. If Alison had faked the whole thing, if she'd sent that message herself, it would pull the threads together.

But why?

She gazed at the board.

"I've had a thought."

"Go on."

"Ollie's paternity."

"It's in doubt?"

"Alison told us he was Benedict's. The ex who died in a climbing accident. But what if he isn't? What if he's really Ian's?"

"You think they've got rid of Maddy so they can be a happy little family without the stepchild?"

Zoe's shoulders slumped. They certainly hadn't looked like a happy family when she'd left them.

"We need two things," she said.

"Well don't hang around here," said Lesley. "Go get 'em."

CHAPTER SEVENTY-ONE

"Connie, come with me." Zoe grabbed her jacket and headed for the door.

"Everything alright, boss?" Mo asked.

"We've got a warrant to search Cleanways. I want to get round there before they've got a chance to destroy records."

"You think he'll do that?" asked Connie.

"He was hiding something, that's for sure. Let's not risk losing it."

Connie followed her to the door. Zoe turned back to Mo.

"I need you to run a check on the forensics."

"Something specific?"

"Yes." She explained to him what she needed: the second of her two things.

"Right." Mo picked up the phone.

"Come on." Zoe led Connie out of the station.

They were less polite this time. Instead of pinging the bell in the reception area, Zoe hammered on the door Colin Clayton had come out of.

"It's DI Finch, Mr Clayton. We're back with that warrant."

No response.

She turned to Connie. "Bastard has buggered off. Stand back."

Zoe waited for Connie to retreat behind the front desk then eyed the door. She pursed her lips and focused on its weakest point. High kicks came easy to her, with her karate training. And the door didn't look all that hefty.

She took aim and it opened on the first kick.

Connie's face was alight. "Impressive."

"I'm a second Dan," Zoe told her.

"What's that mean?"

"Karate. Black Belt. Need to get my third Dan but keep having to put off the assessment."

"Cool."

Zoe shouldered her way through the door. They hurried along the corridor Clayton had led them along last time. A man came out of a door.

"What's going on? I'm calling the police."

"We are the police. I suggest you get back into your office," Zoe snapped.

The man retreated.

The door to Clayton's office was also locked. Two well-aimed kicks got them in.

"Are we allowed to do that?" asked Connie.

"We've got a warrant. Quicker than getting Uniform out."

Connie shrugged.

The office was as chaotic as it had been before. Zoe allowed herself a moment's relief. She'd been expecting it to be empty.

"Right," she said. "Find something we can pack this lot in. I'd rather work through it at the station."

"Boss." Connie slid open a metal filing cabinet. "I think this is what we want."

The top door of the cabinet had a label that said *Staff*. The second drawer said *Accounts*.

Both were empty.

"Shit." Zoe ran her fist through her hair. "Might have known it."

"He's taken what we needed."

"Yes, he bloody has." Zoe turned to scan the room. "No matter. There could be something he missed in this mess. Grab that box over there and start packing things up."

CHAPTER SEVENTY-TWO

ALISON STOOD IN THE KITCHEN, her mind empty. She'd come in here to get some food for Ollie, but couldn't remember what he liked to eat.

"You alright, love? You look tired." Ian was in the doorway.

"He's hungry. I don't know what to get him."

Ian smiled. "Here. Let me."

She nodded and headed back into the living room, where she'd left Ollie lying listlessly in front of the TV. He was still refusing to talk, still barely reacting to them. She clenched her fists as she approached the sofa, his brown hair visible over the arm.

He was asleep. She watched him for a moment, relieved he'd found some peace for a while, then retreated into the kitchen.

"Boiled egg and soldiers," said Ian. "His favourite." He stood at the hob, watching a pan of boiling water.

"He's asleep."

"Oh." Ian turned to her. "That's alright though. Better for him." He approached her, arms outstretched.

She shrugged him off. "How can you be like that?"

"Like what?"

"Happy. Cheerful."

"I"m just glad to have our boy back."

"What about our girl?"

He stiffened. "The police are working on that."

"I thought you didn't trust them."

"We have to."

"I thought you were going to sort it out. I thought you knew better than they did how to get our children back."

"I was wrong."

"So you've given up." She backed away from him, her hips hitting the worktop. She winced.

"It's not like that, love."

She glared at him. "You're happy now we've got Ollie back, but you don't care about Maddy."

"How can you—"

"You think he's yours, don't you?"

Ian raised his shoulders, saying nothing.

"I told you, Ian. Benedict is his biological father. But you're his dad. You're both their dad."

Ian licked his lips. "Are you a hundred per cent sure? I mean..."

"Look at him!" she cried. "He's got Benedict's nose. Can't you see it?"

"His eyes. They're blue, like mine."

"And like Benedict's mum's."

"Alison. Can't you understand how it's felt for me all this time, not knowing?"

"You do know. You know about both of them, and it's never bothered you before."

"Well it does now."

She clutched at the worktop behind her. "I want you to get out."

He took a step forward. She leaned back.

"That's ridiculous," he said.

"I can't deal with you being here right now. Not with the way you feel about Maddy."

"I love her, Al. You know that..."

"Not as much as Ollie!" She spat. "You've never loved her as much."

"That's not true."

"Don't lie to me. Not now, with all this. Just don't."

"Alison," he raised his hands to her face but she batted them away. Her body felt hot, her head fit to burst.

"Go, Ian. I'm not saying for good. But I can't handle being around you right now. I want you to leave."

CHAPTER SEVENTY-THREE

"DNA LAB."

"Hi, my name's DS Mo Uddin. I need a test running on some forensic evidence we've submitted."

"Which case?"

Mo checked the screen. "Case reference FC8578."

"Oh, that rings a bell. Let me check."

Mo drummed his fingers on the desk as the on-hold music kicked in. Across from him, Rhodri stared at his screen, his eyes flickering in a way that showed he was listening.

The music stopped. "You're in luck. We've processed the bags and they're all in storage. Only finished it this morning though."

"Good."

"So what's the test?"

"You should have materials with the DNA of two individuals. Ollie Osman and Ian Osman."

"Umm..." A pause. "Yes. We have."

"Good. I need you to run a comparison check on them."

"You mean you want us to do a paternity test?"

"Yes."

"OK. I can't guarantee the quality of the samples from the child though. There's a note here that they were taken from hair follicles found on his clothing."

"His mum wouldn't give permission for us to take a cheek swab."

"According to this, he's only four. Not surprising, really."

"No. How long will the test take?"

"Depends on your department's budget and how much of it's already allocated this quarter."

Mo sighed. This was what it came down to in the end. He missed the days when this kind of work was done in-house. But now it was outsourced, and there was only so much money to go around.

"I've got authorisation for it to be fast-tracked."

"Good. We can have it done in twenty-four hours."

Mo nodded. He could only hope twenty-four hours was time enough for Maddy, and that this information would give Zoe what she needed to crack the case. She'd been in such a hurry to leave for the cleaning company that she hadn't explained properly.

"Hang on a minute."

Uh-oh. "There a problem?"

"You've already requested this. Yesterday afternoon."

Mo frowned. "No, we haven't."

"Well someone has."

"Who?"

"Hang on."

The music started up again. Mo felt tension build in his gut as he waited for it to end.

"Local CID. Kings Norton. You may as well have a word with them, share the results. Save yourself some cash."

"Can we access those results without them being involved?"

"Sorry, mate. Can't do that."

"If you have the analysis on file, can I access it without having to wait for another test to be run?"

"You're asking me the same question two ways. Answer's the same, sorry. I suggest you talk to Kings Norton."

"OK. Do you have a name?"

He knew what the answer would be.

"DS Amanda Holt."

"Oh." He'd been expecting it to be Ian. But he wasn't stupid enough to order an analysis of his own DNA.

"I suggest you talk to her, sergeant."

"I will. I certainly will."

CHAPTER SEVENTY-FOUR

MADDY FELT like she'd cried herself inside out. After they'd taken Ollie, she'd hammered at the door for what felt like hours, screaming until she was hoarse. When she couldn't stand up any more, she'd stumbled back to the bed and collapsed onto it.

It was light now. She didn't know how long she'd slept for. Her stomach hurt, and her head felt like it was full of wasps.

She went to the door and pounded on it.

"Where's Ollie!"

Silence. She staggered back, slumping onto the bed.

On the desk under the window, someone had left food for her. Weetabix, long since gone mushy. And a glass of orange juice. It looked horrible but she was starving. She ate it greedily, tears rolling down her face.

When she'd eaten it all she went back to the door. She put her ear to it. Someone had come in here while she'd been asleep. They'd left the food.

She had to make herself stay awake, so she could get out next time.

She propped herself up against the wall, sobs running through her body. Her chest felt hollow, her limbs weak.

Pain clutched at her stomach. She ran to the bucket in the corner, throwing up the Weetabix. She retched until her stomach hurt and only bile came out.

When she couldn't sick up anymore, she sat on the floor, wiping her face with her grubby t-shirt. She looked up at the window.

She yanked a curtain open and stared out. A man was crossing the car park. She banged on the window, shouting. He carried on walking.

She balled up her fists against the glass. What if she escaped, and they brought Ollie back to the room? She had to stay here so she could look after him.

Or if they'd taken him to another room...

She ran to the wall behind the bed and put her ear to it. Nothing.

She hammered on it, calling her brother's name. Nothing.

She sat back, panting. Her hands were bruised.

She went back to the window. There was a doll on the desk, next to the empty Weetabix bowl. She retched again as she saw the bowl.

She picked up the doll. It was familiar. A *Frozen* doll. Elsa.

She'd had one of these, when she was little. She'd grown out of it, Mum had given it away.

No. That was wrong. She hadn't grown out of it. She'd given it to her dad, her first dad, the one they didn't talk about. She had a fuzzy memory of him kissing it, sitting on her bed the last night she'd seen him.

She could hardly remember him. Her second dad, Ian, had adopted her. Mum said that meant he was her real dad now. But sometimes she felt a hole inside where she thought her first dad should be.

Was this the Elsa she'd given him, or was it just the woman trying to make this room seem like home?

She turned around. There were no other toys in here. Her posters were on the wall, or copies of them at least. Her books were on the shelf next to the bed, but not the ones she'd got from the library last week. But there were no dolls.

She hadn't had dolls in her room for a while now. Not since her last birthday.

So why was this one here?

Had her first dad put it here? No. He'd died. There'd been a funeral, her nana in black and crying, Mum pale-faced and silent.

She put the doll back where she'd found it. It gave her the creeps. She went back to the bed, determined to escape next time they opened the door.

CHAPTER SEVENTY-FIVE

ALISON STARED out of the back window. Ian had left within ten minutes, his face tight. She'd hated herself, wishing she could find a way to reach him. But every time she thought of letting him stay, she wanted to scream.

Ollie was still asleep on the sofa. She needed to wake him, or he wouldn't sleep tonight. She might as well bring him into her own bed. That would soothe her if not him. She couldn't bear the thought of being separated from him.

She was brought out of her trance by the phone ringing upstairs. The new liaison officer, PC Lark, appeared in the doorway. She'd been hovering in the kitchen, making Alison feel uneasy.

"Want me to get that?"

It was her mobile. "I'll get it. Can you watch Ollie?"

Alison looked back at her son, fearful of leaving him alone with a stranger even for a minute. Especially after what Trish Bright had done. Had this new woman been vetted?

She ran up the stars, grabbed her phone and thundered

down again. She was back in the living room before she answered the phone.

"Hello?" she panted.

Alison nodded to the FLO, wanting her to leave. Ollie stirred on the sofa. She lowered herself down next to him and stroked his wrist, looking into his peaceful face.

"Hello?" she repeated.

Ollie stirred again. He drew a hand across his face, yawning. She smiled at him.

"Who's there?"

A prank caller, no doubt. They hadn't run an appeal but they hadn't kept the kidnapping secret. Impossible with it happening so publicly.

"Leave me alone," she snapped. She shuffled along the sofa to be closer to Ollie. He grunted. *Say something*, she thought. *Tell me what happened to you.*

"Alison?" came a voice at the other end.

"Ian?"

Breathing. Heavy.

"Ian, I don't want to talk right now."

"It's not Ian."

Ollie heaved himself up and leaned into her. His body was warm and soft. She let herself relax into him then stiffened.

She pushed the phone closer to her ear.

"Who is this?"

"Al, I'm sorry."

"Benedict?"

The line went dead.

CHAPTER SEVENTY-SIX

"COME ON, Mo. One last debrief and then you can go home."

Zoe opened the door to the inner office. Rhodri and Connie were already in there, sifting through the paperwork they'd taken from Cleanways. Rhodri had taken off his tie and undone the top two buttons of his shirt. His hair was dishevelled and his face pinched. This kind of work didn't suit him.

"How's it going?"

Connie looked up. "We've categorised everything and now we're working through anything we can find dealing with personnel."

"Is there much?"

"Sorry, no."

The door opened behind Zoe.

"Carl," she said. "What brings you here?"

"Can we talk?"

"Of course."

"In private."

Zoe pointed a thumb in the direction of the door, a sign for the rest of the team to leave. "We won't be long," she said. She turned to Carl. "Will we?" He shrugged.

Mo left last, closing the door behind him. He gave her a meaningful look which she ignored.

"What's up?" She sat in the chair. She needed to decide if this space was going to be an office or a briefing room, and furnish it appropriately.

Carl perched on the desk next to her. He wore a light grey shirt, rolled up at the wrists.

"I've been pulled off Ian Osman," he said.

"Why?"

"Beats me. My DCI gave the order just an hour ago. I wondered if it had anything to do with your case."

"Not as far as I know. I can ask Lesley though."

"If you don't mind."

"Course. Did your DCI give a reason?"

"Not enough evidence, apparently. Which is bullshit and he knows it."

She leaned back in the chair. Carl's face was hard and his eyes dark.

"You think there's something dodgy going on."

He looked up. "I have a theory."

"Go on."

"I think Randle's behind this."

"Why?"

"He's a Superintendent now."

"Still, that doesn't mean he can tell PSD what to do."

"I'm sure he can pull a string or two."

She sighed. "I can't help you, you know. I don't work with him anymore."

"He trusts you."

She grunted. "I'm not so sure about that."

"He brought you in as his right-hand woman on the Jackson case."

"Yeah, because he thought he could push me around."

"But then he found out he couldn't."

"It was too late then. He'd already got me involved."

"Please, Zoe. If you could do some digging for me..."

The door opened: Connie. "Sorry, boss. I just had a thought."

Zoe stood up. "Go on."

"We're getting nowhere with the paperwork. Clayton's taken anything that might point to that hack. But there is a way to find out if Alison was working for them."

"How?"

"It's half six now. They'll be out on a job. There might be some of their cleaners at Hatton and Banerjee. I'll see if I can talk to them."

"How will you get in?"

"I'll find a way."

"Be careful. And take Rhodri with you."

"With respect to Rhodri, this'll be easier if I do it on my own." She twisted her lips. "I'll blend in better."

Zoe considered. "OK. But get Rhodri to drive you, and I want you to text me when you get there. Then every half hour after that. If I don't hear from you, I'll send Rhodri in after you."

"There's no need for that."

"Connie, after what happened when you went looking for Winona Jackson, I don't want to take any chances."

"Rhodri's car'll break down."

"He got it fixed up by the guys in Traffic."

"When?"

"Rhod's good at making friends, he likes to call in favours."

"Yeah." A pause. "OK."

"Good. Let me know how you get on."

Connie nodded and closed the door.

"She's keen," said Carl.

"She's good. Lots of potential."

"So you won't help me."

"I'll keep an eye on Ian for you," she replied. "We're already doing that. But I'm not going sniffing around Randle."

"Fair enough. When this case is done, we should go for that drink."

"We already met in the Kings Arms."

He laughed. "That hardly counts. I want to take you on a date, Zoe Finch."

She allowed herself a smile. "Maybe. Ask me when Maddy Osman's safe."

CHAPTER SEVENTY-SEVEN

CONNIE APPROACHED the back door of Hatton & Banerjee, trying to project as much confidence into her walk as she could. Then she remembered she was pretending to be a cleaner and slowed down. Her mum had done cleaning work for a while, when Zaf was a baby. Annabelle Williams wasn't a woman to slink anywhere, but that had been the closest she'd got.

Rhodri was around the corner in his Saab, which had got them there with no problems. Rhodri had convinced Traffic to give it a tune-up. He'd stroked the steering wheel every time they stopped and looked around his vehicle with pride.

She pushed open the narrow door. A security guard sat at a desk, eating a Pot Noodle.

"Hi," she said.

"Wrong entrance, love. Front's on Colmore Row."

"I'm with Cleanways. Sent to replace Alison."

"Who?"

"Alison Osman."

The guard put down his Pot Noodle. "Hang on." He

picked up a phone. "Hey, Ross. You know anything about a new cleaner to replace one of the girls?"

He stared at her while he waited for the reply, sniffing. She smiled back, her heart racing.

"Alison Osman?" he asked.

"Yeah," she said. Trying to keep her voice steady.

"We ain't got no Alison Osman."

Damn.

"You with Cleanways?" he said.

"They sent me cos they said you were short."

"Yeah, I think there was less of you tonight. Let me check again."

He still had his phone to his ear. "Ross, we need an extra girl to clean tonight?"

He gave her the thumbs-up as the reply came. She responded with a hesitant smile.

He put down the phone and picked up his Pot Noodle. "You're on."

"Thanks."

"Hold on a minute, I need to get you a pass. What's your name?"

"Tracey Sharp."

He eyed her. She didn't look like a Tracey. He nodded, sniffing again.

"You're on the third floor, Mary'll be waiting for you."

"Great." She tried to look like she knew who Mary was.

He turned his back to her and fiddled with a machine. At last he held out a visitor pass on a lanyard. She took it.

He didn't know anything about Alison, but one of the cleaners might.

She hung back as he pressed a button to open the door behind him. "In you pop, love. Have fun."

"Thanks."

His phone rang and she hesitated while he answered it. He raised a finger, gesturing for her to stay put.

Shit. She'd been rumbled.

After a few moments, he hung up. She stared at him, her chest tight.

"Everything OK?" she asked.

"Yeah. Just Ross again. He was checking who you were supposed to be replacing."

"Oh." She waited. "Did he give you a name?"

"There's no Alison Osman. But there is an Alison Tomkin. Guess it's her you're here to cover for."

CHAPTER SEVENTY-EIGHT

ZOE TURNED out of the car park, her mind going over what Carl had said. She'd had her suspicions about Ian Osman, but Randle pulling Carl off the investigation into him just made them more concrete.

Meanwhile, she hadn't heard from Connie in over thirty minutes. She dialled Rhodri.

"Boss."

"You got Connie with you?"

"No, boss. She's in the building still."

"She was supposed to check in with me."

"Maybe she can't. She's definitely in there, though. I can see the door."

"Can you take a look, see who she had to get past?"

"You want me to do it now?"

"Please."

Zoe hung up, turning towards the city centre. Her phone rang again.

"Rhodri."

"Who's Rhodri? Your fancy man?"

She gritted her teeth. "Mum."

"Hello, sweetheart. Haven't heard from you in a bit. Thought I'd give you a call."

Zoe checked the time on the dashboard. Eight-thirty pm. When she'd been a teenager, Annette would be asleep at this hour. She'd got used to looking after herself.

"Why don't you come visit?" her mum asked.

"I'm busy. Work."

"No one's too busy to visit their mum. Especially when she's sick."

"The doctor gave you a clean bill of health."

"What do they know? I had a stroke."

"Mini stroke."

"Hah! What's the difference."

Zoe pulled away from the lights on Harborne Road. Her phone beeped. Rhodri was trying to get through.

"I have to go, Mum. Some other time, yes?"

"You never bloody cared about me."

Give me strength. "Have you been drinking?"

"Mind your own bloody business."

Zoe stared at the phone in its cradle. She was torn between concern for her mum and resentment at the way she'd been treated as a child. Annette Finch hadn't earned the right to be cared for by her adult daughter. Far from it.

The phone buzzed again. "I have to go, Mum. Don't drink any more."

"None of your fu—"

She switched over to Rhodri. "What's happening?"

He was breathing heavily. "She's with me, and she's got news." There was a muffled sound of the phone being passed between the two constables.

"Boss, it's Connie."

"Connie, I was worried about you. You didn't check in."

"Sorry. They let me in and it took a while to get out again without the supervisor spotting me. She'd have known I was an impostor."

"Rhodri says you've got news."

"Yes. There isn't an Alison Osman working for Cleanways."

"You sure?"

"Yes. But wait. There is an Alison Tomkin."

Zoe inhaled sharply. "That's Benedict's surname."

"Would have been hers too, when they were married."

"So she's moonlighting as a cleaner under the name she had in her first marriage."

"And she was there when that hack was sent. I managed to get one of the other girls to tell me who worked what hours, told her I was trying to find out who I could swap shifts with."

"Well done, Connie. You two go back to the station, tell Mo what's happened. I'm going over to the Osmans."

"What are you going to do, boss?"

"I'm going to arrest her."

CHAPTER SEVENTY-NINE

ALISON STARED AT THE TV, letting it wash over her. Ollie was asleep in her bed and she had no idea where Ian was. Frankly, she didn't care.

She heaved herself up from the sofa. She was tired. Every time she looked at Ollie, Maddy's face flitted in front of her eyes. Where was her daughter? Were they hurting her... or worse?

And that call... had it been Benedict? He was dead. He'd fallen into a crevasse on K2. His friends had searched for him and waited as long as they could, in case he found a way out.

He was dead. Her mind was playing tricks on her.

But what if he was alive, and he had Maddy?

Her mind felt like it might explode. If she went upstairs to Ollie, she could fill it with his sweet face, push out the fear.

She knew she was kidding herself.

She'd make a cup of tea. That would keep her hands busy, if not her mind. She'd started chewing her fingernails. Her right thumb bled every time she washed her hands.

The doorbell rang as she passed into the kitchen. She stopped and stared at it.

Ian?

Alison crept to it and put her ear against the wood. She wished they'd had a chain put on, or a peephole.

The bell rang again. She looked up the stairs, worrying it might wake Ollie. She had to answer it.

She took a deep breath and pushed her shoulders back. She opened the door a crack, keeping her hand firm on it.

"Ian?"

"No love, it's me."

Alison staggered back, relief washing over her. "Mum."

"Where is he? He buggered off again?"

Alison shook her head, tears welling. Barbara closed the door, her mouth a tight line. "Where is he?"

"Shh. Ollie's asleep."

Barbara grabbed Alison's arm and steered her into the living room. Halfway there she realised what she was doing and loosened her grip.

"He's up to no good." Barbara let go of Alison and stood in front of her, her arms folded.

Alison squeezed her eyes shut. "It was me, Mum. I asked him to go."

"And he went? Just like that, with one kiddie missing and the other one needing his parents?"

"Mum."

Barbara grunted. "Bloody useless man. Where'd he go?" She reached into her massive handbag and brought out her phone.

"I don't know. Please, mum, leave it. Let me fight my own battles."

"Well, I'm here now. You want me to stay in the spare room?"

Alison's chest tightened at the thought of her mum here twenty-four hours a day, throwing her weight around and making her feel useless. But then she reconsidered.

"Thanks. It'll help Ollie."

Barbara's face softened for the first time. "How is the little love?"

"He's asleep." Alison's voice caught. "Still not talking."

"He'll come round." Barbara put a hand on Alison's arm, gentle this time. "Don't worry."

"What about Maddy, Mum? What if she never comes back?"

"Don't think like that. It doesn't help." Barbara pulled Alison to her and clasped her in a tight hug.

The doorbell rang again, followed by loud knocking. Alison sprang back from her mum.

"If that's him..." Barbara said. She headed for the hallway.

"Mum, please..."

"It's alright, love. Leave it to me."

Alison followed her mum through to the hall. The door was open and DI Finch stood outside. Her heart lifted.

"Maddy?"

DI Finch frowned. "Sorry, no. I need to come in."

"Of course."

Barbara pulled to one side and let the detective through with a look of disdain. Alison stepped forward.

"What is it? Do you know where she is?"

"Sorry, no."

"Then what?"

The detective looked from Alison to her mum and then back again.

"What?"

"Alison Osman, I'm arresting you for child abduction and perverting the course of justice."

CHAPTER EIGHTY

ALISON SHRIEKED. Zoe stepped towards her, pulling hand-cuffs from her pocket. She just hoped she had this right.

"You do not have to say anything," she continued. "But it may harm your defence if you do not say something you later rely on in court."

She clamped the cuffs around Alison's wrists.

"What's going on?" asked Barbara. "This is ridiculous."

Zoe focused on Alison. "Do you have someone who can take care of your son?"

Alison looked at her mum, her eyes filling with tears. Barbara nodded.

"My mum will," she whispered.

"Good. Come with me."

Zoe guided Alison to the front door. She didn't resist. Her face had turned grey and she was breathing in short bursts. Zoe eyed her, worried she might pass out.

"You need to sit down," she said.

Alison nodded. She backed away, dropping to the stairs. She stared ahead of her, blinking, her hands quivering.

"Why?" she asked.

There was movement behind Zoe. Mo had arrived.

"Boss."

"We need to search the house. Secure the scene."

"Adi Hanson's on his way."

"Good." Adi was the best forensic scene manager in the force. If there was evidence here, he'd find it.

Alison was recovering her breathing, still sitting on the stairs. Zoe needed to get her out of here. She turned to Barbara Wilson.

"You'll have to take Ollie to your house for the night. We need access to this house."

"Yes." Barbara's voice was firm, her eyes sharp. She put a hand on Alison's shoulder and started up the stairs.

"No," said Zoe. "We'll bring Ollie down."

'He's my grandson. He's suffered an ordeal."

Two uniformed officers were outside the front door. Zoe turned to them. One of them was PC Lark, the new FLO.

"PC Lark, please escort Mrs Wilson to Ollie's bedroom."

"He's in my bed," muttered Alison.

Zoe nodded. "Take her to Alison's room and let her fetch Ollie. Nothing else, just the boy."

"Yes ma'am."

"What about his clothes? Some toys, at least?" asked Alison.

Zoe hated to make this worse for Ollie. But she had to preserve the scene.

"Sorry. I'm sure your mum keeps some toys at her house for him." She knew that normal grandmothers, ones that didn't drink, did that kind of thing. "You'll have to improvise with clothes for tonight. Once we've conducted a search, we'll let you take some things."

Barbara sniffed and followed PC Lark up the stairs.

"Can I see him, before you take me?" asked Alison.

"I don't think it would do your son any good to see you in handcuffs."

"No." Alison took a step towards Zoe. "Let's go then."

Zoe stared back into her eyes. This was the first time the woman had shown spark.

"Take me to the station. Question me. The sooner you do this, the sooner you'll know I had nothing to do with this."

Zoe said nothing, but led Alison out to one of two squad cars parked on the street. She guided Alison into the back seat then turned to look back at the house.

Barbara Wilson emerged carrying Ollie. He was snuggled into her, barely awake. Zoe hoped he wasn't registering what was happening, that he wouldn't remember this.

"I still can't find Ian." Mo was next to her, having spoken to the driver of the car they'd put Alison in.

"We need to bring him in quickly, before he hears about this," she said.

"We've got an alert out on his car, and I'm working on credit card payments. If he's staying at a hotel, we should find him."

"Where is he? And what's he up to?"

"They must be in it together," Mo said. "Him working the inside, her planting that message."

"And faking the whole thing at Cadbury World."

"She's a damn good actress."

Zoe nodded. "Right. We'll let her stew in a cell for a few hours, then interview her first thing. Let me know if there's any news on Ian."

CHAPTER EIGHTY-ONE

BRIAN LET himself into the flat, careful not to make a sound. There was a loose floorboard behind the front door and he knew to avoid it.

He'd watched the police cars turn up at Alison's house. It had been a while before Alison herself had come out but eventually he'd seen her, being led by that female detective who'd turned up at the climbing centre.

He'd watched from behind a SUV across the road, his heart pounding. Seeing her like this, her face streaked with tears and her hair wild, had brought back memories of how she'd looked after Maddy was born. It had been a difficult birth and Alison had lost a lot of blood. He'd been scared for both of them. And then Maddy had turned out to be a lusty baby, full of energy and with lungs that could melt your eardrums.

He'd waited to see if Ian came out too, but there'd been no sign of him. Had they arrested him already? Instead there'd been Barbara, the awful Barbara, leading Ollie by the hand. Brian had plunged his fist into his mouth at the sight of the boy, trying not to cry.

He'd walked home in the rain, his footsteps heavy. He couldn't face bed, the creeping around and sliding silently under the covers. He and Vic did a lot of that these days. If it wasn't him it was her, coming in late from work. If they wanted to have children, they needed to spend more time together.

He slid into the kitchen and opened the fridge. A beer would take the sting off his evening. As he closed the door, he heard movement behind him.

"Oh. You're still up."

Vic stood in the narrow hallway, her key in her hand.

"Yeah." He lifted his beer. "Want one?"

"OK."

"Late shift?"

She nodded, not meeting his eye. "Hatton & Banerjee."

"That's becoming a regular haunt for you."

"It's easier than the dumps they used to get us cleaning. Cleanways must be going up in the world."

"They need to pay you more." Her pay had been diminishing in recent weeks, while her hours had been increasing. "I don't get why you do that job anyway. What's wrong with the IT work you used to do?"

She frowned. "Let's not talk about it, huh?" She leaned in for a chaste kiss. He grabbed her waist and pulled her in. She smelled of cold air and mints.

"Brian." She pushed him away.

"Brian what?"

"I'm tired."

"You're the one who wants kids."

"I thought we'd agreed we were gonna adopt."

"That doesn't mean we can't have sex," he said.

"Like I said, I'm knackered. Got an early start in the morning."

"More work?"

"Yeah." She turned away from him towards the living room. She flicked the TV on and put her feet up on the coffee table.

He yawned. "I'm off to bed then." It was gone midnight.

"I won't be long."

"Don't be."

She tensed. He shuffled to the bedroom, knowing she wouldn't join him until he'd fallen asleep.

CHAPTER EIGHTY-TWO

THE PHONE RANG out five times before Mo heard the click of his boss picking it up.

"DI Finch." Her voice was muffled. He'd woken her.

"It's Mo."

She yawned. "Aw, shit. Did I oversleep?"

"We've found him."

Her voice perked up. "Where?"

"He's staying in a Travelodge in Walsall. I'm outside now."

"What time is it?"

"Just gone five."

"OK. Don't wait for me. Are you on your own?"

"I've got plenty of Uniform. And Rhodri." He eyed the DC, leaning on Mo's car.

"He'll enjoy this."

"A bit of responsibility for him," he said.

"Good. Do it."

"No problem."

Mo nodded at Sergeant Grice next to him. The Travelodge had thirty windows facing the car park, and as many again facing the street. A McDonalds was next door, a few cars parked up for an early breakfast. He cracked his knuckles then headed for the door to the hotel, knocking quietly.

A middle-aged woman was at the desk inside, reading a book. She looked up, startled. He held his warrant card up to the window.

She composed herself and came to the door, yawning.

"What's wrong?" she asked.

"You have someone staying here who we need to talk to."

"At five in the morning?"

"Would you rather we did this now, or waited till your guests are up and about to see it?"

She blinked at him. "I need to call my manager."

"I've got a warrant, if that's what you're worried about."

"Er, no. I dunno. Can I call my manager?"

"Feel free. But we don't have time to wait. I need you to tell me which room Ian Osman is staying in."

Ian had used his credit card to pay for the room, which meant he'd booked in under his own name. Not paranoid enough to use a false ID, or just unable to pay any other way.

"Err..." She went behind the desk and squinted at a computer screen. Rhodri was already at the door leading to the rooms, peering through it.

"Room 209. Second floor."

"Thanks," said Mo. "Is that the only way in, apart from the two fire doors?"

"Yeah." The receptionist looked at the door to the inside of the hotel as if someone was about to burst through it.

"Good." There were uniformed officers already covering

the fire doors at the back of the building. Ian was going nowhere.

Rhodri pushed at the door.

"I need to buzz you in," the receptionist said.

"Please," said Mo, trying to hide his impatience. He'd had three hours sleep and needed to be at his best later, for the interviews.

The door buzzed and he pushed it open. Sergeant Grice followed him, Rhodri behind.

They were in a small lobby with two lift doors and a flight of stairs towards the back of the building. Mo pointed at the stairs and Grice went first. Mo and Rhodri followed. A PC stayed behind, watching the lift doors.

At the second floor another door separated them from the main corridor. Sergeant Grice looked through it, his movements soundless. He nodded and they followed him through. Another PC came behind them.

Signs on the wall indicated the direction of the bedrooms. 209 was to the left. The PC stayed behind as they headed along the corridor.

At the door to room 209, they stopped. Grice checked up and down the corridor and then nodded. Mo looked at Rhodri, who was sweating. *Calm down, son.*

Mo stepped forward and knocked.

He waited. No answer. He exchanged looks with Grice and then knocked again.

"Police. Let us in, Ian."

The door opened and Ian Osman faced them, wearing a pair of jogging bottoms. His hair was ragged and the skin on his face creased with sleep.

"Ian Osman, I'm arresting you for—"

Ian shoved Mo hard in the chest. Mo held his ground, leaning backwards but not losing his footing.

"I'm arresting you for child abduction and perverting the course of justice. You do not have—"

Ian gave him a look of hatred then lifted an elbow and slammed it into his chin. Mo winced and felt his head snap to one side.

"Stop!" Sergeant Grice grabbed Ian by the arm and spun him round, snapping handcuffs on him.

Mo grabbed his chin and leaned in towards Ian. He wasn't about to let the pain stop him doing his job. "And for assaulting a police officer. Do you need me to finish?"

"No," Ian spat.

"Good." Mo turned to Rhodri. "Stay here. Watch this room, make sure no one comes in, until FSM get here."

"Sure, sarge."

Mo gestured for Grice to follow him and they made for the main stairs. People were emerging from their rooms, disturbed by the commotion. Mo raised a hand to calm them as he passed, wincing as pain ran down his neck.

"Go back to bed, please. Stay out of the corridors."

He heard Rhodri giving orders to the PCs, reassuring more people who'd come out of their rooms to gawp. This was Rhodri's first time securing a crime scene. He'd be fine.

They steered Ian down the stairs, their footsteps light. Uniform were good at this: quiet when they needed to be, noisy as hell when it was warranted. At the bottom the receptionist buzzed them through.

"Thanks," Mo said to her. She stared at Ian.

They emerged into the car park. It was still dark, lights from the bedrooms spilling out into the car park. They'd woken half the place, despite their efforts.

Carl Whaley stood next to Mo's car. Mo felt his stomach clench.

"Sir."

"Why didn't you tell us you were arresting PS Osman?"

"It's in conjunction with a criminal case, not an internal investigation."

"He's force, Sergeant Uddin. You should have told us."

Mo twisted his lips. If Whaley took Ian from them now, Zoe would go ballistic.

"I've got orders from DI Finch to being him in to Rose Road. This takes precedence over any investigation by PSD."

"How d'you know the two aren't connected?"

"Because you'd have told us if they were."

'Touché." Carl surveyed him. This was the first time the two of them had come face to face like this. Mo knew that Zoe was closer to this man than she liked to admit. But this was a kidnapping case. A girl's life was in danger.

"Look," he said. "I can talk to her. I'm sure she'll be OK with you questioning him after we're done."

Carl gave him a look of amusement. "You are, are you?"

"There's a girl missing. We're against a deadline."

"Don't think I don't know. I was the one who questioned PC Bright about that message."

Of course. "Sir."

Carl nodded. "Go on then. Do your worst. I'll talk to Zoe."

CHAPTER EIGHTY-THREE

MADDY WAS THIRSTY.

She'd woken up to find the dirty plate and glass from yesterday still on the desk. A sandwich and glass of milk had appeared after she'd let herself fall asleep again, sometime in the afternoon. She was trying to keep herself awake at night, determined to catch the woman when she came in. But she was too tired.

She picked up the glass, hoping to find some dregs in it. It smelt sour, making her retch. She put it down again, fighting the sickness in her stomach.

The bucket smelt bad. It hadn't been emptied for two days. She tried not to look at it, but she couldn't get away from the smell.

She went to the window and looked out. She'd opened the curtains, hoping the orange glow would help her stay awake. The glow was still there, the sky beginning to lighten. The car park was empty and the street beyond it quiet.

She jumped as the streetlight outside turned off, making the sky seem brighter. What time was it? How long since

Ollie had gone? She'd been hoping he was in another room, that they'd bring him back. But she was having to face up to being alone.

She went back to the bed. She needed to stay still, not use her energy. She could feel her ribs through her skin and had a constant headache. How long were they going to keep her here? Where was Ollie? She hated the thought of him on his own somewhere, with no one to look after him.

The door opened and she sprang round, startled. In the gloom she could only just make out the familiar figure in the doorway. Holding something. A cardboard box.

The woman put the box down on the floor and closed the door again. She didn't look up to see Maddy watching her.

Maddy ran to the door. She tugged the handle. It budged just a bit, then held.

"Let me out! Where's Olly? What have you done with him?"

"He's alright," came a voice. Maddy stiffened. "He's safe."

She threw herself against the door. "I want to see him."

"Shush. Open the box." Footsteps headed away.

Maddy looked down at the box. Food?

Something about it scared her. She crouched down and looked at it, wary. She gripped one of the flaps between her finger and thumb and flicked it, pulling her hand back as it fell open.

She frowned. Had the box made a noise?

She leaned back, watching it. She'd seen a cartoon where someone had put a snake in a box and left it in a princess's bedroom.

She held her breath. The box shifted, just a little.

Maddy's palms were sticky. She swallowed down the bile

rising in her throat. She could go back to the bed, look out the window, ignore the box.

But she had to know.

She flicked the other flap open and leaned back. She held her breath, expecting something to jump at her.

Another sound. Scratching. She peered inside, her heart racing.

There was a cage inside the box, an animal carrier. A face looked up at her from inside it. Two yellow eyes, pointed ears.

Maddy unhooked the lid of the cage and plunged her hand in. She brought it out. She stared at it. It stared right back.

A kitten. Why had the woman left her a kitten?

She dropped it back in the box and went to the door.

"I don't want a kitten! I want my brother back!"

CHAPTER EIGHTY-FOUR

Zoe walked into the interview room, her gaze steady on Alison. A solicitor sat next to her, a woman Zoe hadn't seen before.

Mo closed the door behind them and they sat down. Alison placed her hands on the chair beneath her, her face tight.

"Present are DI Finch and DS Uddin. For the tape, please identify yourselves."

"Alison Osman."

"Hannah Wilson, Alison's solicitor."

Zoe nodded and opened the file on the table in front of her. Mo sat back next to her, surveying Alison. She had her hands twisted in her lap and was staring at Zoe.

"Alison."

"Detective Finch."

Zoe closed her file and eyed Alison. "Have you been lying to us all along?"

"No." Alison's gaze was steady, but her hands clasped tighter.

"Hmm." Zoe flipped open her file. "The CCTV, from when you claim your children were snatched from Cadbury World. You've watched it."

"I have. You were there."

"It shows you walking away from the table with your children. Holding their hands."

"That's not me." Alison's voice was thin.

Zoe took a photo from her file. It was a still from the CCTV. Alison from behind, reaching out for Maddy's hand.

"You have to admit it looks a lot like you."

"Yes. But it isn't me."

Zoe grabbed another photo. This one was from the moment Alison returned. She faced the table, her mouth open.

"Is this you?"

"Yes." Alison exchanged glances with her solicitor. "That is me."

Zoe placed the two photos side by side, facing Alison. "In both of these, you're wearing a grey fleece and green scarf. Your hair's the same. I don't see how you expect us to believe this isn't you."

"Someone must have been impersonating me."

"Who d'you think might want to do that?" asked Mo.

Alison turned to him. "If I knew that, I'd have my children back. Both of them."

So she wasn't going to roll over for them.

"Very well," said Zoe. "So you claim that someone else, who looks exactly like you, took your children while you were buying lunch."

"Yes."

"Can you explain why your children leave with this person? They don't seem worried about it at all."

Alison brought her hands onto the table. "I've been wondering that myself."

Zoe cocked an eyebrow. "Any theories?"

"No."

"No."

Mo leaned forward. "We have a statement from Larry Pierce, who was working security at Cadbury World when Maddy and Ollie were taken. He says he saw you leave with them."

"He's wrong."

"The CCTV has you walking away with them," said Zoe. "And then we have Larry's statement. But you're saying the evidence is wrong."

"It must be."

"OK, so let's move on. This is a printout of the message you sent to yourself on Sunday morning, telling yourself to choose between your children."

"Why would I have sent that message?"

"To make us believe someone else had them. I don't know. You tell me."

"I didn't send the message."

Zoe leaned in. "The message was sent from the offices of Hatton & Banerjee, on Colmore Row. The only people in the building at the time were the cleaners."

Alison shrugged. "So ask them."

"One of our officers spoke to people at the cleaning company, who told us that you work there."

"I already told you I only work at the school. There's no way I could fit in another job."

"Alison, why are you working a second job using your name from your first marriage?"

"What?"

"The cleaning company has an Alison Tomkin working for them."

Alison froze. She stared at Zoe, then turned to her solicitor and muttered in her ear.

"I need a break to confer with my client."

"We're not done yet," said Zoe.

"Five minutes," said the solicitor.

"Very well." Zoe stopped the tape, exchanging glances with Mo as they left the interview room.

In the corridor, she shifted from foot to foot. "Why's she stalling?"

"Why's she doing any of it?"

"Talk to Connie. Get her to find out if they're making any money out of this. Have they done a deal with the papers or anything like that."

"You think that's the motive."

"I don't know. It's complicated by the fact that Ian thinks Ollie's his child. Maybe they want to get rid of Maddy."

"I'm still waiting to hear back from Kings Norton about the DNA test he ordered. But he adopted Maddy too. Would he want to hurt her? Get rid of her?"

Zoe raked her fingernails across her palm. "We need to talk to him. This could be related to whatever Carl's got on him."

Mo nodded. "I'll call Connie." He spoke into his mobile. Zoe watched, her mind racing.

"We don't have enough time," she said.

"You're thinking of Maddy."

"If Hamm's mixed up in this, if his bastards have got her..."

Mo's face was tight. "Petersen and Shand."

Zoe felt her stomach sink. Trevor Hamm had supplied

kids to the Canary paedophile network. They hadn't managed to prove it yet, but she knew it. And Shand and Petersen were still out there.

They had to find Maddy. Fast.

Mo stared at her. He would be thinking the same thing. "You carry on interviewing her. I'll track Hamm down."

"I can't interview her on my own. I want you in there with me."

"What about Rhodri?"

"He's not back from the Travelodge yet, is he?"

"No. Your call, boss. We can pause the interview while we try and track Maddy down."

"You don't think Alison's going to give us anything useful."

"She's denying everything, Zo. You won't crack her."

Zoe raised an eyebrow. "You underestimate me."

"I just don't think this is the quickest way to get Maddy, is all."

"OK. You're right. You go look for Maddy. I'll interview Ian, with Carl."

"Carl?"

"Yes, Carl. He's insisting. And to be honest I think whatever he knows could be helpful. My theory right now is that Hamm has something on Ian, and Maddy's caught in the crossfire. He's given them his daughter to get himself off the hook. Or they've taken her to teach him a lesson."

"*Her* daughter."

"Indeed."

"Maybe she isn't in on it. Maybe it's just Ian," Mo said.

"That doesn't explain the CCTV and the cleaning job."

"No."

"Right."

She pushed the door to the interview room open. "We're done for now. You'll be taken back to your cell."

Alison's mouth fell open.

"You can't hold her for more than twenty-four hours without charging her," said the solicitor.

"Oh silly me, I forgot that." Zoe eyed her. "Don't worry. We'll be back." She turned her gaze on Alison, suppressing her anger at the woman. "But we have more urgent things to do right now, I'm sure you'll agree."

CHAPTER EIGHTY-FIVE

DAVID RANDLE BREEZED into the custody suite, a faint smile on his lips.

"Sir," said the sergeant.

"Sergeant Khan. How's it going?"

"Very well, sir. Bit of a surprise to see you here."

"I like to keep an eye on things. Can't be too distant."

"No, sir."

Randle looked towards the cells. "I hear the Osmans are in custody."

"Yes, sir."

"Have they been interviewed yet?"

Khan straightened. "Alison Osman is with DI Finch right now. Ian Osman is in his cell."

Randle turned back to the sergeant. "He not been interviewed yet?"

"No, sir."

"Hmmm." He surveyed the door to the cells, lightly tugging on his tie.

"Anything I can help you with, sir?"

Randle knew that if he went into that cell, it would be recorded. Standing here, shooting the breeze with the custody sergeant, he could pass that off as a routine visit. Just about. But if he spoke to Ian...

Then, if he didn't speak to Ian...

"Very well," he said. "Thanks for the chat."

"Sir." Khan looked puzzled. Randle gave him a tight smile then pushed out of the custody suite, scanning the corridor. There were cameras all along here, keeping the prisoners under surveillance as they were moved around the station.

He walked to the interview rooms, careful to look as if he was taking a stroll around his old base. He smiled at everyone he passed, exchanging quick greetings. The big gun back from Lloyd House to keep in touch with how things were on the ground. Maybe that was the kind of superintendent he'd be. It could be useful.

He rounded a corner to see a slim man in his late sixties walking towards him. Edward Startshaw: Trevor Hamm's solicitor, and Bryn Jackson's too. Surely he wasn't acting for Ian Osman?

"Detective Chief Inspector Randle." Startshaw narrowed his eyes. This was the man who'd threatened Randle when they'd been investigating Jackson's murder, who'd tried to get him to call off his dogs. Hamm's foot soldier.

"Detective Superintendent."

"Of course. Congratulations." Startshaw's voice was cold.

"You're here to represent someone?" Randle asked.

"I don't imagine you need to ask me that."

"No."

"Well, then," said Startshaw. "It was... interesting to bump into you."

Randle grabbed Startshaw by the elbow. The solicitor jerked out of his grip. "I wouldn't do that if I were you."

Randle leaned in. "What's he saying?"

"He hasn't been interviewed yet."

Startshaw looked pointedly up at the camera in the corner. Randle stood back, squaring his shoulders.

"It's all in hand," Startshaw said.

Randle nodded. Hamm had told him to get to DS Osman, to wheedle himself a spot in the interview if he could. But with Startshaw muttering in the guy's ear, that was hardly necessary.

"He'll need a Federation rep," said Randle. "Professional Standards are sniffing around."

"Don't worry about that."

"I won't."

Randle glanced up at the camera then turned on his heel and headed back towards Lesley's office. That would be the official reason for his being here. He just had to think of something he wanted to talk to her about.

CHAPTER EIGHTY-SIX

Mo PULLED up outside Trevor Hamm's apartment building. He'd moved since the death of his wife Irina. A drowning, that had been recorded as death by misadventure but most likely had been murder.

This apartment was further south, near the cricket ground. It was part of a modern block that rose up next to Cannon Hill Park. Hamm was on the top floor. Of course.

The desk was staffed by a petite blonde woman with an insincere smile. Mo showed her his warrant card.

"I need to speak to one of your residents."

"This is an exclusive building, sergeant. I'm sure there hasn't been any trouble."

"He lives in apartment sixty-one."

"Oh." Her face dropped.

"You look surprised."

"It's nothing."

"It doesn't look like nothing."

Unease passed across her face. How much did she know about Hamm? "He moved out."

Damn. "He's only been there a month."

She shrugged. "Cleaners went up there earlier. Found it empty."

"Can you let me in anyway?"

"I'm not sure if I..."

He took a breath, eyeing her badge. He smiled. "Pam. D'you mind if I call you Pam?"

"Of course not. It's my name."

"Have you been following the Osman case?"

She gasped. "Maddy and Ollie. Twitter's full of—"

"This is why I'm here."

Her gaze flicked upwards, her mouth falling open. "You think they're up there?"

"I can't tell you specifics. But if you can let me in..."

"Of course." She opened a drawer and placed a key card in his hand. "Sixth floor, left hand door."

"Thanks, Pam."

She chewed her lip. "Those poor kids."

Mo hurried to the lift, tapping his foot as it rose. At the top was a large carpeted hallway, a floor-to-ceiling window giving views of the park. Each of the two side walls had just one door.

He put the key card in the slot, holding it in place. He knocked on the door. Once, hard.

"Police!"

Not waiting for an answer, he leaned into the door and pushed it open.

Beyond it was a wide hallway, the only furniture a built-in cupboard with a vase of wilting flowers.

"Is anyone here?"

His voice echoed in the empty space.

He continued forward. Doors led off either side of the

narrow hallway, but ahead the apartment opened up into a vast living space. Glass filled the walls, a view of the park on one side and the cricket ground on the other.

The room was empty. The polished oak floors spread out in front of him, without so much as as a stick of furniture.

He ran back through the hallway, flinging each door open in turn.

"Maddy!" He called. It was a long shot.

He ran through bedrooms, hurling open cupboard doors, crashing into ensuite bathrooms. Everywhere he turned was empty. No Maddy. No Hamm.

He trudged back to the door. As he waited for the lift, he dialled Zoe.

Voicemail. She would be in with Carl, interviewing Ian.

"Hamm's done a runner, boss. No one at his apartment. No sign of Maddy."

He got into the lift, his mind a blank. Where was Hamm? Had he taken Maddy somewhere?

He thought back to the Osman house, the scaffolding. He knew where he was going next.

CHAPTER EIGHTY-SEVEN

THE KITTEN WAS SCRATCHING at the walls, chasing something Maddy couldn't see. She leaned against the wall, watching it. It was a cute little thing, grey with dark stripes under its eyes. If Mum had brought her that, to share with Ollie, she'd have loved it.

If she was honest with herself, she'd have argued with Ollie over it. He'd have been rough with it, grabbing its tail and pulling its whiskers. She'd have shouted at him. But still, it would have been better with him to enjoy it.

The kitten approached her and sniffed her foot. Maddy flinched, not wanting to fall under the creature's spell. It looked up at her and made a soft mewling noise. She smiled.

"Why are you here?" she asked it. It mewed in response.

She put out a hand and it pulled back, wary. She wiggled her fingers and it reached its head out, bringing its nose closer but not its body. Sensible cat. Maddy wished she'd been wary at Cadbury World. But the woman had said she was their aunt, that it was a surprise. Maddy knew her mum had a sister who lived in Australia. The woman looked so much like her mum, it had been easy to believe her.

The kitten walked away. There was a corner under the window, away from her bucket, where it was in the habit of peeing. The smell was sharp, different from the smell of her own urine in the bucket. She hadn't used it since yesterday. And it had hurt last time, her pee too dark. Mum got cross with her when her pee was too dark, told her to drink more water.

She'd give anything for a glass of water right now. She'd never grumble and say she preferred Pepsi again.

The door rattled and the kitten jumped almost out of its skin. It ran under the bed, a streak of grey and silver. Maddy wished she could fit under there with it.

She pulled herself up onto the bed and huddled against the wall, her eyes on the door. It opened slowly.

"Hello." The woman was here again, wearing that hoody. She'd been wearing a fleece at Cadbury World, Maddy had thought it funny that the two so-called sisters dressed the same.

She pushed the hood down and Alison gasped. She looked nothing like her mum now. Her eyes were narrow and uncaring. She'd looked different at Cadbury World. Nicer.

"I've got news." The woman's voice was soft but her eyes were hard. She scanned the room, looking for the kitten.

Maddy said nothing.

"Where is it?" the woman asked. Maddy's gaze lowered.

The woman dropped to the floor and peered under the bed. Maddy eyed the door. Did she have time? She remembered what had happened last time, the way the woman had chased her. She still had a bruise on her arm where she'd been grabbed.

"Where's Ollie?" she asked, trying to push courage into her voice.

The woman stood up. "He's safe."

"Where is he?"

"You don't let up, do you? He won't like it if you're sullen."

"Ollie won't?"

"You'll find out. Come on."

"What?"

"Come on. We're moving."

Maddy stared at the woman. Moving? Where? Would she be with Ollie again?

"Where are you taking me?"

"You'll find out." The woman's eyes crinkled. "You'll like it. Promise. I've got a surprise for you."

The kitten had been the last surprise. Before that, losing Ollie.

"I don't like surprises."

"This one's special. Better than a kitten. Come on."

Maddy strode up. If there was a chance she was being taken to Ollie, she had to go along with it. She took deep breaths, her heart racing.

"Is the kitten coming?"

"Not just yet. But don't worry, you won't lose it." The woman sounded irritated, like Mum when Ollie hassled her for sweets. "Come."

Maddy followed the woman out, praying she wouldn't hurt her.

CHAPTER EIGHTY-EIGHT

"DI Whaley."

"DI Finch." Carl stood back to let Zoe into the interview room. She bristled, making sure not to touch him as she passed.

Ian was already inside. Zoe was taken aback to see Edward Startshaw sitting next to him. She exchanged a look with Carl.

"DI Whaley and DI Finch present," said Carl.

"Edward Startshaw and my client Ian Osman," said Startshaw. His suit looked new, and his grey hair had been cut into a neat crop. He was barely recognisable as the man who'd sat next to Margaret Jackson when Zoe had interviewed her with David Randle.

Zoe was determined not to let Carl take over. "Ian," she said, "We need to talk to you about Maddy."

Ian gave Carl a look of contempt. "What's he doing here?"

Carl cleared his throat. "I'm from Professional Standards, Ian. If you're involved in the abduction, we have an interest."

"You bastard."

Carl raised an eyebrow. "That how you talk to all your DIs?"

"Not the ones that are on the level."

Zoe leaned forward. "DI Whaley is here because as a serving police officer, Professional Standards have an interest in your part in this case." She flicked her gaze from Ian to Startshaw. Choice of solicitor could never stand up as evidence...

"You need to do better than that, DI Finch," said Startshaw. "My client's been told this is solely about the disappearance of his children."

"It is," she said. "For now."

She met Ian's stare. "You got that note. You know today's the deadline. So I'm sure you'll be happy to help us."

Ian looked at his solicitor, who nodded. "Of course," he said, his gaze steady on Zoe.

"Good. Do you know where Maddy is?"

"Of course not."

"We have reason to believe the Facebook message you received about your children was sent by your wife. We think the two of you are working together."

"No idea what you're talking about."

Startshaw leaned forward. "My client deserves to know the nature of the accusations against his wife, if you're looking at a conspiracy."

"We'll get to that when we're ready," said Carl. Zoe clenched a fist under the table.

"She didn't send that note," said Ian. He ignored Startshaw's restraining hand. "I know what you think. But we'd never hurt our kids. We'd never do that."

"You refer to them as 'our' kids, Ian," said Zoe.

"I adopted them both after their birth father died."

"Benedict was birth father to both of them?"

Ian coloured. "Yes."

"You sure about that?"

"That's what Alison told me."

"Despite the fact you and Alison were in a relationship before Benedict died. Before Ollie was conceived."

"Do you think she might have lied to you?" said Carl.

Ian's eyes widened. "What are you saying?"

"Ian, did you commission a DNA analysis on your own and Ollie's biological material two days ago?" Asked Zoe.

"I don't see what that has to do with the accusations," said Startshaw. He whispered in Ian's ear.

"No comment," said Ian.

"Use of police resources for personal gain," said Carl. "You stand to lose your job, and your pension. Not to mention possible criminal charges." He leaned back, folding his arms.

"No comment," Ian repeated.

"OK," said Zoe. "What about the roof work you're having done on your house? The kitchen you had put in a year ago."

"What about them?"

"That's a very expensive kitchen."

"We saved up."

"Did you?"

"Yes."

Carl pulled a sheet from a file. It showed a summary of Ian and Alison's bank records for the last two years. A joint account, two personal accounts with salaries going in, and a small pot of savings.

"See, there's no record of it in your bank statements," he

said. He pushed the sheet across the table and Startshaw grabbed it.

"We paid by card."

"No record there either." Carl pulled out a second sheet.

Ian shifted in his chair. He licked his lips. "No comment."

Zoe stared at him. "Ian, if what you say is true and you aren't hiding Maddy somewhere, that means she's in danger."

He blinked back at her. "Yes," he croaked. He looked at Carl, his eyes dark.

"Which means you'll want to do everything you can to help us find her." She watched his reaction. "Which we need to do today."

Ian hoisted himself up and then shuffled back down again. Tears came to his eyes. "Yes."

"So, once again. Tell us why your wife was working for a cleaning company under her first husband's name."

"She was *what*?"

So he didn't know, she thought. "Cleanways cleaning company. Your wife worked for them under the name Alison Tomkin. They clean Hatton & Bannerjee in Colmore Row."

Ian frowned. His nostrils flared. "What's that got to do with anything?"

"Hatton & Banerjee was the source of that Facebook message. It didn't come from PC Bright at all, but then you already knew that."

"I thought it wasn't the kind of thing Trish did, but then..."

"Then what?" asked Carl. "Go on."

Ian glanced at Startshaw, who looked confused.

"Trish and I fell out. Back when we worked together in

Coventry. I thought she might have sent it as a hoax, to get back at me."

"Must have been something pretty serious you did for her to take that kind of revenge," said Carl.

"Yeah."

"What did you do to Trish Bright, Ian?" asked Zoe.

"I made a pass at her. DC Zahid Shah's leaving do. We were all pretty wasted. Alison was absorbed in Ollie, didn't want to know me. I got a bit fixated on Trish."

"Why didn't you tell us about this, when Trish was assigned to your family as FLO?" Zoe asked.

"I didn't want anyone to know what had happened."

"Ian, what did you do to Trish? Was this 'pass' actually an assault?"

He tugged at his collar. "God, no. Nothing like that. No, not at all. It was just... embarrassing. She kissed me back, just for a moment. Then she pushed me off like I had the pox. We never spoke about it again, and I got a transfer a month later."

"You've moved around a lot in your police career, haven't you?" said Zoe.

"I've followed opportunities."

"Or you've run away from cock-ups like this," said Carl.

Ian eyed him. "It was only the once, never again. I'm not an idiot."

Carl shook his head. "How do you know Stuart Reynolds?"

Ian paled and turned to his solicitor, then back to Carl.

"Who's he?"

Zoe rolled her eyes. "He's the man fixing your roof."

"Oh. Yes. Of course. It's easy to forget that sort of thing. Alison's been the one doing all the..."

"How do you pay him, if not through your bank account or your credit card?" asked Carl.

Zoe put a hand on Carl's arm.

"Ian, do you know a man called Trevor Hamm?"

Startshaw cleared his throat. "I don't see what any of this has to do with the children being kidnapped."

"Oh it has a great deal to do with it, Mr Startshaw," said Zoe. "I think you know that."

"You can't just—"

Zoe was becoming impatient. If he was as innocent as he claimed, why wasn't he helping them? "Does Trevor Hamm have Maddy, Ian? Have you pissed him off, and he's taken your daughter to punish you?"

"No," whispered Ian. "I promise you. I've got no idea where she is."

"Does Alison?"

Ian's Adam's apple bobbed. "I don't see why she'd do something like this."

"Why did your wife fake the abduction of Ollie and Maddy, Ian?" asked Zoe. "What do the pair of you have to gain?"

"Nothing." he straightened. "If we'd done that, why would we have sent Ollie back?"

"I think you know why," said Carl. "You believe that Ollie is biologically yours. You sent for a DNA test to prove it. Maddy, on the other hand..."

"That's monstrous. Maddy is my daughter. So what if she doesn't share my DNA? I love her."

"Where is she, Ian?"

"I don't know." He wiped his face. "I swear to you, I don't know."

CHAPTER EIGHTY-NINE

REYNOLDS CONTRACTING WAS QUIET. Mo leaned on the door and peered through the glass, rattling the handle.

He banged on the door again. "Police! We need to talk to you."

Nothing. He stopped rattling and listened, hoping to hear people working out back. There was a van at the front, the familiar logo on its side.

It was a squat building with two floors. Venetian blinds obscured the upstairs windows.

He headed round the side. A tall fence barred his way, fringed with nettles. *Damn.*

"Excuse me?"

Mo turned to see a woman staring at him. She wore overalls covered in paint splatters. He waded through the undergrowth back to her.

"Do you work here?"

"I'm in the unit next door. Brushworks Decorating. Can I help you?"

"I'm looking for Stuart Reynolds." He showed her his card.

"That bastard."

"Oh?"

"Uses this place like a fly tip. Have you seen round the back of there?"

"I can't get round."

"I'll show you." She beckoned for him to follow.

Reynolds being an inconsiderate neighbour had no bearing on the case. But if it allowed him access round the back...

"We need to hurry," he told her. "I don't have a lot of time."

"OK, hold your horses." She unlocked a narrow door into the next unit and ushered him through. "Back there." She pointed to a back door. Paint pots were piled against one wall. The room was surprisingly clean given the state of the woman's overalls.

Mo pushed the back door open. Behind it was a bare concrete yard, surrounded by the same blue fencing he'd seen at Reynolds's unit. A gate at the back gave onto a narrow roadway.

He walked to the fence bordering Reynolds's unit. Like this one, it was neat and tidy. A wooden shed sat in one corner and a gate at the back was secured with a chain.

He turned back to the building. "I think you've got confused," he began, making his way back to the woman.

The door he'd come through was locked. Mo hammered on the wood. "Hello? You've locked me out."

An engine started up on the other side of the building. There was no sound from inside.

He'd been played.

He tugged at the door once again but it wasn't budging. He hammered, louder this time. No answer.

He grabbed his phone. Stuart Reynolds was hiding something, and Zoe needed to know about it.

CHAPTER NINETY

"WE NEED to do this quick. The clock's ticking."

Zoe was in the inner office with Rhodri and Connie. Lesley stood against the door, sipping a coffee and watching. Carl stood behind Zoe, fidgeting.

"Yes, boss," said Rhodri.

"Ian swears blind he didn't take Maddy and Ollie," Zoe said. "So does Alison. I don't know if they're telling the truth, but Carl's going to carry on putting pressure on them. Meanwhile, we think Trevor Hamm might be involved."

Connie's face fell. "You think those bastards have..." Her hand came to her mouth. "That's why they've still got Maddy. She's twelve."

Zoe tried to push the thought from her mind. "We have to hope we're wrong. That it was just her parents trying to make a fast buck, and that they've got her somewhere safe. But we can't take any chances."

"We should get right round to Hamm's, boss," said Rhodri. "Get Uniform in."

"It's not as easy as that. He moved a month ago, to a flat

overlooking Cannon Hill. Mo's been there, and he's gone."

"Shit," muttered Rhodri. Connie put a hand on the wall to steady herself.

"Mo also went to Stuart Reynolds's unit. He's been doing some work for the Osmans, we think it's the same arrangement as ACC Jackson. No money changing hands, Hamm commissions it as payment for services rendered."

"What kind of services?" asked Connie.

"He works in CID," said Carl. "He could have been tampering with evidence, planting false leads, getting information to Hamm and his associates. Anything really."

"Evidence in the Canary case?" asked Connie.

"Maybe," said Zoe.

"We haven't got time for this," said Lesley. "Keep the catastrophising for after we've got the girl back."

"Ma'am."

Lesley put a hand over her mug as the door opened behind her.

"Mo," said Zoe. "You OK?"

Mo eyed the DCI and nodded. He approached Zoe. "Just bloody embarrassed is all. Can't believe that decorator tricked me like that."

"You get her details?"

"Well I know where her business is. Nothing else. And it's probably a front."

"No sign of the kids having been in those two units?"

Mo shook his head. "Adi's team are still there, but there's nothing so far."

"What about Hamm's flat?"

"I searched the place." Lesley raised an eyebrow. Mo spotted it, blanched, then focused on Zoe. "But you're right, Forensics might be able to find something I can't."

"We'll need a warrant for that," said Lesley. "You can't just go blundering in there without the proper procedure."

Zoe clenched her teeth. "With respect, ma'am..."

Lesley held a hand up. "Don't worry. I'll sort it. You get on with finding Maddy."

"Thanks." Zoe turned back to her team. "So. Carl's going to interview Alison. Put pressure on her, make her think Ian has given her away. That leaves us with the organised crime angle. We need to pay a visit to Shand and Petersen."

Lesley sheeshed out a breath. "I bloody hope you're wrong on that angle."

Zoe nodded. "Me too, ma'am." Heat rose in her chest. "We need to find out more about what Alison and Ian have been up to. Mo, find out if they've been doing anything out of the ordinary recently. Go back to neighbours. Alison's head teacher, colleagues. The grandmother."

"Nasty piece of work," said Rhodri.

"That doesn't make her a criminal," said Zoe. She pictured the way Barbara Wilson had looked at her. "Not necessarily."

"No, boss."

"Anyway. You and Connie, get more information on the pair of them. Where they go when they're not at work, who their friends are. Anywhere they might be keeping Maddy. Carl's going to see what he can get in interview, but we're not hopeful. Go back over their social media records, emails. everything. Anything out of place, tell me."

"Right, boss." Connie looked determined.

"What about you?" asked Mo.

"I'm going to be knocking on the doors of our two favourite paedophiles."

CHAPTER NINETY-ONE

BRIAN DIDN'T HAVE work today. Truth was, he was worried Rick was thinking of letting him go. He was a bloody brilliant climber, better than anyone at that stupid wall would ever know. But teaching wasn't his thing. He got impatient with the students, with their fear of a piddly little climbing wall and their inability to climb something that to him would have been a gentle stroll just a few years ago.

There was no such thing as a gentle stroll for him now. The fracture he'd suffered in his right leg saw to that. If he'd been able to get it treated quickly it would have been OK. But three days of agony dragging himself down from the mountain, followed by two weeks watching the infection kick in, had taken their toll. The bone had partly rotted away and he would always walk with a limp.

He could climb, but only the lowest grades. Embarrassing, really.

He got out of bed, wincing as his right foot hit the floor. Until he'd taken his painkillers, the days were a struggle.

He'd bought a carbon fibre brace online, expensive and shipped in from the States. When he wore it, he could pass as normal. Uninjured, if not all that agile.

So long as he never took his beanie off, and revealed the state of his ears.

He paced into the kitchen and opened the drawer containing his tablets. The brace felt constricting for the first half hour after he put it on, and he was glad he didn't have to go out this morning. The shock of seeing Alison led away by police had got to him. He'd seen the news stories, the social media outcry. He knew about Maddy and Ollie. What he found impossible to believe was that Alison would ever hurt them. It had to be that bastard Ian.

He filled the kettle for a cup of herbal tea – caffeine didn't play nicely with the drugs – and sat at the kitchen table, waiting for it to boil. He had a sudden memory and stood up, ignoring the discomfort.

In his bedroom he opened the drawer at the bottom of the wardrobe. It was here, hidden under his decorating clothes. Where Vic wouldn't look. She kept most of her clothes at her own flat anyway, repeatedly telling him he needed more storage. If they had kids together, they'd need to decide which flat to give up. Maybe get a house.

He rooted around at the back of the drawer. He remembered her giving it to him before he left for the mountains, her eyes wet. Something to remember her by. He'd had it in his rucksack when he'd fallen. The elderly woman who'd coaxed him back to health and brought a proper doctor to treat him had found it when he was unconscious. It had been sitting on a chair waiting for him when he woke, a jolt to his senses.

He pulled the clothes hiding it aside, his heart picking up. He pulled the drawer out and tipped it upside down, clothes strewing the floor.

It was gone. The Elsa doll. The one his daughter had told him to keep with him and think of her. It had been taken.

CHAPTER NINETY-TWO

Zoe took a deep breath before opening the door of her Mini. She'd parked a few doors along from Howard Petersen's house. A fair distance on this wide road in Four Oaks. Petersen owned a stationery supply company and a group of web design agencies, but she imagined this house had been paid for by other means.

She strode up the long driveway, taking in the porticoed entrance and the tall conifers. The kind of house that was supposed to look classy, but in reality looked tacky.

She tugged on a metal rod that activated the doorbell. A bell sounded from a distance away, loud and insistent.

She shrugged her shoulders, an urge to wipe her hand clean coming over her.

A woman in a white apron answered the door. She was short with wiry black hair and an expression that would melt granite.

"Can I help you?"

"I need to speak to Mr Petersen."

"I'll need to see if he's in. Who can I say is calling?"

"Detective Inspector Zoe Finch."

The woman didn't flinch. "One moment, please." She closed the door on Zoe, who frowned at it.

Howard Petersen had received a suspended sentence for money laundering. He was restricted in his movements, had to report to a probation officer every month. Zoe knew that he was expected to be home, and that he was also expected to respond to a visit from the police.

The door opened. "Come in."

She followed the woman through a wide hallway adorned with vases of brightly coloured flowers, to a comfortable sitting room looking over a lawned garden. The garden was long and wide, with well-stocked flower beds. The room had feminine touches: ornaments, a shaggy rug, more flowers. Zoe wondered what kind of woman stuck around after her husband was arrested for abusing children.

"Detective Inspector."

She turned to see Howard Petersen in the doorway. He wore a sweaty t-shirt and running shorts, a towel draped around his neck.

"I was on the treadmill," he said. "What d'you want?"

"I need to know where Trevor Hamm is."

"I'm the last fucking person who'd know that." He threw himself into a pale leather armchair, his long legs stretched out in front of him. He patted his forehead with the towel.

She stood over him. "He's disappeared. I believe you know where he is."

He dumped the towel in his lap. "Like I say, no bloody idea. He's not exactly flavour of the month round here."

"Howie, can I get you a... Oh." A woman stood in the doorway. Brown-haired, with make-up more suitable for a night on the town. She looked about fifteen years younger than Petersen.

"Mrs Petersen?" Zoe asked.

"Who wants to know?"

"Detective Inspector Finch. Force CID."

Mrs Petersen's gaze flicked to her husband. "He's been here all day, every day, since the trial. You've got nothing on him."

Zoe approached her. "Has he had any visitors?"

Again the woman's eyes went to her husband and back to Zoe. "No."

Zoe turned to Petersen. "Hamm's been here, hasn't he?"

"If that man ever tries to come here..." Mrs Petersen's voice was sharp. Either she was shaking with rage, or she was a damn good actress.

"You know the terms of your sentence, Mr Petersen," she said. "No association with your co-defendants."

"Trevor Hamm wasn't a co-defendant."

He was right. Hamm had managed to slip out of their grasp. But if Hamm was in touch with Petersen, Shand would be too.

"You haven't seen Jory Shand at all?"

"No!" cried Mrs Petersen. "He's been a good boy. Leave him alone."

Zoe ignored her. "Have you heard of Maddy and Ollie Osman?" she asked Petersen. His face darkened.

"Those poor babies," said Mrs Petersen. "Their mother must be..."

Zoe raised a hand. "You've heard of them, yes?"

"Of course we've heard of them." Petersen's teeth were gritted.

"If you helped us find them, I'm sure your probation officer would be happy."

"Those fuckers are never happy. And I don't know where those kids are. Why should I?"

Mrs Petersen shuffled to her husband's side. She stroked her long fingernails down his arm. "Leave us alone. We've done nothing wrong."

Zoe raised an eyebrow at Petersen. His wife can't have been that stupid.

"If Hamm gets in touch, you tell us. Straight away. If you get so much as an inkling of where he is."

"An inkling?" Petersen stood up. "Of course." He returned her gaze, his face impassive. "I'm only too happy to cooperate."

Yeah, right.

"Anything else?" asked Mrs Petersen.

"No." Zoe sighed. The clock was still ticking.

CHAPTER NINETY-THREE

CONNIE AND RHODRI sat in silence in the office, focused on their work. Connie was jealous of the bosses, out chasing leads in the real world. But she knew that scouring the internet could be more efficient, and that it would help the DI and the sarge do their jobs. And besides, last time she'd gone running after a lead hadn't gone well. She and the sarge had been knocked out cold by Simon Adams, one of Hamm's men. She still felt pain in her leg, even though it had healed enough for her to be out of plaster.

Ian and Alison's computers were on her desk, along with their phones. Rhodri was trawling their social media accounts on his own workstation and she was searching through these again. Yala in Forensics had done this already, there was little chance she'd come up with anything.

She scrolled through Ian's phone contacts. He'd made two calls to an unknown phone the week before the abduction. The phone was an unregistered pay as you go mobile. A burner phone. Yala hadn't been able to trace it.

They'd tried calling the number, but there'd been no

reply. No cell mast ping, no voicemail. The phone was out of action.

It was pointless, but she wanted to give it one last try. This time, she'd use her own phone.

She keyed the number in and waited. The phone rang out. Once, twice, three times. When it got to six rings she was about to hang up.

The phone clicked. She held her breath.

"Who is this?"

Connie felt her stomach plummet. She held the phone by her fingertips as if it was on fire.

"What's up?" asked Rhodri. She held her finger to her lips, her breathing shallow.

"Don't call this number again, please." The line went dead.

Shaking, she rang it again. No answer.

"What's up. Connie? You look like you've seen a ghost."

"The voice."

"What voice?"

"On the other end. The number Ian rang, the burner."

"What about it?"

"I've heard it before."

CHAPTER NINETY-FOUR

ZOE KNEW that a visit to Jory Shand would be as fruitless as the one to Howard Petersen had proved. She wasn't ruling it out, but she had other fish to fry.

Luckily, the information she needed had been on the Companies House website.

She walked up the path to Stuart Reynolds's white-rendered house in Northfield and waited. The house looked neat and tidy, recently painted. The wide porch had a collection of healthy-looking plants and a bike with pink tassels on the handlebars.

The door opened. Stuart Reynolds stared back at her, his face hard.

"What you doin' here?"

"We tried to find you at your office."

"Having a day off. Not a crime, is it?"

"Depends what you do with your free time."

He scowled at her. "Fuck off."

She put a hand on the door. "I need to ask some questions about one of your clients."

"What I do for my clients is confidential."

"Even when they're police officers?"

"Work is work."

"Except your police officer clients don't pay you, do they?"

"No idea what you're on about."

"Assistant Chief Constable Bryn Jackson. Detective Sergeant Ian Osman. Both have had work done by your company. Neither of them paid."

"I don't do work for free."

"Your accounts are on record at Companies House."

"Yeah. And you'll see payments coming in for all those jobs."

"True." Reynolds was good at covering his tracks. Better than his clients. "But the problem is, neither Jackson or Osman's bank accounts show any record of them paying you."

He shrugged. "Not up to me how they manage their money."

"Who pays you, Stuart? Is it Trevor Hamm?"

"Don't know what you're talking about."

"Why don't you let me in. I don't imagine you'd want your neighbours seeing this."

He grunted and stood aside. She passed him, surprised at how easy that had been.

She entered a living room whose walls were covered in floral wallpaper. A pink fleece was slung over a chair and there was a family photo over the mantelpiece, one of those ones designed to look like a painting. Zoe stood in the centre of the room and turned back to Reynolds.

"I'd offer you a seat, but I don't want you stopping," he said.

"Don't worry, I'll make this quick."

"Fuck you will."

"Just tell me where Trevor Hamm is and I'll get out of your hair."

"Why should I know?"

"He's one of your best clients. You did that bespoke wardrobe for him, the one you were working on last time we met."

When she'd visited his unit for the first time he'd been working on a teak wardrobe for Hamm's flat in Brindley-place. She'd spotted it in the crime scene photos after Hamm had staged a break-in to his flat. It had helped her make the link between Hamm, Reynolds, and Jackson.

And now Osman.

"No idea where he is, sorry darlin'. Wastin' your time."

She narrowed her eyes.

"If Trevor Hamm's paying for you to do up Ian Osman's house, just what is it that Osman's doing for Hamm?"

He barked out a laugh. "You're asking the wrong bloke."

Zoe's phone rang in her pocket. She ignored it.

"Don't you think you better get that?" he said.

"I'm talking to you."

"Wasting your time, more like." He leaned towards her. His breath smelt of salt and vinegar crisps.

"A girl's life is at stake," she said. "Now, I've got a hunch that you don't know quite how unpleasant your so-called biggest client is. You're a nasty pice of work who likes to talk to people like they're something you trod in, but I don't reckon you're the type who'd be involved in abusing vulnerable kids."

His pupils dilated. "You're talking bollocks."

"Ian Osman's daughter is missing, Stuart. We think Hamm's got her, and he's going to give her to some filthy fucker who deserves to be in prison. If you know where Hamm is, you can help us stop that."

He blinked. "You're lying."

Her phone rang again. *Be patient.* She pulled it out of her pocket and glanced at it: Connie.

She turned back to Reynolds. "How old is your daughter?"

"None of your business."

"That picture over the mantelpiece. She looks about three in that, but you look a fair bit younger. I guess she's a teenager now. Same age as Ian Osman's daughter."

"She's none of your business." He clenched his fists. He was sweating.

"Tell me where he is. I can tell my bosses you cooperated with us." She paused. "And it'll keep girls like your daughter safe."

He looked down at the carpet. "He's not doing that sort of thing."

She cocked an eyebrow. "How d'you know?"

"I just do, OK?"

"So you know about other stuff he's up to?"

'I'm not saying anything, alright."

"Stuart. If Trevor Hamm gives Maddy Osman to abusers, you'll be responsible. I hope you can live with that."

She turned and left the room. She opened the front door, not looking back. Hoping this would work. The house was silent behind her, no sound of the door being closed.

She checked her phone. A text from Connie. *Call me, Urgent.*

"Alright."

Zoe turned to see Reynolds standing in his front garden. He glanced up and down the road as if expecting Hamm's guys to jump out of a bush.

"Yes?"

"I can tell you where he is."

CHAPTER NINETY-FIVE

"You alright, Con?"

"I'm trying to get hold of the boss."

"She's knocking on doors. Probably can't pick up."

"Yeah." Connie put her phone down and sighed. She picked it up again and started texting.

Rhodri turned back to his own screen. He needed to focus. He was running through the Osmans' social media accounts, looking for anything the week before the kids had been taken. Trying to trace their movements.

Alison had sent a message to the climbing centre, booking Maddy in for a lesson. He wondered what it would be like, learning to do something that had killed your dad. Then he wondered how much the kids knew about Benedict.

He flicked onto the climbing centre's Facebook page and then through to their website. There was a slideshow, photos of kids learning to climb, adults hauling themselves up walls. Lucky buggers.

He stopped on a photo of four men on top of a crag somewhere. One of them was Rick, the manager they'd spoken to. Next to him was a skinny guy with a beanie in his hand. Chunk were missing from both his ears. Rhodri winced.

He looked in closer.

"Connie?"

"Yeah." She was putting her phone down, staring at it as if it would talk to her.

"Have you got a photo of Alison Osman's ex?"

"There's one on the board."

Rhodri went into the inner office and checked the board. On the top row, separated from the Osman family, was a photo of Benedict Tomkin. He had dark hair and a scruffy beard. The tops of his ears were missing.

"Shit."

Rhodri grabbed the photo and ran back to his desk. He held it up to the screen.

He scrolled through the rest of the slideshow, looking for more. He delved further into the website, seeking out galleries, videos, anything.

On the page advertising their outdoor climbing days was a video of a climb in Derbyshire. Birchen Edge. Four professionals were in it, with a dozen punters. One of them had that scruffy beard and the beanie again. He leaned in. There were red marks on one of his ears, just below the line of the hat.

"Whoah."

"What's up?" asked Connie. She had her phone to her ear.

"It's Benedict. He's alive. And I've met him."

Connie threw her phone down. "You've what?"

"I need to tell the boss."

"I can't get her."

"No." He hesitated, gazing at the screen. "I won't be long."

Rhodri jumped out of his chair and grabbed his coat, his heart thumping in his ears.

CHAPTER NINETY-SIX

CONNIE STARED AT THE DOOR.

Rhodri had leapt out of his chair and shot through the door like his life depended on it.

She went to his desk. His monitor was still on the website he'd been looking at. The climbing centre. What was he doing investigating that when they had Trevor Hamm to track down?

The door opened. She looked up, about to lay into Rhodri. She stopped herself when she saw it was DI Whaley. She stood up straight. She'd never been alone with him.

"Sir."

He smiled, his eyes glinting. He was muscular but slim with eyes you could get lost in. His skin was light brown, unblemished. The sort of man her mum would describe as *fine*.

"Connie. How's progress?"

She frowned, unsure how much the boss would want her telling him. She seemed to be working with him on this case, but Connie had spotted the tension between them. She still didn't know why he'd left Force CID so abruptly after the Jackson case.

She swallowed. She couldn't keep this to herself.

"I've got something, sir."

"Show me."

She stood up. DI Whaley was in her way. She waited for him to move, uneasy. He pulled to one side and muttered apologies.

Should she be telling him this?

The boss wasn't picking up. Neither was the sarge. Someone had to know.

"You've been interviewing Ian Osman." she said.

"Yes."

"About suspected corruption?"

He said nothing.

"I've found a phone number."

"Go on." He leaned over her. He smelt of musk.

She grabbed the phone in its evidence bag. "He made two calls to an unregistered mobile the week before the kidnapping."

"And we don't know whose they were."

"Well..." She eyed him. Could she trust him?

"Go on, constable. If it helps us find Maddy..."

He was right. "I called the number," she said.

He raised an eyebrow.

"It was answered," she continued. "I recognised the voice."

He put a hand on the basck of her chair. "Who?"

She pursed her lips. This was going to get her in so much trouble with the boss.

"Connie, tell me. Please."

OK. "It was Detective Superintendent Randle, sir."

His face froze, his mouth half open. He seemed to stop breathing.

"Sir?"

He straightened. "Well done. Leave it with me."

He almost ran out of the office. Connie watched, her mind racing. Had she done the right thing?

CHAPTER NINETY-SEVEN

"Boss."

"Mo, where are you?" Zoe was on the Bristol Road, heading into the city centre.

"Hamm's flat. Just come from Reynolds's unit."

"Did you find anything?"

"Nothing so far at Reynolds's. Adi's setting up now here."

"Is it still as empty as it was when you found it?"

"Seems to be. But you know what Adi's like."

"He'd find a speck of dust in a thunderstorm."

"Let's hope so," Mo replied. "Where are you?"

Zoe slammed on her brakes, only just spotting the lights at the university turning red.

"Zo?"

"Sorry. I'm on my way to you. Be ready for me to pick you up."

"Where we going?"

"I know where Hamm is."

"How d'you find that out?"

"Reynolds told me."

A whistle. "Jeez. How did you manage that?"

"He's got a daughter."

"I see. Where is he?"

"The Canalside hotel."

"Seedy."

"Yeah. Perfect for Hamm's brand of depravity." Her stomach dipped at the thought of Maddy there.

"We have to be quick," Mo said. His voice was thin. "You want me to head over there?"

"I'm nearly with you. Be out front, wait for me."

"No problem."

She heard him muttering to someone in the background. Adi Hanson, most probably.

The lights turned green and she hit the accelerator.

CHAPTER NINETY-EIGHT

THE CLIMBING CENTRE was quieter than it had been last time Rhodri was here. Two groups of men were in the main climbing area and a couple sat in the cafe, laughing over their drinks.

Rick Kent was at the front desk. Rhodri walked up to it, trying not to show urgency.

"Hi, I was here a few days ago, with my boss."

"You booked a climbing session?" Rick turned to his computer.

"No." Rhodri leaned in. "We're police. Remember?"

Rick pursed his lips. "I remember."

"We talked to you about Benedict Tomkin."

A nod. "Poor bastard."

Rhodri shook his head. "He's not dead."

"Of course he's dead."

"Uh-uh." Rhodri pulled out his phone. He already had the slideshow ready. "This is him."

"That's Brian."

"How long has he worked here?"

"Two years, maybe a bit more. I'd have to check. His name's Brian Parrish. That's not Benedict."

"You never met Benedict."

"No, but..."

Rhodri flicked through his photos. "This is Benedict."

Rick squinted. "Looks a bit like him, but so do lots of people."

"Does Brian ever take his beanie off?"

"He did, in that film."

"When he's here, at the centre."

"No. But climbers like their beanies. It's not exactly..." Rick's shoulders fell. "He's hiding it. He doesn't want to be recognised."

"Exactly."

"That's a big accusation you're making. Brian needs to be able to give his side of the story."

"Is he here?"

"It's his day off." Rick's expression hardened.

"Where does he live?"

"I can't give out private information—"

Rhodri lowered his voice. "I'm a police officer. And I'm looking for Benedict's daughter. She was kidnapped."

Rick paled. "Yeah."

"I think a man who hides his identify might have something else to hide."

"Surely you don't think Brian would hurt his own daughter."

"Maybe not hurt her. Maybe take her. Take her back."

Rick shook his head. "I still don't think..."

"Look. I can get this without your help. But you can make it a hell of a lot quicker." Rhodri brought up a photo of

Maddy. "She could be in danger. If Benedict – Brian – hasn't got her, he might help us find out who has."

"He wouldn't hurt her."

"How d'you know? What's he told you about himself?"

A pause. "Not much." Rick looked at the computer screen, coming to a decision. "OK. But don't tell him, OK?"

Rhodri mimed zipping his lips. "Lips are sealed, mate. Now give me his address. Please."

CHAPTER NINETY-NINE

Mo turned back to Adi.

"Was that the lovely Zoe Finch?"

Mo rolled his eyes. "She's picking me up in five minutes."

"No problem."

They were in the large living space in Trevor Hamm's penthouse flat. Pam, the receptionist who'd been so helpful before, hovered outside in the hallway, clearly worried she'd done something wrong.

"Can you get rid of her?" Adi said. "She's going to contaminate my scene."

Mo went out to the hallway, a gentle smile on his face. "Hello again, Pam."

"Is everything OK? I hope there won't be trouble."

"We'll keep out of your hair as much as possible. Try not to disturb your other residents."

"Oh. Good." She allowed herself a smile.

"But I need you to go back downstairs for me."

"Oh. I thought you might need me..."

"We need you to keep an eye on the front entrance. Tell

me if Hamm comes back. Or anyone who visited him." He cocked his head, trying to appear conspiratorial.

"Oh, yes. Of course. I'll do that."

"Thanks. And while I'm on it, we'll need a description of any visitors he did have. Someone will get a statement from you."

"No problem." She shivered. "He did have quite a lot of visitors."

I bet, thought Mo. He pulled his phone out and brought up a photo of Ian Osman. "Was this man one of them?"

She squinted, leaning in. Her breathing was shallow.

She looked up at Mo. "No. Sorry. I don't remember him."

"That's OK." Mo put his phone away. Nothing was ever that simple.

"Sergeant Uddin!"

He turned to see Adi waving him into the flat.

"Gotta go," he told Pam. "You guard the front door. OK?"

She grinned. "OK."

He turned back into the flat. Adi had moved into a bedroom, two of his white-suited FSIs examining something on the floor. One of them was scraping up samples and depositing them in evidence pots.

Adi nodded towards his colleague. "We've found blood residue. And semen."

Mo followed his gaze. "Much of it?"

"No. The place has been cleaned pretty thoroughly. But they've left traces. We'll analyse the samples, see if we can get a DNA match."

"Right."

One of Adi's colleagues was coming out of the ensuite bathroom.

"DS Uddin, this is Yala Cook," Adi said.

"We've met," she said. Mo nodded recognition.

She turned to Adi. "You need to see this."

Adi followed her back into the bathroom, followed by Mo. The space was tight and echoey, and Mo could hardly see what they were looking at.

"Bastard." Adi's voice was stern. He pulled out of the way so Mo could see.

The lid of the toilet cistern had been lifted. Yala pulled something from it. A length of striped material.

"What is it?" Mo asked.

"It's a tie," Adi said.

"Why would Hamm put his tie in there?"

Adi turned to him, his eyes flashing. "Does Hamm have kids?"

"No. His wife died just a few months after they married."

"I thought not."

"Why?"

"Because this isn't a man's tie. It's a school tie."

CHAPTER ONE HUNDRED

ZOE HAD HALF a dozen missed calls from Connie and a text. As soon as she ended the call with Mo, she dialled.

"Connie. Sorry I couldn't pick up, I was interviewing Reynolds."

"It's OK, boss. I know what it's like."

"What is it?"

"I dialled the number on Ian's phone. One of the burners. The ones Yala had no joy with."

"You wouldn't be calling me unless *you* had some joy with it."

"Yes, boss."

"Go on then. Whose is it?"

"I'm not sure how comfortable I feel talking about this on the phone."

"Why? Who was it?"

Connie's breath came down the line, heavy and fast.

"Connie. You have to tell me."

"I already told DI Whaley, boss."

"OK. So is he following it up with Ian?"

"I imagine so. He stormed out of here pretty fast after I told him."

"You're making this sound like it's huge, Connie."

"It could be."

"So. Who was it, then?"

More heavy breathing. Zoe resisted the urge to shout at the DC. She clutched the steering wheel and waited.

"It was the Detective Superintendent, boss."

Zoe didn't need to ask which Detective Superintendent.

"OK," she said. "Don't tell anyone else. If DI Whaley asks more questions, you run it past me."

"Did I do the wrong thing, boss?"

"No. I'd have told him myself. But I'm glad you told me."

"Good."

"Right," said Zoe. "Anything else on the Osmans? Their movements the days before the kidnapping?"

"I think Rhodri found something."

"Think?"

"He got all jittery then ran off. Not sure where he went."

"He did what?"

"Sorry. I didn't even get a chance to stop him. He was a bit of a state."

"OK. I'll track him down. Meanwhile I want you to check the Canalside Hotel."

"You think Maddy's there?"

"She might be. Trevor Hamm is."

"No." Connie's voice was barely a whisper. "You found him."

"I'm going there now with DS Uddin. Find out what you can about the place and text me with it. I might not be able to pick up."

"No problem."

"And Connie?"

"Yes?'

"Don't worry about DI Whaley. He's on our side."

"Yes, boss."

Zoe hung up. She'd arrived at the Hemisphere building where Hamm's flat was, but Mo was nowhere to be seen. She dipped her head down to look up at the building through the windscreen.

Mo, where are you? This wasn't like him.

She picked up her phone then thought better of it. If he was still in there, it would be for a good reason.

She passed a smiley blonde woman in the foyer and made for the lift. At the top, forensic equipment spilled out of the flat and she could see cameras being set up.

"Mo?" she called. "Adi?"

Mo emerged from a door on the left. He looked like he'd been punched.

"What is it? Who's here?"

Mo shook his head. "He's a sick bastard."

"I know that."

Adi appeared behind Mo. His eyes, the only part of his face currently visible, brightened at the sight of Zoe. "DI Finch, as I live and breathe. Good to see you."

"You too, Adi. What's going on? What have you found?"

Adi looked her up and down. "You're not suited up."

"I left it in the car. Didn't think I'd have to..."

"Stay there."

Adi disappeared through the door.

Zoe looked at Mo. "You weren't out front."

"You'll understand why, when you see this."

Adi re-emerged holding an evidence bag. He held it up for Zoe, reaching across the threshold. She took it.

It was a school tie, black and red stripes. A crest near the tip. There was a smear of lipstick on the back. Her stomach hollowed out.

"Oh my God," she whispered.

"Yeah," replied Adi.

She looked back at him. "You go over this place like there's no tomorrow. Find anything we can use to take this bastard down."

"Don't you doubt it," said Adi.

"Good. Mo, we need to get him. Hurry."

CHAPTER ONE HUNDRED ONE

ZOE AND Mo jumped into her car.

"You find anything else?" she asked him.

"Not yet. We only just found that."

She bit her bottom lip, thinking of Maddy. She pushed her foot down on the accelerator.

"If he's got her," said Mo, "she probably won't be at the hotel."

"I know."

They stared ahead, both lost in thought. Both hoping Mo was wrong.

"Shit," she said. "I need to call Rhodri."

"What's he done this time?"

"He's gone chasing off after something. Connie said he left the office in a hurry."

"I'll do it. You focus on the road."

She braked at the lights where Edgbaston Road met the Pershore Road, muttering under her breath.

"Put him on speaker," she said.

Mo nodded, his phone at his ear. After a moment he

pressed a button and laid it on his lap. Rhodri's voice came over the speaker.

"Sarge."

"Rhodri, I'm with DI Finch. Where the hell are you?"

"Sorry, sarge. Boss. But Benedict Tomkin didn't die."

Mo glanced at Zoe. She indicated to turn onto the Pershore Road, cursing the traffic.

"What makes you think that?" she asked.

"When you and me went to the climbing centre, boss, d'you remember the guy on the desk?"

"Wearing a beanie indoors. I remember him."

"That's him. He's changed his name. But it's him alright."

Zoe ran over the visit to the climbing centre in her mind, trying to recall the man's face. But she'd been too distracted by the ridiculousness of wearing a woolly hat inside.

"How d'you know?" asked Mo.

"I spotted his photo on the website. The climbing centre have got videos. He wears that beanie to hide the frostbite damage to his ears."

Now *that* Zoe could remember. Benedict Tonkin had lost the tips of his ears on an expedition to Annapurna, a year before the trip to K2.

"Where are you?" Mo asked.

"I'm just leaving the climbing centre, heading for Brian's flat."

"Who's Brian?"

"That's what he's calling himself. Brian Parrish."

"When you get there," said Zoe, "you wait. Call Connie, arrange backup from Uniform. I don't want you going in there on your own."

"What if he's got her, boss?"

"I don't think he's got her."

"He might have wanted to get her back. It'd explain why he let them have Ollie."

Zoe exchanged glances with Mo. If Ian believed Ollie was his, then Benedict could have come to the same conclusion.

If this was a case of a heartsick father wanting his daughter back, then Maddy wouldn't be in danger. Zoe hoped.

"Like I say, Rhod. Sit tight. Watch his flat, and wait."

"What about you?"

"We're about to go and arrest the city's nastiest bastard," said Mo.

CHAPTER ONE HUNDRED TWO

When Maddy got into the car, she found the kitten already waiting for her, in a cage on the back seat. She poked her fingers through the bars, watching it sniff her skin. She smelt bad, she knew.

The woman closed the door behind her then got in the front. They were in a scruffy road with tall buildings either side and a row of shops opposite. Half of the shops were boarded up. Maddy shivered and huddled down into the seat.

"Don't worry, Maddy love. Everything's going to be alright. He's going to be so happy to see you."

"Who is?"

"You'll find out."

Maddy clutched her arms around herself as the car started. She hadn't brought her hoody and her skin had goosebumps.

"Are you taking me to Ollie?"

The woman looked in the rear-view mirror. "Shush. Be

patient." Her eyes crinkled. Maddy shifted in her seat and looked out of the window.

They left the scruffy street and drove onto a dual carriageway. This felt more familiar. The tall shapes of the city centre were up ahead. Cars surrounded them. She placed her hands on the glass. Could she get someone's attention?

"Don't do anything stupid," the woman said. "This is a fast road."

Maddy curled her fingers around the door handle, wondering if she dared try. Something inside the door clicked and she pulled her hand away as if she'd been bitten.

"That's better." The woman's eyes were cold in the mirror, not crinkling anymore.

The car picked up speed and so did the traffic around them. They were on the motorway leading out of the city now, the route Mum took when they were going to the shops. Maddy scanned the cars, hoping to see Mum's blue Fiesta.

"Where are you taking me?" She needed a wee and her stomach hurt.

"I told you to be patient." The woman brushed her short hair back. It was a lot like Mum's. "Jeez, you don't let up, do you? He'd better appreciate all this."

The kitten moved in its cage. It was balled up in a corner, mewling softly. It didn't like being in the car, or the cage. Maddy knew how it felt.

She poked her fingers though the bars. "Hush, now. You're safe. I'll look after you."

She'd said that to Ollie, she thought. She wiped tears from her eyes, hoping they hadn't hurt him.

CHAPTER ONE HUNDRED THREE

ZOE PARKED on double yellow lines and jumped out. Mo went to the boot and grabbed two stab vests. The Canalside hotel was in Digbeth, a down-at-heel establishment with fading paint on its door and a wide crack across the front window.

She elbowed the door open, warrant card ready in her pocket. An elderly man sat at the tiny front desk, smoking a roll-up.

"Police," she said. "Stay where you are and don't make any phone calls."

There was movement behind her: Force Response. She felt the tension ease in her chest.

"What's the score?" The sergeant scanned the room, his eyes resting on her.

"Suspect may be armed. Definitely a lowlife. Trevor Hamm."

"Right. I'm Sergeant Ford. You are...?"

"DI Finch."

"Inspector. We'll go up first, you follow. We don't want to take any chances."

"Fine."

He nodded to his colleagues, one of whom started up the narrow stairs.

"What's goin' on?" said the man at the desk. His cigarette had fallen to the floor and was burning a hole in the flock carpet.

"You've got a Trevor Hamm staying here," said Zoe. "Tell me which room."

"Never 'eard of 'im bab."

She reached across the desk. There was a thick file full of receipts. She flicked thought it, searching for Hamm's name. No sign.

"OK," she said. "Which is your largest room?"

"Why, you wanna rent it with yer boyfriend 'ere?" He threw a grin in Mo's direction.

"Just tell me."

"My clients' business is their own concern."

"D'you want these officers to bust every door in the place open? Because they will."

The man blanched. "Alright. Fucking pigs."

"Well?"

"Yeah, yeah. It's the top floor. Whole thing's the owner's flat. He let one of his mates borrow it like."

"Thank you."

She gestured to a uniformed constable, who stepped in to make sure the man didn't go anywhere. Sergeant Ford was already at the top of the first flight of stairs. Zoe followed, her footsteps light.

At the top of the stairs was a dim corridor. A light flickered on, on a motion sensor maybe. They peered up and down. An officer stayed behind and they continued upwards.

They repeated this routine until they got to the fourth and top floor. The single door facing them had three visible locks and a host of bolts on the other side, no doubt.

Zoe and Mo stood back while three constables came through with the enforcer. The door took two slams and it was open.

"Police!" Sergeant Ford called. He and his colleagues hurried in, splitting up to cover the rooms. Zoe stood outside, time ticking. She plunged her hand into her pockets, nerves shredded.

"In here," Ford called from inside. "Two males."

She saw her own emotions mirrored in Mo's face. Relief, elation, hope, dread. She went in, two constables moving back to let her through.

Trevor Hamm sat on a balding green sofa. Simon Adams, who'd broken bail after the Jackson case, was next to him. In front of them was a bottle of whiskey and two glasses. Hamm looked up at her, his face a mask of innocence. She eyed Adams, who wore a look of defiance.

"Where is she?" Zoe barked.

"Where is *who*?" Hamm replied.

"Maddy Osman. Is she here?"

Hamm stood up. Sergeant Ford pushed him back down to the sofa. "No idea who you're talking about." He returned her gaze.

"There's no one else here, sarge." One of the constables was behind her. Zoe gritted her teeth and clenched her fists.

"You bastard, you tell me where she is or I swear I'll—"

Mo's hand was on her arm. "Boss."

She yanked her arm away but stopped talking. *Focus*, she

told herself. She remembered what Lesley had said to her when Shand and Petersen had gone free. Procedure. Good policing. *We build a case.*

She certainly wouldn't balls it up by giving Hamm reason to make a complaint.

She stepped towards him. "Trevor Hamm, I'm arresting you on suspicion of child abduction and trafficking. You do not have to say anything, but it may harm your defence if you do not say something which you later rely on in court."

CHAPTER ONE HUNDRED FOUR

RHODRI SAT IN HIS CAR, impatience gnawing at him. He'd done as he was told. Chosen a spot with a view of the flat, parked up, sat tight.

He hated it.

If Benedict had Maddy, she could be in there. Her mum wanted her back. He knew what his mum would be like if his little sister disappeared. They'd thought she'd gone missing once, back when she was fourteen. But she'd only been playing silly buggers. He'd found her at the bus stop and given her a tongue lashing, prepared her for what she got from their dad.

The street was quiet, just the occasional car passing and person walking along. It ran alongside the cross city train line, Gravelly Hill station just a hundred yards away. Two trains had been and gone while he'd sat here. It was killing him.

His phone buzzed.

"Sarge."

"Where are you, Rhodri?"

CHAPTER 104

"Doing as I'm told. Watching his flat. No sign of backup yet."

"OK. The DI's on her way. She'll be about fifteen minutes."

Shit. He hoped he wasn't in trouble.

"Yes, guv."

"You stay where you are till she gets there, alright?"

"Did you get Hamm?"

"We did. No sign of Maddy here though."

Rhodri's gaze flicked back to the door to the house that held Brian's flat. *That's because she's here,* he thought.

"We did get more than we bargained for though," said Mo. "Stick Adams was with him."

"That bastard. Nice one."

"Yeah. Let's just hope we can make it stick, eh? It'll all be about the forensics now."

A car drove towards him, a squat Mini that made him think of the DI and her pride and joy, the bottle green Mini she drove everywhere. Rhodri watched as it crept along the street, slower than the cars that had passed so far. He wondered if Brian was in it.

"Gotta go, sarge," he said. "Might have spotted something."

"Go easy, alright? I don't want you getting a broken leg like Connie did."

"Don't worry, I'll be a good boy."

"Hmmm." The line went dead.

Rhodri looked in his rear-view mirror. The car had disappeared. This road was chock-full of parked cars, he'd been lucky to spot someone coming out of this space. If the driver of the Mini was looking for somewhere to park, they could be a while.

The car reappeared behind him, returning from the far end of the road. It crept along, definitely looking for somewhere to park. Rhodri slid down in his seat and watched as it passed. Inside, a woman scanned the road, looking from side to side.

At last she must have spotted a space. The car pulled in about fifty yards in front of Rhodri. He sat up, watching the spot where it had disappeared.

A woman crossed the street, the same woman he'd seen in the car. He held his breath. She walked towards Brian's flat, looking behind her every couple of seconds as if she knew she was being watched. He wore a grey hoody and her face was obscured.

Rhodri slid down in his seat again.

She went up Brian's path. Rhodri perked up, holding his breath. She pulled a key out of her bag and went inside.

He leaned on the window, trying to get a better view of the windows. The house had two flats. She could be Brian's neighbour. He hadn't thought to ask Rick if Brian was married or had a girlfriend.

He chewed his lip, thinking. He could saunter up there nice and casual like, knock on the door and pretend to be selling something. But then what? How would he find out if Brian was in there? If Maddy was in there?

The door opened and the woman emerged. She was alone. She'd pulled down the hoody and he could see a green scarf beneath it. She looked annoyed. Rhodri watched her retrace her steps, heading back towards her car. She crossed right in front of his car, looking up and down the road again. Not at him. She was looking for someone.

As she passed in front of his car, she turned her head and

their eyes met for a second. He pulled his gaze away, his face hot.

He knew that face. Pale skin, long dark hair, large eyes. That scarf she wore.

But it was impossible. They had her in custody. Didn't they?

So what was Alison Osman doing here at her ex-husband's flat?

CHAPTER ONE HUNDRED FIVE

ZOE NODDED to Rhodri as she drove past his car. This street was full and there was nowhere to park.

She didn't have time to waste searching. She pulled up at the double yellows next to the station and got out.

She climbed into Rhodri's car. "Which flat?"

He pointed. "That one. I saw someone go in."

"Benedict?"

"No, boss. Is Alison still in custody?"

"Yes. Why?"

"Because I reckon she's got a twin."

"Go on."

"A car was driving round, looking to park. Then she got out and went into that building. She looked just like Alison. She was even wearing the same scarf."

"What scarf?"

"The green scarf. The one in the CCTV."

Zoe turned to him. "Rhodri, are you sure about this?"

"Course I am, boss. Wouldn't be telling you otherwise."

"Did you get her plates?"

CHAPTER 105

"Sure did." He showed her his notebook.

"Well done. She drove away?"

"Yeah."

She leaned into the windscreen, her fingers clutching the dashboard. "If she came out, then chances are he's not there. But who is she?"

"Dunno. But that there's Benedict."

A man wearing a striped beanie walked along the street from the station. He carried a bag of shopping and looked tired. His steps were sluggish.

"That's the guy from the climbing centre," Zoe said.

"It's Benedict," said Rhodri. "I'm sure of it."

"OK then." She pushed the door open. As Benedict reached his flat she crossed the street. She was right behind him as he put his key to the lock.

"Brian Parrish?"

"Er, yes." He turned, lowering his arm. He looked confused.

"Previously known as Benedict Tomkin," she said.

His face crumpled. "Who are you?"

"Detective Inspector Finch, West Midlands Police. I think we'd better go inside, don't you?"

He glanced up and down the street. *Oh no you don't*, she thought, hoping Rhodri was in a good position to help stop him if he ran. But then Benedict heaved out a sigh and unlocked the door.

His flat was small but tidy, thin curtains diffusing the low sunlight from the street. He put his shopping bag on a table and turned to her.

"How did you track me down?"

"My colleague did. Through the climbing centre."

He winced. "Damn."

"Going to work there, sounds to me like you wanted to be found."

He shrugged.

Rhodri came in behind her, sniffing the air. Zoe could smell perfume.

"Where's Maddy?" she asked Benedict.

"I was hoping you could tell me that."

"Have you got her here?"

"Boss." Rhodri pointed to a photo on a side table. On it was a picture of Benedict and Alison.

"She remarried, you know," Zoe said. "Not much point keeping her photo."

Benedict turned to it. "That's not Alison. That's my girlfriend, Vic."

CHAPTER ONE HUNDRED SIX

"DON'T TELL HER, ALRIGHT?" Benedict said.

"Tell her what?" Asked Zoe.

"If Vic knew she looked just like my ex-wife, she'd have a meltdown."

"Does she know you have an ex-wife?" said Rhodri. "Is she even your ex-wife anyway?"

"Alison lives a mile and a half away in Erdington," said Benedict. "You think I'd tell Vic?"

Zoe ran over the CCTV in her head. The cleaning company. The threads were coming together. "Where is she?" she asked. "Vic?"

Benedict shrugged.

"She was here," said Rhodri. "She came in, then left."

"She's got a key," said Benedict.

"She live here?" Zoe asked.

"Sort of. She's got her own place, other side of town. She sleeps here most nights, though. Not so much lately."

Zoe eyed Rhodri. Her heart was racing.

"Give us her address," she said.

"Why? You going to tell her I'm not who I say I am?"

"She already knows," Zoe replied. She'd worked for the cleaning company as Alison Tomkin. "But right now, I think Vic has your daughter."

Benedict almost toppled backwards. "Madison?"

"We believe it was Vic who took her."

"What about Ollie?"

"He's with his gran."

"Barbara." He blew out air. "Why isn't he at home? That old witch..."

"He's not at home because we thought... no, I'm not telling you why he's not at home." Zoe felt an urge to punch this man, who'd lied to so many people. "Just tell us where Vic is."

Zoe turned at the sound of a key turning behind them. It was muffled, coming from the building' main door. Rhodri stared at her, his chest rising and falling.

"It's her," he whispered. Zoe gestured for him to move away from the door. She slipped in behind it.

"Please don't..." said Benedict.

The door opened and a woman walked in. She was taller than Alison. But otherwise they could have been twins. She spotted Benedict and a smile broke across her face.

"I've got a surprise for you," she said. "Early birthday present."

Benedict shook his head. "Vic, I don't..."

Vic turned to see Zoe standing behind the door. Zoe put out a hand to grab her.

"Where is she?"

Vic turned back to Benedict, her eyes ablaze. "You bastard! I thought you'd be pleased!"

She pushed the door in Zoe's face and ran out of the

room. Rhodri went to grab her but missed. Zoe ran after them both into the hallway.

There was a flurry of movement in the outer hallway. Vic pushed a girl towards the door. The girl held a cage.

"Maddy!" Zoe cried. The girl shrieked.

"Come on!" Vic urged. She dragged Maddy outside. Maddy kicked her and Vic screeched. "Stop it! God, I don't know why I bothered." She slammed the door in Rhodri's face.

Rhodri yanked the door open and ran out. Zoe followed. Vic was dragging Maddy across the road. Maddy dropped the cage and it made a yowling sound. There was a small grey pile of fluff in it. A kitten? This woman had pretended to be Alison. She'd abducted Maddy, and then she'd given her a kitten?

"It's no use, Vic!" Zoe called. "You won't get away."

Maddy cried out again. She turned to Vic, who paused to stare into the girl's eyes. Maddy screamed and then bit Vic on the arm. Vic yelped and jerked away. Maddy seized the opportunity to run off down the street.

Shit.

Zoe turned to Rhodri. "I'll go after Maddy, you get Vic."

She sprinted after Maddy, calling her name, shouting that she was police. Front doors opened as she passed and people emerged from their houses. Behind her she heard more shouting: Rhodri and Vic. She hoped he'd got her.

Maddy was about five houses ahead of her, heading towards the station. Zoe picked up speed, eyeing the train line below them. *Oh dear God*, she thought, her mind tight. *Slow down.*

Maddy took a quick look behind her then swerved out into the road. She made for the entrance to the station.

Zoe could hear a train approaching. If Maddy got on it, they might never find her.

"Maddy, stop! I want to take you home. To your mum."

Maddy glanced over her shoulder. "She said *she* was going to be my mum!"

"She lied. It'll be OK. Just stop."

Maddy was on the ramp down to the platform, gravity and momentum pulling her forward. Zoe ran after her. The train was nearing.

Please, no.

Maddy was almost at the bottom of the ramp. She turned to look at Zoe, her hair flying out behind her. She tripped, stumbling over a crack in the tarmac, her own feet, Zoe couldn't be sure.

Maddy cried out, her hands flying out in front. She tumbled to the ground and landed at the feet of a woman pushing a stroller up the ramp.

"You alright, love?" the woman asked. She looked up at Zoe. "You need to keep a better eye on your daughter."

Zoe gave her a breathless nod then bent to crouch next to Maddy.

"Maddy, I'm a police officer. My name's Zoe. I'm here to take you back to your mum and dad."

CHAPTER ONE HUNDRED SEVEN

ZOE REACHED out for Maddy's hand as they walked back to the house, but Maddy pulled away. She shook her head, eyeing Zoe warily. Zoe couldn't blame her.

"We're not far from your home, Maddy. I'm going to take you to your gran's. Ollie's there. We'll be five minutes."

She couldn't even take the poor girl home. Her mum was in custody, her dad too. She'd call Carl, have Alison released. With Ian, she wasn't so sure. He was Carl's problem now.

The cage with the kitten was still in the middle of the road. Zoe was grateful no cars had come along.

"Can I keep it?" Maddy asked.

Zoe picked it up. The kitten meowed at her, its eyes wide.

"Sure. We'll put it in my car."

Rhodri had Vic in handcuffs. The two of them were sitting on a low wall outside the flat. Brian stood in the doorway, staring at Maddy.

Had he seen her, while all this was going on? Did he

know what his girlfriend had done? *A surprise*, she'd said. *For your birthday*. Zoe shivered.

"That's my dad." Maddy's voice was small.

"I thought Ian was your dad?"

A frown knotted Maddy's brow. "You can have two dads, I guess."

Benedict shuffled from foot to foot, his hands fidgeting. He was a bag of nerves.

"You want to talk to him?" she asked the girl.

Maddy shook her head, her eyes on the ground. "I want to go home."

It was for the best. Maddy had been through enough, without dealing with the reappearance of her dead father.

"You wait for me in the car, huh? I'll be two ticks. Here." She handed over the cage and opened the passenger door. Then she considered. Could a twelve-year-old travel in the front?

Of course she could. Nicholas had done it.

Maddy slid into the car and sat gazing at the kitten. She wiggled her fingers at it, her forehead pressed to the bars. Zoe watched her smile at the kitten. She looked OK now, but there would be a hell of a lot for her to unpack. She'd need professional help.

She turned to Rhodri. "I'm taking her to her gran's. Can you wait here for Uniform?"

"They were supposed to be here ages ago."

"You can't just do this," said Vic. "This is bloody humiliating, sitting out here in the street."

"You done the honours, DC Hughes?"

"Arrested her for child abduction."

"And the rest." She turned to Vic, her voice hardening. "Considering what you did, I think a bit of embarrassment in front of the neighbours is going to be the least of your worries."

This woman thought she was giving her boyfriend a gift. Instead she'd taken Maddy's innocence and broken a family in two.

She heard an engine behind her. A squad car.

"About bloody time," said Rhodri.

"Take her to Harborne," said Zoe.

"Yes, boss." Rhodri yanked the handcuffs and led Vic to the waiting car.

Zoe walked back to her own car, her chest tight. Taking Maddy to her grandmother would be a joy and a heartache at the same time. He only hoped they could get Alison home soon.

She stopped before getting in the car. She grabbed her phone.

"Boss?"

"Rhodri was right, Mo. Benedict's alive. He's got a girl-friend who's the living spit of Alison, and it was her who took them."

"So she was the one in the CCTV?"

"And at Cleanways. It was Rhodri who put it together."

"Good on him." *Yeah. Connie too*, she thought. Except the information Connie had uncovered was more sensitive.

"It means we've got nothing on Alison," she said. "Can you tell Carl, get her released and brought to her mother's asap."

"Sure thing. What about Ian?"

"That's up to Carl."

"Yeah."

Zoe hung up and got in the car, throwing Maddy the most confident smile she could muster.

CHAPTER ONE HUNDRED EIGHT

CARL PARKED his car beneath Lloyd House and headed for the lift. It had been a long day. Working with Zoe had been a bonus but seeing the look on Alison Osman's face when they'd told her Maddy was safe and sound... That was priceless.

The lift pinged open at the fifth floor. He hesitated, considering what Connie had told him. He waited for the doors to close and pressed the button again.

He got out to find the tenth floor a buzz of activity. Mainly civilian staff: secretaries, legal advisors, PR people. This was where the high-ups worked, along with their protective bubble of civvies.

David Randle's office was on the west side of the building. Carl turned towards it.

He stepped back into the lift. All he had was a DC saying she'd recognised his voice. Zoe's suspicions during the Jackson case. His own gut instinct. It wasn't enough. It hadn't been enough when Randle was a DCI. It was nowhere near enough now he was a Superintendent.

He pressed the button for the fifth floor and travelled down, his mind foggy. He'd call Zoe later, see if he could persuade her to have that drink.

"DI Whaley." Superintendent Rogers was standing outside his office. Waiting?

"Sir."

"How did it go?"

"We've got a strong case against Ian Osman, sir. But we could use him."

"Not out here."

Carl let his boss go into the office first. Inside, Rogers closed the door. "Explain your plan."

"There's strong evidence he had contact with Stuart Reynolds. Reynolds is definitely one of Hamm's men."

"Hamm's already in custody."

"You know his type. He'll get a good lawyer. He'll be back on the streets in a couple of weeks."

Rogers pursed his lips. He knew Carl was right.

"And besides," said Carl. "It's not Hamm we're after. Let Force CID worry about him. He can lead us to corrupt officers. If he had Jackson in his pocket, there'll be others."

Rogers raised his eyes to the ceiling. Who on the tenth floor was involved in all this? Carl hated the way Jackson's corruption had been shoved under the carpet. No point, he'd been told, seeing as the man was dead.

"Ian might be able to give us information," Carl said. "He might know about other corrupt officers, even indirectly. I say we offer him a deal."

"What kind of deal?" asked Rogers.

"Hamm doesn't know we suspect Osman. As far as the world's concerned, he was questioned over the disappearance of his kids. Nothing more."

"You think we can use him as a plant."

"For him, it's either that or lose his job. Maybe criminal proceedings. I think he'll take it."

"You think he's got the bottle for it?"

"Only one way to find out."

Carl watched his senior officer, hopeful. Rogers scratched his chin.

"We'd be putting him at risk. Just because he's bent, doesn't mean..."

"I'll take personal responsibility, sir. Make sure we assess and mitigate the risk before sending him in there. And he'd only be doing what he's already done."

"Plus talking to us. That can get you killed, when people like Hamm are involved."

"We need a way in, sir."

"Let me think about it."

Carl knew that was the best he could get. "Sir." He pulled out of the office and headed back to his own desk, taking his phone from his pocket and dialling Zoe.

CHAPTER ONE HUNDRED NINE

"ZOE. WELL DONE."

Lesley was in the team office, Mo, Connie and Rhodri behind her. Zoe walked in, looking around at her team. There was a bottle of sparkling water on Mo's desk and glasses.

"You took a kid back to her family," he said. "I think we're allowed to celebrate."

Zoe smiled. She eyed the water. Only Mo would remember that champagne wasn't the right thing. "Thanks."

"What's that, boss?" Rhodri eyed the object Zoe was carrying.

She hoisted the cat carrier onto his desk. Connie leaned over it, her eyes bright.

"Maddy's kidnapper gave it to her. Trying to win her over, I guess. I told Maddy she could keep it but her gran was having none of it."

Rhodri looked horrified. "Why not?"

Zoe shrugged. "She said it would bring back memories. Didn't want it crossing the threshold." She peered at it. It was rubbing against the back of Connie's hand through the bars of the cage. "Guess I'll have to call the RSPCA or something."

"You could always keep it," said Mo.

"Me?"

"Company for you, when Nicholas goes to Uni."

She eyed the kitten. Could she trust herself, looking after this scrap of fluff?

Connie opened the cage. She reached inside, as gently as if she were handling fine crystal, and pulled the kitten onto her shoulder. It mewed, blinking at them.

Zoe allowed herself a smile. "It is quite cute."

"Go on," said Connie. "I'll look after it when you're working late."

"You live the other side of the city from me."

"My brother's at your house all the time. I'll get him to do it."

"Until he goes to Uni."

"You'll think of something."

The kitten mewed. "Fair enough." Zoe reached out and scratched it under the chin. It stuck its little head out and closed its eyes.

"It likes you," said Mo.

"It likes a bit of fuss," she replied.

"Anyway, since we've got the kitten's parentage sorted... a word, please?" Lesley stood by the inner office, her arms folded.

Zoe dropped her hand. *What's up?* She glanced at Mo, who shrugged, then followed Lesley into the office.

"What is it, ma'am? A problem?"

"Close the door."

Zoe did as she was told. Lesley perched on the desk, her legs out ahead of her.

"What's happened?"

"Ian. He's been released."

"*What?*"

"PSD said they didn't have enough to pursue the case."

"But he was working with Stuart Reynolds. Who's part of Hamm's organisation. We've got a solid case..."

"It's not our case, Inspector. It's PSD's. And they say it isn't good enough."

"So he goes back to his job like nothing happened?"

"Seems that way."

Zoe slumped back against the partition. "That's not like Carl."

Lesley shrugged. "Not his call, I imagine."

"Right."

"But that aside, well done. This was your first case as SIO, and you did good."

"Thank you, ma'am."

"I know you had a lot of balls in the air. You handled them without a wobble."

"Well, I wouldn't say that..." Zoe thought of the evening she'd come to Lesley, worried she was getting nowhere. Of the conversation she'd had with Mo in his kitchen.

"The important thing is, you caught the right ball."

"DC Hughes deserves the credit for that. He was the one that worked out Benedict was alive. To be fair, we had no idea that wasn't Alison on the tape until we saw the photo of Vic in Benedict's flat."

Lesley stood up. "Zoe, will you just take praise when it's offered to you? Yes, your team made a significant contribution. But they're *your* team. They work hard for you. Well done."

Zoe felt heat creep up her neck. She resisted the urge to add something about the work other members of the team had done: Connie on the background information, Mo in Hamm's flat.

"What's happening with Hamm?" she asked.

"He's in custody. You and I will be interviewing him together."

Zoe raised an eyebrow.

"I've worked other cases he's had fingers in, Zoe. We need to link it all together, build a watertight case. If there's a way Hamm can wriggle out of this, he'll find it."

"Yes, ma'am."

"And there's another piece of news."

Not more. "Go on."

"DI Dawson's coming back."

Zoe felt her body slump. DI Dawson was her old boss, Mo's old boss too. It was him she'd temporarily replaced when she'd been an acting DI.

"His secondment's over."

"Yes," said Lesley. "Seems it went well enough for brass to be happy, but not so well they've made an opening for him in the Met. You'll be colleagues."

"Yes, ma'am." Dawson would be resentful of her promotion. She'd have to work hard to make sure he didn't act like he was still her senior officer.

"He'll need a team," Lesley said.

"Not..."

"Not all of them, no. But the four of you were his team, before you were promoted."

Zoe felt light and heavy at the same time. Who was she going to lose?

"I think DS Uddin is best placed to move across to Frank's team."

"Mo?"

"Yes, Zoe. You get to keep DC Hughes and DC Williams. Two for you, one for Frank."

"Mo and I have worked together for years."

"I know. Pair of you are as tight as that kitten out there's arse."

"He's..." *He's my best friend* wasn't the right thing to say.

"If you keep Mo, Dawson gets the two constables."

Zoe looked out at the team. Connie was at her desk, the kitten rubbing its head against her computer monitor. She stroked it as she stared ahead at the screen. Rhodri had taken a glass of sparkling water to his desk and was sifting through paperwork. No cheap lager today, she thought. Mo had been watching her, but shifted his gaze as she caught his eye. Did he know?

Mo could deal with Dawson. He had more experience of the man.

Zoe sighed and turned back to Lesley. "As you say, ma'am."

CHAPTER ONE HUNDRED TEN

ALISON WATCHED her children playing together. Maddy had brought some Lego down from her room and was helping Ollie build a tower. He giggled every time it fell down.

Maddy had a haunted look in her eyes. Alison had caught her staring into space when she thought no one was looking.

What had she gone through, in that flat? What had that woman, who'd pretended to be a new mum to her, done?

Alison shivered and pulled her cardigan tighter. She heaved on a smile and went to join them. Ollie looked up and smiled as she knelt on the floor next to him. She placed a kiss on the top of his head and put a hand on Maddy's shoulder. Maddy stiffened.

"Higher!" said Ollie. He'd started talking as soon as Maddy came home, but had said nothing about his ordeal. All they had was what Maddy knew. She had no idea what had happened to him between leaving that room and being brought home. He'd been dumped in a phone box, photographed. How long had he been left there? What had been going through his mind?

The doorbell rang. Alison sighed and pushed herself up. The press had been out there for the last three days, since Maddy had come home. Her mum had told her to sell her story but she was having none of it.

She peered through the peephole the police had put in for her and gasped. She stepped back, wiping her hands on her trousers. Her palms were damp.

She turned to the door and looked through again. A man stood outside, wearing a woolly hat.

She didn't have to open it. She could pretend they weren't in.

Another man got out of a car opposite. A journalist. He shouted something and ran across the road to the house. He'd spotted her visitor. Had he recognised him?

Alison didn't want the press involved.

She opened the door. He straightened as she did so, his face pale.

"You'd better come in." She eyed the journalist, who stopped at the end of the path.

Benedict slipped through the door, careful not to make contact with her. She closed it firmly.

"What do you want?" she asked. She checked the door to the living room was closed. *Don't come out. Nothing to see.*

"I wanted to say sorry."

"Sorry for pretending to be dead, or sorry for taking Maddy and Ollie?"

"I had nothing to do with that, Alison. You have to believe me."

"You lied about your own death. How can I believe a word you say?"

"It's complicated."

"Yes, it's bloody complicated," she hissed. "I don't even know if my marriage to Ian is legal now."

"I've been away more than three years. Even without the assumption of death, we're legally estranged."

"Yes, but I married him in..." She stopped. She didn't want Benedict knowing when she'd started seeing Ian.

"Is Ollie his?" Benedict asked. His breathing was shallow.

"He's his in the sense that Ian is his legal father now, and is the man who's bringing him up."

"You know what I mean."

She closed her eyes. "No. You're his father. His biological father."

"I'd like to see them, if you'll let me."

She glared at him. Maddy had gone through the horror of her dad dying. Ollie had never known him. And now he wanted to rip those wounds open?

She shook her head. "They've been through enough."

"Not now, maybe. But someday?"

She stared at him. He was still the same Benedict she'd fallen in love with. She'd adored his sense of adventure, his irrepressible nature. As a husband, that had made him worse than useless. But looking into his eyes now, she could remember what had drawn her in.

But she'd chosen Ian over him. Ian was reliable, steady. He loved the children. He didn't care that they didn't share his DNA. He'd be their dad, whatever it took.

"I can't think about it right now," she said. "Maybe when they're a bit older, better able to handle it."

"They're my kids, Alison."

She felt like she would burst with rage. "You forfeited all right to them when you faked your own death."

"I didn't fake it. I was given up for dead. It was months before I made it home. I came here and saw you with him. I spent months watching you, wondering if I should contact you. I saw how happy you all were."

"You used a fake name."

"I thought it would make things easier for you."

"Do you know I booked Maddy in for a lesson at the climbing wall? What would have happened if you'd taught her? Were you planning on snatching her away?"

His face crumpled. "No, Al. Never. Vic was a monster. I didn't know that when I met her."

The door opened: Ian. He took one look at Benedict and launched himself at him.

Alison pushed herself between them. "No, Ian! He's just leaving."

Ian let her pull him off. He was panting and his hair was dishevelled. He smelled of sweat and cold metal.

"Has he seen the kids?"

"No," she said. She grabbed Ian's shoulders and span him round to face her. "You're their dad. I told him to leave. He's no threat to you."

Ian's eyes flashed at her. She met them with as much calm as she could. *Believe me*, she thought. *Trust me*.

He turned to Benedict. "I think you should go."

"You're right." Benedict cast a sad glance towards the living room and let himself out of the front door.

Alison felt tension seep out of her body. She wrapped her arms around her husband. "You're back."

"Yeah."

'Why did they keep you so long?"

"I don't know." He sounded distracted. He would be wanting to see Maddy.

"Come on." She smiled into his face. "They're through here."

CHAPTER ONE HUNDRED ELEVEN

ZOE LEANED on her front door, her limbs heavy. The kitten was on the mat by her feet, in its carrier.

Her phone buzzed: Carl. *When are we going for that drink?*

She thumbed it off. She wasn't in the mood for Carl, after what Lesley had told her.

She picked the cat carrier up and carried it into the living room. *Let's see what Nicholas makes of you*, she thought.

She froze as she entered the room.

Nicholas was on the settee, twisting round to look at her. Zaf was next to him.

And opposite them, on the threadbare armchair, was Zoe's mum.

Zoe flicked a glance at her mum then back to Nicholas. She walked to the back of the settee and ruffled his hair. "I got you something."

She plonked the cage on the back of the settee.

"A kitten!" Zaf cried. He sprang up and threw himself around Nicholas, reaching for the cage. She let him take it and open the door. The kitten cowered inside. It had had enough of new people for one day, she reckoned. She didn't blame it.

"Nicholas, can you help me in the kitchen please?" she asked. She ignored her mum.

"Er..." Nicholas looked at Zaf and shrugged. Zaf grinned at him, pulling the kitten out of its hiding place.

In the kitchen, it was all she could do not to round on him. She tried to project casualness into her voice.

"What's she doing here?"

"She turned up about an hour ago. She's been asking Zaf about his art. Seems she knows a lot about it.

Annette Finch had cast herself as a bit of a bohemian, back in the day. Art, poetry, literature. Until the booze had rendered her too stupid to think about any of it.

"I don't like her being here," she hissed.

"She's OK. She just wanted to see you."

Zoe drew in a breath. She didn't want to pass her resentment of her mum down to Nicholas, didn't want him to feel the tension that she'd grown up with. She nodded, slowly.

"Come on," he said. "I'll put the kettle on. I've got a lasagne in the oven." Nicholas was a great cook. He had to be, since Zoe couldn't get fish fingers right.

She looked at him, thinking of Alison. The expression on her face every time she'd gone round there, the momentary hope. Losing a child like that... and she was about to lose him, in a way. To university, and adulthood.

"Go in," he said. "Keep an eye on that kitten."

She twisted her lips and gritted her teeth. Today she'd chased after a terrified child, apprehended a deranged kidnapper, and dealt with the return of DI Frank Dawson. None of that was a match for trying to be polite to her mum.

She shuffled into the living room. Zaf had the kitten on his lap and was scratching it under the chin, muttering to it. Annette watched, her eyes sparkling. She didn't have the dullness that came over her when she'd been drinking.

There was no way she'd given up. She just hadn't started for the day yet.

"Mum," Zoe muttered. She eased herself onto the sofa next to Zaf.

"Zoe, love."

Don't call me love. Zoe watched Zaf with the kitten. He reminded her so much of his big sister.

She turned to her mum, all her senses ablaze. She hesitated.

"Nicholas has made a lasagne," she said. "Would you like some?"

READ ZOE'S PREQUEL STORY, DEADLY ORIGINS

It's 2003, and Zoe Finch is a new Detective Constable. When a body is found on her patch, she's grudgingly allowed to take a role on the case.

But when more bodies are found, and Zoe realises the case has links to her own family, the investigation becomes deeply personal.

Can Zoe find the killer before it's too late?

Find out by reading *Deadly Origins* for FREE at rachelmclean.com/origins.

Thanks,
Rachel McLean

READ MORE DI ZOE FINCH BOOKS

CPSIA information can be obtained
at www.ICGtesting.com
Printed in the USA
LVHW031327040920
664825LV00001B/9